Crenshaw stretched and began her lecture. "The Macdonalds are still trying to decide whether to attempt to take over the universe. They view humanity as their major stumbling block.

"The peace faction believes that humans are wildly variable, geniuses balancing out morons so that if push comes to shove in interstellar-political terms, the bright humans are going to kick the living hell out of Alt Bauernhof.

"Based on Alt Bauernhof's unfortunate experience with career diplomats and the Contact Survey Corps, the militarists believe that humans are too dumb to live, much less dominate the galaxy.

"The balance of power is held by the faction that has a third theory. Since most humans are too dumb to live, a secret master race must be guiding humanity's destiny. Variants on that theory include The Aryan Master Race Theory, The Inscrutable Oriental Master Race Theory, the Jewish Princess Master Race Theory, and—last but not least—the VMR, or Vampire Master Race, Theory.

Crenshaw began examining her nails. "We may have planted a story or two to the effect that the vamps run Earth. And, since the two of you are the only vampires the Macdonalds have been able to identify, the Macdonald leadership is very interested in taking a look at you . . ."

By Robert Frezza
Published by Ballantine Books:

A SMALL COLONIAL WAR
McLENDON'S SYNDROME
FIRE IN A FARAWAY PLACE
CAIN'S LAND
THE VMR THEORY

THE
VMR THEORY

Robert Frezza

A Del Rey® Book

BALLANTINE BOOKS • NEW YORK

A Del Rey® Book
Published by Ballantine Books
Copyright © 1996 by Robert Frezza

http://www.randomhouse.com

Library of Congress Catalog Card Number: 96-96761

ISBN 0-345-39026-1

Manufactured in the United States of America

First Edition: December 1996

10 9 8 7 6 5 4 3 2

On Confederation Secret Service

The beer joint we were in qualified as a dimly lit dive, one of many that litter the alleys of Rio, the imaginatively named capital of Brasilia Nuevo. Beer joints and spacers go together, like Fred and Ginger or magnets and iron filings, which still doesn't explain why the messes I get myself into always start out in bars.

As the floor show involving four-legged animals and dancers of indeterminate gender threatened to spill over onto our table, I asked my partner, Catarina Lindquist, "How long do we plan on waiting for our contact to show?"

"Ken, Navy Intelligence special agents are notoriously unpunctual." She tipped down her sunglasses. "You aren't getting cold feet, are you?"

Catarina and I have a complicated relationship, in that my life has developed complications since I met her. "Did you have to spray-paint 'Positions Available' on the sign advertising 'Live Sexy Revue,' and do they amputate toes for frostbite?"

The corner of her mouth turned down. "I've heard it said that it is better to die on your feet than to live when they freeze."

1

Catarina employs very bad puns, partly because she adores them and partly because I don't.

"Couldn't we just go back to the ship and watch a movie?" I pleaded. "I picked up a new remake of *Casablanca*."

Her eyes surveyed the row of bottles behind the bar. She said in a deceptively mild voice, "How about if we watch 'Tequila Mockingbird' instead?"

A sharp throbbing pain appeared between my eyes. "My head hurts."

She stroked my forehead solicitously. "I'm sorry. Is it a real pain or is it a—"

"No. It is *not* a champagne." I sucked in my breath. "Let's give this guy five more minutes."

Catarina smiled and laid her hand firmly across my arm in case I got a sudden urge to jump. She said, "Ken, sherry, you jest. This den of giniquity isn't much of a bar-gain, but this is a pretty big space *port*. Wine not give our man another hour? Beer in mind that if we don't rum into him here, our chances of cognacing him aren't very rosé," thus proving that she was indisputably liquor on the uptake than I was.

She then politely thumped me on the back until I stopped choking. I considered jumping, but leaping out of a ground floor window is not an ideal way to attempt suicide.

The bartender came over. "Senhor, you are very pale. In this establishment it is customary to choke after drinking and not before." He tilted his head. "You don't look well at all."

Like bartenders on other planets where they run armed guards on the beer trucks, bartenders on Brasilia Nuevo avoid difficulties with the police by arranging for their customers to die elsewhere. I waved my arm at him. "It's okay. I usually look this way. How about two bottles of mineral water?"

"*With* the caps on," Catarina stipulated.

The bartender mopped his forehead nervously. "I will see what I can do."

As he departed I asked Catarina, "What will our contact look like, anyway?"

"Navy Intelligence undercover types try to blend in." She nudged me. "Kind of like 'Guido' there."

Short and swarthy with greasy black ringlets and lots of gold chain, "Guido" looked more local than the locals did. Pausing to twirl a toothpick in his mouth, he sauntered in our direction. "Senhor, senhorita, you are spacers, I see." Carefully enunciating each word, he asked, "Do you happen to have a match?"

Catarina kept a straight face and said with equal care, "No, neither of us smoke. But I could supply you with a lighter."

"That is all right. Tobacco is illegal, so I am trying to quit. Allow me to introduce myself. I am Sandy Francisco."

I gritted my teeth. Our last undercover agent had introduced himself as Newt York. I decided to jump in before the cloak-and-dagger stuff got out of hand. "Pleased to meet you, Sandy. I'm Ken MacKay, captain of the merchant vessel, *Rustam's Slipper*. This is my partner, Catarina Lindquist."

Sandy took a seat and placed a good commercial voice scrambler on the table to make sure nobody would eavesdrop. "By coincidence, I have a cargo I wish to ship off planet. A few tons of fertilizer. What good fortune it is I ran into you," he repeated by rote.

Rear Admiral Lydia Crenshaw, the sector commander, has a sense of humor similar to Catarina's, and the old bat personally selected "a few tons of fertilizer" as our code phrase. My ship, *Rustam's Slipper*, affectionately known as *The Rusty Scupper*, is a Kobold-class freighter. I had her rebuilt after a !Plixxi* warfleet tried to turn her into junk during her brief and reluctant career as a Confederation Navy warship, although an unbiased observer would have concluded that she was junk years before the !Plixxi* shot holes in her. As a result of a recent change in government, she now serves as the unofficial flagship of the !Plixxi* Navy, in part because we used pieces of the previous flagship to patch her up. As reconfigured, she boasts five holds, an almost new set of Madsen drives, and an AN-33 missile launcher in Number One Hold which I decided to keep after I saw the quote on what it would cost to take it out. We haul stuff from planet to planet, and my rates are very affordable.

I reluctantly launched into my sales pitch. When I finished, Sandy scratched his head and stepped out of character. *"Rustam's Slipper?* Where have I heard that name?"

I explained modestly, "We helped fight off some Plixxi ships at Schuyler's World." I left the tongue-click off the beginning of the word !Plixxi* and the charming hoot-whistle off the end. Actually, Catarina and I could have billed our crew as the gang that couldn't shoot straight, but that's another story, which has since become a very bad movie.

"Oh, I didn't make the connection." Sandy wagged his finger. "You're *that* Ken MacKay. I thought you were older. You know, the guy who played you in the movie—"

"I *feel* older," I explained.

Sandy looked at us with something resembling respect. "Let me buy you two a drink."

"We'll have to pass, but thanks for the offer," Catarina said tactfully.

Sandy slapped himself on the forehead. "Oh, that's right. I remember reading that you two are vamps. You should wear your capes."

I winced. "Call it McLendon's Syndrome, please."

Vamp is short for vampire, and McLendon's Syndrome is distantly related to the kind of vampirism you read about in books with naked women on the cover. The disease is a slow-progressing bacterial disease like leprosy. Maybe three percent of the population has a genetic predisposition for it, and being one of the lucky few is as close as I'm ever going to come to winning the lottery. Thanks to McLendon's, Catarina has an alabaster complexion and platinum hair, while I have the functional equivalent of a prison pallor and mousy, colorless hair.

Catarina gave Sandy a crooked smile. "Please understand that the disease is similar to porphyria and that there's nothing supernatural about it. Ken and I do not sip blood from the living or sleep in tubs of Transylvanian night soil." She accuses people who think that vamps drink blood of "circulatory reasoning."

"Tomato juice is enough to make me queasy," I interjected, "and my friends only call me 'the living dead' because I fall asleep at parties."

Contrite and genuinely curious, Sandy said, "Sorry, I didn't realize you were sensitive about it. The disease slows down the aging process, doesn't it?"

"Researchers think that the disease encourages promiscuous cell replacement and cushions the impact of glucocorticoids on the body, so theoretically Catarina and I would live longer than normal people if we quit doing jobs for Admiral Crenshaw," I explained, "but it isn't something you want to catch. The two of us have every food and skin allergy known to man."

"Sunlight? Garlic?" Sandy reflected.

"I can get sun poisoning on a cloudy day," I said glumly, "and thinking about a Korean restaurant is enough to make my sinuses swell."

McLendon's is nothing to fool with. Every month, it seems like you read in the tabloids about some poor, whacked-out vamp who abandoned a home and a job and ended up on the streets, living in a cemetery with his or her possessions piled into a shopping cart.

"What about the Rats? Are you still having problems with them?" Sandy asked, taking a break from playing spy.

"Call them Rodents, or Plixxi, please. Some of my best friends are Rats, including the new Poobah, Bucky Beaver. He made me an honorary captain in the Plixxi Navy. He made Catarina an honorary rear admiral, which may suggest that I'm hurting for friends." I stepped on Catarina's toe so she wouldn't repeat the line about her rear being admirable.

Sandy waved his free hand for emphasis. "Didn't I read somewhere that the two of you got mixed up in the succession war they had about six months ago?"

Catarina and I exchanged glances. "Well, yes—Bucky accepted a challenge from his youngest surviving demi-brother, who uses the name Mordred, but a succession war on Plixxi is considered harmless entertainment, like an election. Each pretender buys up supporters for a couple of weeks, and whoever has the most edged weapons is declared the winner, while the loser leaves town on a fast-riding beast."

"It's considered a bad omen if someone other than one of the principals gets killed." Catarina touched her finger to her nose. "Fun's fun, Sandy, but we need to get down to business. Where does Admiral Crenshaw want her fertilizer shipped?"

Sandy looked embarrassed. "Alt Bauernhof."

The planet has several other names, some of which are printable. It's a place that nine out of ten tourists would recommend to people they actively dislike, mostly because the Macdonalds live there.

Macdonalds were the first intelligent nonhuman species mankind stumbled across, unless you count dolphins and lawyers. They look like wizened little gnomes, and being a proud and aggressive bunch, they weren't too thrilled to find out that they were number two in the known universe. The Confederation formed the Contact/Survey Corps specifically to uplift them. The Macdonalds have long considered this a mortal insult since Contact boys tend to be long on altruism and short on smarts. Having put several generations of steady military progress under their belts, they've reached the point where they want to conquer new worlds, and they'd probably try if they weren't tolerably certain that the Confederation Navy would kick their tails. Except at the government-to-government level, this causes a certain amount of friction, and I personally haven't forgiven them for covertly financing the flare-up with the Rodents that nearly cost Catarina and me a chance of living long enough to retire.

Sandy stood up. "It just so happens that this place has

a back room, where Admiral Crenshaw is waiting to fill you in on the details."

I nodded. "I'm not feeling very good."

"You do look pretty awful," Sandy observed. "Have you tried vitamin B-12? My girlfriend swears by it. And maybe some calcium and vitamin C for your skin. Well, I hope I'll see you again!"

"Me, too," I said with more enthusiasm than I felt.

As he walked away I looked at Catarina out of the corner of my eye. "You know, I just remembered something I left back on the ship."

She took me gently by the arm. "Come on, Ken. It'll be nice to see Lydia."

We found Admiral Crenshaw in the back room in a very loud muumuu, playing solitaire. Crenshaw is a very big, very overbearing black lady. The navy hierarchy keeps trying to bury her behind a desk somewhere. I keep hoping they'll succeed.

She shoved her cards aside. "Catarina! Good to see you! Pull up a chair. You, too, shorty." Crenshaw was Catarina's Tac Officer at the Naval Academy, and the two of them have a free and easy relationship that Lydia has not asked me to share. "I knew if I sent an errand boy to relay orders to your boyfriend here, he'd tell my messenger to take a flying leap."

"What's this about sending us to Alt Bauernhof?" I asked, cautiously seating myself next to Catarina. "The Macdonalds don't let Confederation ships visit their planet."

"Technically, you're not a Confederation ship. You have Rodent registry," Lydia said patiently.

"Yeah, but everybody who can afford the price of a newspaper knows that Catarina is ex–Navy Intelligence,

I'm a lieutenant in the reserves, and that rust trap of ours fought the only naval battle worth the price of popcorn in the last fifty years. Aren't the Macdonalds going to figure we're still on the navy payroll?"

"Ken," Catarina explained gently, "the Macdonalds know that we're N.I. We know that they know we're N.I. They know that we know that they know we're N.I. After that, it gets complicated."

"The Macdonalds transship a lot of goods from Confederation worlds through here, and they send a freighter about once a month. That ship had an unfortunate mishap a few days back—it should take a month to fix the damage. The Macdonalds either have to hire you or send out another ship. So they need you." Crenshaw's smile widened. "They're also curious about you."

Little alarm bells went off in my head. "Say again?"

Crenshaw stretched. "The Macdonalds are still trying to decide whether they want to attempt to take over the universe."

"Ambitious little devils," I said gloomily.

"They view humanity as their major stumbling block and have three competing schools of thought about us." Crenshaw folded her hands and began acting professorial. "The peace faction espouses theory one, which is that humans are wildly variable, with geniuses to balance out the morons so that if push comes to shove in stellar-political terms, the bright humans are going to kick the living hell out of Alt Bauernhof."

"Sounds reasonable to me," I commented.

"The militarists lean toward theory two, based on Alt Bauernhof's unfortunate experience with career diplomats and the Contact/Survey Corps, to the effect that humans are too dumb to live, much less dominate the galaxy. As one leading scholar of the school expresses it, if you take a human out in the rain and let him look up, he'll drown trying to talk."

Catarina nodded. "They have the Contact boys pegged pretty well."

"Now, as much as I would personally enjoy promoting peace through superior firepower with the Macdonalds, my orders are to try to quietly nudge them in a peaceable direction. The ones who believe in theory three hold the balance of power, and that's where you two fit in," Crenshaw concluded.

"What is theory three?" I asked, closing my eyes.

"Theory three is that since most of the humans the Macdonalds have seen are too dumb to live, there must be a secret master race guiding humanity's destiny. Variants on theory three include the Aryan Master Race Theory, the Inscrutable Oriental Master Race Theory, the Jewish Princess Master Race Theory, the Everyone-of-Consequence-Who-Ever-Lived-Was-Gay Master Race Theory, and—last but not least—the VMR or Vampire Master Race Theory."

I looked at her suspiciously. "You wouldn't have helped them come up with this Vampire Master Race Theory, would you?"

Crenshaw began examining her nails. "We may have planted a story or two to the effect that vamps run Earth."

I considered that a pretty nasty dig, considering how things run on Earth. "Swell."

"The two of you are the only vampires that the Macdonalds have been able to identify, and your little escapade on Schuyler's World did wonders to promote the VMR Theory, so the Macdonald leadership is *very* interested in taking a look at you."

"Swell," I said.

Crenshaw leaned over and pinched my cheek. "I just love it when you're enthusiastic, MacKay. I keep wondering what Catarina sees in you." She paused. "I've asked her to get her eyes checked."

To fill an otherwise pregnant silence, I asked, "What are we actually supposed to do on Alt Bauernhof?"

"We need you to get one of our local agents out, a scientist who works on their naval armaments. Call him Dr. Blok." Crenshaw passed across a thick packet of materials. "He's under suspicion, and we haven't been able to contact him."

I glanced through the pictures in the packet. "Have you tried an ad in the personals?"

Crenshaw said pointedly, "Catarina darlin', will you get your dopey boyfriend here flying straight? Blok is important. Everybody except the Foreign Office knows that the Macdonalds are building up their navy quicker than rabbits breed. We need the details from Blok. If the two of you can smuggle him out in that bucket of bolts you laughingly call a ship, we'll be in a position to have the Foreign Office tell the Macdonalds to stop. Or else." She smiled at the prospect of "or else."

"If we fly in with the lights on our hull practically spelling out 'Confederation Naval Intelligence,' Blok should try to get in touch with us," Catarina observed for my benefit.

"Ma'am, shouldn't we have a plan or something?" I asked timidly, glancing through the packet.

"MacKay, if I actually gave you a nice, detailed plan, would you actually follow it?"

"No, but I'd *feel* better."

Crenshaw showed me her teeth in what was intended

to be a reassuring gesture. "MacKay, the minute I met you, I knew you were a natural for intelligence work."

"Not real bright," I admitted.

"Like I said, a natural." She chucked me under the chin. "You know, MacKay, I made the connection between you and the VMR Theory about fourteen seconds after you volunteered your services to Navy Intelligence by threatening to bite me on the neck if I didn't fix your ship and let Catarina ship out with you. And yes, I do hold grudges."

I nodded and looked at Catarina, who was practicing her Mona Lisa smile. "Uh, what are the odds on the Macdonalds peaceably letting us go after we arrive?"

"The whiz kids and computers back on Earth say that there's at least a nineteen percent chance," Crenshaw said jovially. "Bunch of wishful thinkers, aren't they? Concentrate on getting Blok out. Any other havoc you cause while you're there is pure profit. Given your talent for creating mayhem, I figure you'll convince the Macdonalds that if there is a Vampire Master Race, it's nothing to mess with."

I asked Catarina, "You have any idea how we're going to get out of this alive?"

"Just remember, shorty," Crenshaw cautioned, "you're doing this for truth, for justice, for peace and eternal fellowship in the galaxy, and I forget how the rest of it goes."

"Why do I feel like this is PBS pledge week?" I thought for a minute. "What can I tell my crew?"

"Nothing. They're not cleared for it."

"That settles it." I decided to see what would happen if I tried to avoid getting killed for a change. "Catarina and

I may have volunteered to go off on suicide missions, but I can't drag my crew into this blind. Count me out."

"Ken—" Catarina said.

I didn't wait for her to finish. I've learned to move quickly when the situation demands it, and I headed for the door before Crenshaw could twist my arm, either figuratively or literally. As I emerged into the saloon, the bartender caught me by the elbow. "Senhor, I am so very sorry. We have not a single bottle of mineral water in the house with a cap on. Have a beer instead." He grimaced as if the words were being pulled out of him with tongs. "On the house."

"Thanks, I appreciate the offer, but I'm in a hurry and—"

His eyes narrowed. "You refuse my kind offer. You disdain my kind offer." He raised his voice. "You perhaps don't like our beer, senhor?" Several persons in the vicinity began eyeing me.

"Well, it's not that I don't like beer—"

"Then you will drink!" He raised his fist. "To Brasilia Nuevo!"

The crowd repeated it. Like a lot of colonial worlds, Brasilia Nuevo would be severely underpopulated if they made potential immigrants pass intelligence tests. It's also one of those places where Diogenes would have been well-advised to ditch his lamp and walk around with a floodlight chained to his wrist. Smiling cordially, I drank.

Discovering I was allergic to something or other in the beer, I promptly threw up. I gather it would have been safer to spit on the local flag.

Next to Detroit, Newark, and Washington, D.C., Brasilia Nuevo is the most heavily armed society in the galaxy, and people here have the habit of firing guns in the air to celebrate special occasions like birthdays, funerals, Tuesdays, and Thursdays. Fortunately, the police arrived within four or five minutes to form a human wall and escort me off into protective custody.

Unfortunately, my stock plummeted when they found Catarina's spray paint in my pocket. Rio's hoosegow proved to be less than desirable; having been in several jails since becoming acquainted with Catarina, I consider myself something of a connoisseur. The local vermin weren't nearly as cute as the rats you find most places, and the little red eyes glaring out at me made me feel unwelcome. Catarina appeared about an hour later.

"Is this one of those good news, bad news sorts of things?" I asked.

She nodded.

"What's it going to cost to get me out of here?"

"That's the bad news, I'm afraid. One of the people you threw up on was an alderman. Also, the locals have a well-developed and possibly well-deserved inferiority complex. The local beer is about the only thing they have to be proud of, so it assumes religious significance in the local culture."

She paused to allow me to digest this. Colonial planets tend to be provincial. On many of them, drinking beer is the most popular form of recreational activity. On some of them, it's the only form of activity.

"After the police took you away, the crowd in the bar formed themselves up into a lynch mob." She shrugged. "I bought a few rounds, so it's likely to be three or four days before they navigate from there to here, but I don't think the municipal government is going to let me bail you out."

"Hmmm," I said.

She looked around my cell. "The place could use some wallpaper. Lots of company?"

"The constabulary mentioned that they like to nibble on your toes if you fall asleep, but otherwise they're fairly harmless." I asked hesitantly, "What was the good news?"

"Lydia and I followed you out, and after she finished chortling, I talked her out of court-martialing you. She offered her good offices in getting you sprung, although she recalled both of us to active duty and made me promise to keelhaul you if you act up again. She says we can tell our crew everything except Dr. Blok. Would you consider reconsidering?"

"I assume you've already briefed and polled our ship-mates. How many of them voted to come along?"

"All of them, although Wyma Jean's cat deserted."

I exploded. "They all want to come? For heaven's sake, what a bunch of idiots! Of course, they'd have to be to work for us."

"True. Most spacers don't like to work for people with communicable diseases, like difficulty with cash flow. Anyway, we've already received an offer through the Macdonald consulate, and Bunkie jacked them up to twice standard rates in real money, half in advance. We can sign the contract and start loading whenever you want."

"Okay. When can I get out of here?"

Catarina pulled a chocolate bar out of her purse and handed it to me through the bars. "You'll be out in no time."

Observing the guards nudging each other, I was not

unduly surprised to find a hacksaw blade stuffed inside the wrapper.

We caught a shuttle, thoughtfully laid on by Lydia, up to Rio's little space platform, where my purser, Bunkie Bunker, and my supercargo, Harry Halsey, were scurrying trying to load the stuff the Macdonalds wanted shipped and locate things that might pay for us to carry on our own account.

Bunkie is a diminutive ex-yeoman we stole from the navy who will undoubtedly end up as CEO of a very large company if she ever gets serious about a career and quits hanging around Catarina and me. Harry, who could pass as the "after" photo in a steroid commercial, is also ex-navy, but the navy asked him to leave. He usually tells people that a supercargo is a kind of space cadet, and they believe him. He sold his bar on Schuyler's World to give me some much needed working capital, and on Schuyler's World, where bouncing drunks is considered an art form, I've been told by people interested in that sort of thing that he practically invented the cross-body headlock toss, which makes him very good at helping Bunkie negotiate contracts on planets like Brasilia Nuevo.

After signing where Bunkie told me to sign, I went back to check on the cargo the Macdonalds had waiting. Finding that they hadn't committed any overt violations of Confederation law, we took on seventy pallets and about a hundred tons of industrial solvent through the four-centimeter tubing that extends from Brasilia Nuevo's space platform to a ground station just outside Rio. Because it's bad luck to have industrial solvent sloshing around trying to dissolve the hull, we did so carefully, and I hoped that Rio's station master would remember to clean out the hose before somebody tried shipping flour.

This accomplished, I went back to see how Catarina was making out back in Stores. "How are we doing?"

"We're stocked up and almost ready to roll." She smiled impishly. "I bought some fresh fish for dinner tonight."

I stopped to peer into a little tank where Mr. Fish and several family members were lethargically swimming around. "How do you plan on fixing it?" I asked, tumbling into her trap.

"You like tempura. How about some battered cod?"

"Sure," I said thoughtlessly.

"Okay." She pulled out a fish and tossed him into my arms. "Smack him around." It took several seconds to register, after which the fish and I both started gasping for oxygen.

"I know I shouldn't bait you, but think of it as my squid pro quo for getting you out of jail," she explained.

"I'm eel-equipped to handle this sort of thing," I countered, hoping that somebody would suspend her poetic license.

"Reel-ly, Ken. You're floundering."

Minnie, one of our two Rodent watch-standers, appeared, sparing me further piscatorial torment. Minnie is an attractive young member of her species, which means she looks something like an upright schnauzer. "Friend Ken, sir, the manifest checks, payment cleared, and Rosalee says we're ready to rock and roll."

Generally speaking, !Plixxi* are friendly, courteous, kind, cheerful, thrifty, less than completely truthful, and thoroughly irreverent. They resemble furry bowling pins, and they shed, which is hell on drains aboard ship. The ones who deal with humans adopt human names. Our friend, Bucky Beaver, the current Poobah occupying !Plixxi*'s Semi-Sacred Cushion, named himself after the principal character in a popular set of children's stories, while our two, who were selected from among his nieces and nephews and stand about twentieth in the line of succession, picked "Minnie" and "Mickey." While no one is quite sure what the !Plixxi* did for amusement before they encountered mankind, I for one would be very interested in finding out.

"Uh, thanks, Minnie. Ask the port master if we can shove off in half an hour."

"Sure thing."

As she waddled off, I complained to Catarina, "What happened to a brisk salute and 'Aye-aye, captain, we're ready to lift ship'?"

Catarina wiggled her nose. "I think it stopped about the time they took 'Tere Simms: Queen of the Spaceways' off the air." The fish was adjusting to the situation better than I was, so she popped him back in the tank and we went forward.

I sent off a quick message to Catarina's friend, Father Yakub, on Schuyler's World. If anyone has a private pipeline to the Big Guy in the Sky, it's Father Yakub, who runs a surprisingly successful mission to Schuyler's World's numerous feebleminded. Father Yakub has done some heavy-duty praying on our behalf in the past, and I figured a little more might not hurt. Then I joined my other three watch-standers, Rosalee Dykstra, Clyde Witherspoon, and Wyma Jean Spooner, on the bridge.

Rosalee, a journeyman spacer, is a large woman who reads Kant and Hegel for pleasure and wrestles cops and medium-sized crocodilians for fun. Clyde and Wyma

Jean are still apprentices. Clyde is a former navy criminal investigation undercover agent with an undercover agent's taste in clothing, while Wyma Jean, blond and buxom, has been making up for an underloved and unhappy childhood with a vengeance.

As we watched Brasilia Nuevo fade into the distance, Wyma Jean observed, "If ships like ours stopped operating, planets like this would be cut off from civilization. Of course, it might be a while before people here noticed."

Catarina had the second watch, and I had the third. Minnie and Mickey were still fairly new on board. As we approached our black hole for the run to Alt Bauernhof, Catarina and I introduced the two of them to the joys of high-speed maneuvering in a lumbering old freighter, just in case.

Mickey proved an apt pupil. "Friend Ken, Minnie and I greatly appreciate the honor you have done us by consenting to make us part of your crew," he commented as he practiced cutting power in to the side impellers.

"Uh, sure." The fact that his uncle Bucky was footing his salary out of the Royal Privy Purse may have influenced my decision just a little. "How did you guys pick the names Minnie and Mickey anyway?"

"After careful consideration, we concluded that the names 'Florence Nightingale' and 'Horatio Nelson' were a trifle pretentious. As Bucky says, 'When the humble and lowly cry out for bread, give them cake to eat.' "

"Uh, right. Uh, how is the cabin working out?"

"We are very happy with our accommodations. You should not worry so, friend Ken."

The *Scupper*'s eight cabins are laid out in pairs separated by a central living area. Rosalee Dykstra had installed them in the cabin opposite hers, which left the other six cabins for me and Catarina, Harry and Wyma Jean, and Bunkie and Clyde. Two humans cooped up together like that would have killed each other in about a week, but Minnie and Mickey seemed to be doing fine.

"You two spot any new surprises from the rebuild team?" The Rodent engineers who fixed up the *Scupper*, bless their furry little hearts, thought of spaceships as big toys that people let them play with.

"No, friend Ken. The gold-plated shower heads seem to be the last such extravagance, although admittedly they have a pleasing aspect which helps to assuage the monotony of space. Do you know, friend Ken," he said, looking straight at me, "when I was a mere pouchling looking up at the stars at night, I would often dream of traveling among them. I find that actually fulfilling this dream intoxicates me with joy."

"Uh, right."

Mickey's delicate muzzle quivered. "Perhaps I should not say this, but it has always been a goal of our species to prove ourselves worthy junior partners of humanity in its quest to bring enlightenment to the universe. I earnestly hope that Minnie and I will meet with your full approbation in this endeavor."

"Uh, right."

When the Contact/Survey Corps reached !Plixxi*, Mickey's great-grandfather was the semi-hereditary ruler of a medium-sized principality. A budding John Rockefeller, he quickly learned enough English to flimflam the Contact boys out of a "small" industrial development loan which enabled him to unify the planet by buying out the competition. The rest, as they say, was history. Since then, the brighter members of the family have gone into politics, while their less gifted brethren have mostly stuck to ordinary piracy.

Harry and Wyma Jean materialized on the bridge, arm in arm, and Wyma Jean leaned over the back of my chair. "Ah, Ken—stop tickling, Harry!—Ken, can I, ah—"

"No, I'm not going to trade watches with you. See if Rosalee is willing to switch. She's probably in the galley."

"Okay." She kissed Harry with a loud smacking sound. "While we're in the galley, do you want a piece of cake, sweet pea?"

"Only if you feed it to me, snookums."

I coughed politely. "We're having dinner in about an hour, so don't spoil your appetites."

Harry and Wyma Jean giggled and headed aft.

I looked at Mickey. "Why am I saying that? Either one could eat a horse in one sitting and come back for the saddle."

"Actually, friend Ken, I am not quite sure why you are saying that." Mickey twitched his whiskers. "Oh, I see, you are asking me a rhetorical question! But actually I thought that horses were quite large, and I understand that they use a great deal of wood and metal in making saddles. Perhaps Mr. Harry could, but I doubt Miss Wyma Jean's abilities in that regard."

"Look up 'hyperbole.'"

"Oh! Certainly." Mickey pointed his nose at me inquisitively. "Friend Ken, I have been meaning to ask you a question. I have been watching Harry and Wyma

Jean for several weeks now without coming to a firm conclusion. Is behavior like that normal for humans?"

"Humans in love sometimes act like that. Of course, I'd be hard-pressed to say that Harry is completely human. Come to think of it, she and Harry have been cooing nonstop for four months now, which is amazing when you consider that Harry thinks an overnight relationship is long-term."

"Oh." Mickey paused to consider the implications of this. "What is love, friend Ken? I have read the definition in the dictionary, but it does not seem to apply."

"That's a tough one." I thought for a minute. "When you do stupid things for someone you care about, and you do them anyway, knowing that they're stupid—then you're in love."

"That does not make a great deal of sense."

I nodded vigorously. "That's the point."

Mickey paused to digest this. "Is this more hyperbole, friend Ken?"

"No. Definitely not."

Mickey let it ride. "Friend Ken, I have been meaning to ask why you humans originally decided to move out into space."

"That's another tough one. Some people wanted to rekindle the pioneer spirit by exploring strange new worlds—you know, to boldly go where no man has gone before—while other folks wanted to free themselves of the exactions of organized government without moving to a place like Arkansas. The Uniform Ancient Burial Sites Preservation Act probably had as much to do with it as anything."

"What was this?"

"Well, the World Congress passed it to keep people

from accidentally digging up old grave sites, but it's pretty hard to find a spot on Earth where someone isn't buried. After folks began filing lawsuits to keep anyone from building anything anywhere, most people said, 'To hell with paying off Indians, let's mess up some other planet.' "

"Is this anything like being in love?"

"It's similar."

Mickey's whiskers twitched. "Friend Ken, what is it like being a vampire?"

I thought hard for a moment. "It's kind of hard to describe. It's a strange feeling really—to think that if you play your cards right, you might be humming along fifty years after most of the people you know are dead, and to know that half the people you run into think that you sleep in a coffin and suck blood out of people's arteries. You're constantly aware of a vast gulf that separates you from the rest of humanity."

"It must be like being admitted to law school," Mickey observed thoughtfully. "Friend Ken, I was wondering . . ."

"Yes?"

"As you know, humans brought the priceless boon of civilization to !Plixxi*." He paused. "After seeing several human worlds now, I was wondering if perhaps we could return the gift by bringing the priceless boon of civilization back to humanity."

"Let me think about that awhile."

Clyde Witherspoon showed up a few seconds later to take over the board, so Mickey and I toddled off to Sunday dinner.

Sunday dinner is one of the few times we all get together, so after grace and the obligatory toast to the navy, I rapped the table for silence. "Okay, everybody. In a couple of days we're due to arrive on Alt Bauernhof. I know there's an element of danger here, but I also know that you all are dedicated professionals. I just wanted to say—"

"Ken, sir? Food's getting cold." Harry rubbed his hands together. "We're having pasta!"

"But we have pasta every Sunday." Catarina and I are allergic to nearly everything, and Minnie and Mickey get stewed on sucrose, so it isn't as though we have a lot of choices.

Harry blinked twice.

I shrugged. "Skip it. Dig in."

We did. Things went smoothly until I made the mistake of asking Wyma Jean, "I hear you taught Minnie, Mickey, and Bunkie how to play that stock market game of yours. How did it go?"

Wyma Jean stiffened in the act of helping herself to more salad. It dawned on me that the three short people had begun taking her to the cleaners. "Maybe I don't win, but at least *I* don't look like a schnauzer," she sniffed.

Minnie, Mickey, and Bunkie all turned their heads and looked at me expectantly.

Catarina winked. I dabbed at my chin with a napkin and thought for a second. "Well, only if you clean up afterward."

The three short people nodded in unison. A few seconds later Wyma Jean was wearing three plates of pasta carbonara.

Catarina and I disappeared into the galley as the food fight began in earnest, with Harry and Wyma Jean unloading on the little people and Rosalee cheerfully taking on all comers.

"Wyma Jean got a little saucy in there," Catarina commented.

I shuddered. "I just hope this bunch frightens the Macdonalds half as much as they frighten me."

A moment later the noises stopped and Rosalee appeared, tastefully decked out in spaghetti like Medusa with yellow snakes in her hair. "We're finished."

I looked to Catarina for support. "Thanks. We'll be in in a minute."

As Rosalee shut the door I shuddered again.

Catarina patted me on the arm. "Look at the bright side, Ken."

"And that is?"

"I'll let you know when I figure it out."

"When you were talking with Lydia, did she let slip any helpful hints?"

"Yes. She said that the local beer is red and the natives call it 'beer of the angels.' Try and say nice things about it."

"How bad is it?"

"They flavor it with calcium cyanimide, so no one's quite sure."

"Ah, right."

The latest remake of *Casablanca* turned out to be the worst one yet. Sam was an android, the Nazis looked Oriental, and the actress playing Ilsa had a monster set of breast implants and swayed from side to side when she walked.

I keep hoping that somebody'll dig up Ingrid Bergman and clone her.

Where Angels' Beer is Red

As we made our final approach to Alt Bauernhof's main space station, I eyed the warships orbiting the Macdonald capital city of Klo'klotixa and told Catarina, "If this works out the way I expect, all I want is a simple headstone, no viewing."

She punched me lightly on the shoulder. "Ken, the Macdonalds know that if they do anything to us, they'll have major diplomatic problems—"

"Be sure and chisel that on the headstone."

"—so they have every reason to treat us politely, at least until they catch us at something overt."

Rosalee and Wyma Jean ignored the exchange and eased us into our assigned berth until the magnetic field brought us to a stop.

As soon as we had a tight seal on the boarding ramp, Catarina, Bunkie, and I put on breathing masks and stepped briskly through the ozone bath to the station's quarantine area, where a big sign in English and Sklo'kotax read HAPPY STAY KLO'KLOTIXA. FOR THE TWELFTH FIVE-YEAR PLAN, YOU MUST MAINTAIN GOOD SPEED AND RHYTHMS!

"Catchy jingle," Catarina observed.

I nodded. "It sounds like something my ex-wife would

26

dream up to sell toothpaste. Darn! They sure like it warm here."

"Sir, it's not the heat, it's the humidity," Bunkie explained.

Barefoot customs inspectors were waiting for us, dressed in the tight leather collars that symbolized their service to the state and reminded me of Christmas in San Francisco. Around the galaxy, creatures designed to fill the same environmental niches end up looking similar, and through a quirk of nature, the Macdonalds came out looking more like human beings than they probably wanted to.

They had four-fingered hands, plantigrade feet, bottle-shaped lower abdomens, and cartilaginous internal bracing, which allowed them a reasonably upright stance. Their goggle eyes were pushed together for good stereoscopic vision, and they had fleshy nasal bulbs for Jacobson's organs on their faces, ranging in size from a cute, pug one on the young female scrubbing the floor to dipsomaniacal monstrosities on the males.

I was immediately struck by the way their jug ears artistically framed their low-slung foreheads. Protective oil gave their grayish skin a glossy sheen, while modified gill slits in the folds of skin over the throat allowed them to breathe, although I noticed they kept their mouths open for maximum respiratory efficiency. In short, it appeared that nature had conspired to make Macdonalds the butt of every Polish joke known to humankind.

As we stepped up to the desk, the two officials wearing the fanciest outfits moved forward together and almost bumped into each other. Body language among bipeds being something of a universal constant, it was readily apparent which of the two handled customs on a regular basis, and which of the two outranked the other.

While they were sorting it out I whispered to Catarina, "Secret police?"

"Maybe. The Macdonalds have a Navy Intelligence Service, an Army Intelligence Agency, a Joint Army-Navy Intelligence Board, a Bureau of Planetary Security, a Central Security Service, the Secret Police, and the Special Secret Police, so it's sometimes difficult to tell the players without a scorecard."

The flashier of the two interrupted in singsong English, "Please present your papers. Do you have anyt'ing to declare?"

Macdonald palates can't accommodate a "th" sound.

"We have nothing to declare," I announced cheerfully.

Bunkie handed over our papers, and the two Macdonalds spent a few minutes with their tongues hanging out scanning our documents for flaws. Finally, the little one opened and closed his eyes rapidly three or four times, which was the equivalent of a shake of the head, and fancy-pants reluctantly said, "Your papers are in order. Tee atmosphere on t'is space station is hazardous to your well-being. Breat'ing masks are available in tee gift shop."

"Uh, thanks." I pointed to the mask I was wearing. "But we're already equipped." Although Alt Bauernhof's atmosphere has a respectable oxygen content, it also has more carbon dioxide and hydrogen sulfide than is healthy, not to mention what Macdonalds smell like.

Clearly annoyed that I was screwing with his memorized lines, he glowered at me and hitched up his sagging trousers with a free hand. "You will report to office 512 to arrange for off-loading of cargo. You will be escorted to office 512."

"Thank you," Catarina said smoothly, tucking her arm firmly in mine and moving me along smartly before he lost either his temper or his pants.

Office 512 sent us to office 845. Office 845 sent us to office 653, which lingered over our bills of lading before finally stamping them and sending us to office 513 for payment. As Catarina had expected, the Macdonalds were in a hurry to get the stuff and had decided to cut most of the usual red tape.

As we headed for office 513 I noticed three Macdonalds in wigs, sunglasses, and silver spandex waiting for their guitars to come in. "Elvis must be turning over in his grave."

"Oh, no, sir," Bunkie rejoined, "the Scribbs Institute estimates that Elvis turning over in his grave would register 5.9 on the Richter scale, and no such disturbance has been reported."

"Thank you, Bunkie."

Predictably, the boys in office 513 tried to stiff us on the money they owed by substituting payment in local currency for payment in real money. Since Macdonald currency isn't worth spit off Alt Bauernhof, and probably isn't worth spit *on* Alt Bauernhof, this was not an acceptable substitute. I let Bunkie negotiate, and we finally compromised on payment of half the balance in commodities, half in local currency, and waiver of all import taxes and port, exchange, and handling fees, which is pretty much what I expected.

Being unduly burdened with local currency that we would have to spend during our stay or use for toilet paper on the trip home, an impulse struck me—it felt like

Catarina's left elbow—and I dropped a wad of cash into the soup bowl in front of a Macdonald seated with a white bandage over his eyes and what looked like a begging license pinned to his head covering. "There you go, old codger."

His Jacobson's organs quivered, and he reached into the basket to finger the cash. "You are most gracious, effendi."

"Your English is pretty darn good," I blurted out.

"How much wood could a woodchuck chuck if a woodchuck could chuck wood? One learns to speak passable English if one wishes to work t'is corner, effendi. It is not impossible."

Bunkie nodded agreement. "Sir, with practice, Macdonalds can utter voiced bilabial nasals without nasal passages, and voiced and voiceless palato-alveolar affricates without an alveolar ridge. That's pretty impressive."

"That's 'm,' 'j,' and 'ch,' " Catarina announced, in case inquiring minds wanted to know.

"In fact," Bunkie concluded, "the only thing Macdonalds have trouble with are voiced and voiceless dental fricatives and, of course, German vowel sounds."

"Thank you, Bunkie."

Bunkie executed a crisp salute. "You're welcome, sir."

The blindfolded Macdonald touched his head to the floor. "I am honored by your presence and cash, effendi."

"Uh, I'm Ken MacKay. Pleased to meet you, honored."

Catarina stopped leafing through our messages and raised one eyebrow. Some days, I'm fractionally slow on the update. Some people claim those days are Sunday through Saturday, inclusive.

"I am Wipo." The blind Macdonald touched his head to the floor. "But you are tee famed Ken MacKay! It was foretold you would come."

"By who, er, by whom?"

"By tee men who make up shipping schedules. T'ey speak to each ot'er in tee halls."

"Oh," I said, moderately deflated.

Bunkie looked back toward the six Macdonalds who were attempting to look casual as they followed us from office to office.

"Wipo," I said, "you wouldn't happen to know who these guys work for, do you?"

"Sorry. Not all of tee various security agencies confide in me."

"Ah, thanks," I stammered. As we headed back to the ship followed by our escort, I asked Catarina, "What's our next move?"

"We need to get dressed." She waved one of our messages. "We have a party to attend dirtside."

A horrible thought struck me. "Oh, my God. We're going to have to give our crew shore leave while we're here."

Spacers traditionally let off steam dirtside, and the steam my bunch generated could power oceangoing vessels. Rosalee shed her inhibitions after the *Scupper* changed owners, and Harry had none to begin with, so the two of them had approximately the same impact on a town as Attila and his Huns. While most of the places we visited took this sort of thing in stride, I had a feeling the Macdonalds might get a little upset.

Catarina looked up into the artificial lighting. "You're right, but there's no way around it—it's in their contracts, and it'll look strange to the Macdonalds if we don't let them go."

Bunkie patted me on the wrist. "Be brave, sir."

I looked at her. "Uh, Bunkie, would you consider—"

She shook her head. "No, sir. Somebody needs to supervise the Macdonalds unloading the cargo, so I'm going to stay up here where it's safe."

"All right," I sighed, and I heard Catarina mutter something that might have been a prayer.

After we got back, Clyde volunteered to help Bunkie watch the ship. I gathered the liberty party on the bridge to read them the riot act. Pulling the prybar out of Rosalee's pocket, I banged the deck plates. "All right. Everybody listen up."

An expectant hush fell over my merry band of Visigoths. I've noticed that holding a blunt instrument in a suggestive manner is the best way to appeal to my crew's better nature.

"First things first, gang. No riots. None."

"Not even a little one?" Rosalee wheedled. Strangers often chat with her on the street, probably on the theory that if they don't, she might attack.

"Not even an itsy-bitsy, little one," Catarina said firmly.

"That brings me to the subject of cops—no picking fights with the cops." I folded my arms. "This is not a Confederation planet. If you so much as look at a cop cross-eyed, they'll throw you in the slammer."

"It'll take about twelve of the oily little toads," Harry muttered under his breath.

"Don't even think about it," Catarina admonished him sternly. "They'll shoot you, and they'll send us a bill for the ammunition."

"What a bunch of weenies," Wyma Jean said.

I banged the deck plates again with my borrowed prybar. "That brings us to the next item. No insulting language. Do not refer to the locals as 'oily toads' or 'greasers,' and avoid singing songs that they might find offensive. There's one song the Macdonalds are particularly sensitive about, and singing it is a felony offense. Even saying 'E-I-E-I-O' is enough to land your tail in jail. So let's not."

"Bunch of party poopers," Rosalee muttered.

"One moment," Catarina interrupted. "Harry, are you packing?"

Harry owns a 12mm Osoro, the kind of weapon that almost qualifies as a handgun but can do double duty as antiaircraft artillery and, if you're as big as Harry, you can almost conceal it. "Yes, ma'am," Harry admitted.

"Sorry, Harry. It stays, or you do."

"Aw, come on, if I leave it, I'll practically be unarmed down there!"

She smiled. "That's the idea."

Harry solemnly handed it over to Clyde.

"Think of yourselves as guests here. Pretend you like these people. Make friends," I said.

"And don't get caught," Catarina added.

On that high note we trooped off to the commuter terminal. Like most planets with a real space station, Alt Bauernhof ran regular shuttles from the station to the surface, and Bunkie had booked us seats.

"Don't you worry about a thing while you're at that party, Ken," Harry assured me as we watched the station recede on the overhead vision screen, "we're going to do cultural stuff."

Minnie and Mickey nodded their heads up and down in unison, which confirmed my worst fears.

On the viewscreen a small rocket gracefully leaped away from the space station. Descending, it reached an appropriate orbit over the planet, where it unfolded into a dazzling display of multicolored light which hung in space spelling out its message in a cursive script.

"I'm not sure," I said, studying the flowing Macdonald lettering. "It's either for antacid or tooth powder."

When the shuttle grounded, Catarina and I picked up our baggage and watched our happy henchmen hop into an animal-drawn taxi and speed away, in a manner of speaking, into the sunset.

A fresh set of shadows nonchalantly took up positions, watching us. "You know, I'm beginning to think that you-know-who didn't think through all of the angles on sending us here."

Catarina shook her head. "I'm afraid she did."

I shuddered. "Well, what's the an-play for onight-tay?"

"First, let's stop at the embassy and make sure we have rooms." Alt Bauernhof didn't have much of a tourist trade, and the Confederation Embassy was the only place on the planet that maintained an Earthlike atmosphere and served human meals.

Catarina flagged down a taxi, a ground car this time, and showed the driver the address for the embassy. As the driver whipped across two lanes of traffic to make a left-hand turn the wrong way up a one-way street, I asked him, "Do you speak English?"

"New York!" he said, waggling his tongue.

Twenty minutes later, after we made him pull over, we figured out that he couldn't speak English *or* Sklo'kotax.

I asked Catarina, "Do you think—no, forget the question. He couldn't have."

"New York!" he said, waggling his tongue.

Eschewing further discussion, Catarina got out and flagged down the Secret Police who were surreptitiously following us. "We need a lift to the Confederation Embassy," she explained, opening the door and climbing in.

The two operatives in the car looked at each other.

Catarina added, "If you get us there in ten minutes, we won't tell your boss how much we appreciate your assistance."

Cop Number One looked at Cop Number Two, who lolled his head helplessly and moved us out of there at a high rate of speed.

The traffic was light, so we zipped along, passing street vendors who cheerfully waved fingers and other appendages, and badly whitewashed buildings that suggested the Macdonalds stressed functionality over aesthetics. The architectural style was half-baked, and so were the mud bricks. The combination made the downtown edifices resemble a collection of diseased horse droppings.

"Local building style, or did someone visit Washington during the pigeon season?" I inquired.

"It is tee unquenchable desire of tee common people to avoid any foreign influences," Cop Number Two said awkwardly as we passed one enterprising citizen with a White Sox baseball cap on his pointy little head.

We pulled up in front of the Confederation Embassy with two minutes to spare, and our secret policemen blew bubbles of relief.

"We appreciate this very much," Catarina said, peeling off a few bills from my wad. "Do you accept gratuities?"

"Of course not!" the driver said indignantly, reaching for the cash.

Catarina winked at me. "We should be back in about half an hour."

As they drove away I asked her, "Is this wise?"

"Would you rather chance the cabs?" She tucked her arm in mine. "Come on."

The Marine guards at the gate saluted and passed us through the pressure doors to a reception room decorated in a charming mixture of middle Versailles and early motel. The second secretary, a portly man with a black toothbrush mustache and the turtle-in-shell look you associate with career diplomats, was waiting for us. Rising from behind his desk, he greeted us without any evident signs of warmth. "I am Second Secretary Mushtaq Rizvi. I bid you welcome to Klo'klotixa." He glanced at his watch. "I have asked the third military attaché to be present for this discussion."

He gave us wristband Sklo'kotax-English dictionaries so we would know useful phrases in the local language, like "Where is the rest room?" and "Would you please stop torturing me?" and a moment later the third attaché walked in.

Catarina's eyes lit up. "Why, it's Mailboat Bobby Stemm. So this is where Lydia parked you. How nice to see you!" she said with absolutely transparent insincerity.

Bobby Stemm hunched his shoulders, looking slightly less than pleased to see us again.

Bobby had reached Schuyler's World on a mailship a few days before Prince Genghis's invading Rodent hordes showed up. On arrival he tried to order us to surrender to Genghis's less than tender mercy on the theory that giving up would embarrass the navy less than getting ourselves blown away. Although Bobby's golden profile belongs on a recruiting poster, it was not his finest hour. He ended up wearing the proverbial egg-yolk mascara after we whipped Genghis. The navy being somewhat sensitive about its image, after Bobby was depicted as cowering under a couch in the movie loosely based on our exploits, his career took a sharp nosedive.

He said, with obvious trepidation, "With the second military attaché indisposed, Secretary Rizvi asked me to be present."

"Indisposed. Irate husband?" Catarina inquired sweetly.

Bobby unbent slightly. "Well, yes. Fortunately, a terrible shot."

"It's nice to see that attaché duty hasn't changed."

Bobby reached over and shook my hand gingerly. "Good to see you again, MacKay. I understand you're a vampire, too. How does one catch McLendon's Syndrome?"

I gave him a toothy grin. "Shaking hands works for me."

Bobby yanked his hand back, and Catarina leaned over the desk. "Bobby, if we're going to be working together, I should mention that I had them backdate my promotion to lieutenant commander to be absolutely certain that I would be senior to you. Got that?"

"Yes, ma'am." Stemm nodded his head up and down like a puppet.

"Lieutenant Commander Stemm has informed me that you are here at the request of Navy Intelligence," Rizvi said sternly. "I must insist on being kept apprised of your activities. Negotiations between the Foreign Office and the Klo'klotixa government are at a delicate stage, and Ambassador Meisenhelder has instructed me to avoid anything which might upset them."

Catarina smiled crookedly. "Of course."

Rizvi relaxed visibly. "Lieutenant Commander Stemm has also informed me that the two of you have McLendon's Syndrome. Ah—"

"Yes, we're vamps," Catarina said cheerfully, tapping her sunglasses. "But there's absolutely nothing to worry about unless someone gets us upset and unsettles our endocrine balances."

Under certain circumstances, meaning when our endocrine balances get mucked up, vampires can sometimes perform incredible feats of hysterical strength. Catarina proceeded to tell them how on Schuyler's World I came out of a coma to beat an assassin half to death with a pillow, bend her pistol in half, and tear a hospital apart looking for chocolate chip cookies.

"We will try to ensure that you are properly taken care of." Rizvi wiped his forehead. "The ambassador is, however, concerned about the level of interest the Klo'klotixa government is taking in the so-called 'Vampire Master Race Theory.' "

"I trust the ambassador has taken pains to assure them that there is no truth to the theory whatsoever," Catarina said.

"Naturally the ambassador did so, in the firmest possible language," Rizvi said stiffly.

"That must have impressed the heck out of them," I commented. A second or two later I felt a sharp, stabbing pain in my ankle.

Rizvi coughed judiciously. "You might also find it

interesting that a Ms. Gwen Shurie has accepted an offer of employment from the Klo'klotixa government and is expected to arrive from Earth shortly. Captain MacKay, I understand that you know her."

"Not true!" I protested. "Ask anyone! If I knew her would I have married her?" As long as Gwen is twenty or thirty light-years away, she's one of my favorite people. I'm not quite as fond of her when she's on the same planet.

Catarina interrupted. "Ken's ex-wife is an advertising executive. Why would the Macdonalds hire her?"

"In opinion polls, Confederation citizens rank this planet's inhabitants just above reporters, politicians, and child molesters, and the government is interested in sprucing up its public image," Stemm said. "However, the timing of this is suspicious given their intense interest in the so-called Vampire Master Race Theory."

"She's suing me," I groaned.

"Hmmm," Rizvi said, licking his lips. "Ahhhh."

"It's not what you think. She was working for one of the big firms, and after we whipped the Rodent Navy and ended up in the newspapers, she bragged about the connection to her clients."

"I can see that her clients might have thought her obtuse for severing the connection prior to your becoming famous," Rizvi reflected.

I shook my head. "No, they had better reasons for thinking she's dippy."

Catarina cleared her throat.

"Oh, yeah. Where was I? Anyway, after the news leaked that I was a vamp, the kimchee hit the fan. She lost a couple of big accounts, her agency fired her, she sued them, they countersued, and then *both* sides sued me on the legal theory that I intentionally inflicted emotional distress by continuing to be alive."

Noticing the puzzled looks on Rizvi's and Stemm's faces, Catarina explained, "Gwen's home of record is in California."

California law tends to be a little weird. The California courts recently garnered notoriety for awarding split decisions where both sides in a lawsuit paid damages to each other. It gave new meaning to the phrase "equal protection under the law," and it worked about the way you'd expect.

"Anyway," I said glumly, "I'm trying to stay a jump ahead of her process servers. Between Gwen and the people who are trying to sue me over stuff that happened on Schuyler's World, I expect I'll be in court for as long as I live."

"Or longer," Catarina observed.

Rizvi folded his hands primly. "Well, hopefully you'll restrain your litigious instincts while you're here on Alt Bauernhof, Mr. MacKay."

I realized that he was making a joke when Mailboat Bobby started chuckling dutifully. After Bobby concluded his spontaneous outburst of hysterical mirth, Rizvi continued, "As part of our standard in-briefing procedures, I must caution you and your crew members to refrain from providing the inhabitants here with any books on the index of prohibited books. We have provided your computer with a complete listing, and you can simply key in titles to find out whether they are prohibited."

"What kind of books are on the index?" I asked.

Rizvi shifted his bulk uncomfortably. "Mainly works

of a religious, philosophical, political, or, ahem, fictional nature."

I scratched my head. "Does this mean no romance novels?"

Rizvi gave me a forbidding stare. "Mr. MacKay, the restrictions on destabilizing literature were originally instituted to prevent the mores of a primitive and pastoral people from being contaminated and overwhelmed by Confederation culture. Over the last half century, teams of psychologists brought in to study the situation have repeatedly advocated continuing this ban, due to the extreme literalism that imbues Klo'klotixag society and the violent competitiveness the Klo'klotixag manifest toward mankind."

I shuddered at the vision of Macdonalds competing with humans to write trashier romance novels.

"Moreover, it would be highly destabilizing to Con-federation-Klo'klotixag relations for the Confederation government to have to, er, admit to the practice at this late date."

"Ah, right." Having experienced the Bucky Beaver phenomenon first-hand on !Plixxi*, it was hard for me to disagree, although I suspect that most teams of psychologists would like to prohibit humans from reading works of a political, religious, philosophical, or fictional nature. "To ask a dumb question, why are the Macdonalds so competitive with humanity?"

Rizvi gazed up at the ceiling. "Please, Mr. MacKay. You really should refer to the natives here as the Klo'-klotixag after the principal extended clan grouping."

"Sure thing." I looked at Catarina.

"Would you two like to answer his question or should I?" Catarina asked in a sugary voice.

Stemm and Rizvi looked at each other and hesitated. Then Stemm said, "Well, the diplomatic service favors the so-called Freudian Theory."

"Does that mean they want to marry their mothers, or does that mean they resent the gratuitous uplifting the Contact boys gave them?" I queried.

"Although there is a certain animus toward the Contact/ Survey Corps, the Freudian Theory postulates a resentment based on certain physical disparities," Stemm discoursed. "It's, ah, somewhat personal, if you comprehend my meaning."

Obviously I didn't, so Catarina elaborated. "The Macdonalds are very humanlike in most respects."

I nodded.

"However, they're not humanlike in all respects. According to anthropologists, male Macdonalds muster double-headed penises about so big." She held up her ring finger and flexed it. "To add insult to injury, I understand they tend to fire their cannons in about ten seconds flat."

A light dawned. "You're telling me that given full disclosure and complete freedom of choice, half the female population would emigrate," I said, dimly grasping the essential fact that the so-and-so's had little so-and-so's.

"Precisely," Catarina said.

Rizvi looked discomfited, but he added one stern warning. "Mr. MacKay, although the Klo'klotixag have adopted some Confederation customs, understand that this is merely a veneer over their essentially alien nature. They have embraced some of mankind's most despicable vices without acquiring even the thinnest patina of Terran civilization."

"Like Los Angeles, huh?"

Rizvi blinked. "I shall look forward to reading your reports." He consulted his watch. "Ambassador Meisenhelder sets certain hours in which he prefers not to be disturbed for routine business. In a minute or two we can get you in to meet him."

Before I could find out which soap operas he watched, Catarina asked pointedly, "How does the ambassador feel about the Klo'klotixag military buildup?"

Rizvi and Bobby Stemm exchanged looks. "Ah, Ambassador Meisenhelder believes strongly that the current militant phase is due in no small measure to the psychic insecurity these people have been subjected to in being exposed to Confederation civilization," Stemm said without enthusiasm.

"To counter this," Rizvi added, "the ambassador is passionately committed to making even the lowliest Klo'klotixag citizen feel that he or she is the ambassador's equal."

I had no doubt the ambassador could succeed. Before I could mention this, I felt another stabbing pain in my ankle. I decided to look impressed instead.

"Shall we go in now?" Rizvi said, apparently disinclined to continue the conversation.

Meisenhelder turned out to be a pleasant man with long hair to comb over his bald spot and a weak handshake to go with his weak chin. All in all, he seemed like a nice, sincere kind of bureaucrat, sort of a poor man's Heinrich Himmler.

He tapped his nose. "MacKay? MacKay? Now where have I heard that name before? Ah! Weren't you the author of that book *Coming Out of the Coffin*?"

Catarina shook her head and smiled sweetly. "Ghost-written."

The civil service has gone downhill since the courts ruled that the government can't discriminate against the mentally challenged in hiring and promotions, thus allowing nitwits who can't change a lightbulb the opportunity to climb the career ladder. Unfortunately, I quickly gathered that the Foreign Office makes sure its lightbulbs get changed by promoting its nitwits into policy-making positions. After the ambassador unburdened himself of a few pointless anecdotes, Rizvi cleared his throat. "Miss Lindquist, Mr. MacKay, Lieutenant Commander Stemm can show you to your rooms now."

"That's all right, we can find them." Catarina rose to her feet. "Thank you very much for your time, Mr. Ambassador."

When we got out into the hall, I said to her quietly, "I notice you never mentioned Dr. Blok."

"Dear me." Catarina tossed her head. "It must have slipped my mind."

"I also notice you promised Rizvi that you'd report our every move."

"I intend to give him a full report about two weeks after we leave orbit."

I stopped beside a room. "Two thirteen. This looks like one of ours."

The lock responded to her voice print, and she pushed the door open. "If we hurry, we can still catch the reception we've been invited to." She reached into her bag and pulled out a couple of cartons of Leopard Milk protein supplement and some celery. "We're not going to have time to eat, but I brought some things to tide us over."

I stared at my celery with distaste. "You could have brought food."

"Not to worry."

A moment later a member of the kitchen staff appeared, wheeling a cartload of chocolate chip cookies straight from the oven, with the compliments of Secretary Rizvi, who had been more worried by some of the things we had said than he let on.

I bit into one. "I take back what I said. You're a genius. Who are we receptioning with anyway?"

"The Klo'klotixa-Terra Friendship Society."

"The Secret Police, huh."

"Most likely the *Special* Secret Police, which means lousy hors d'oeuvres. Here, go ahead and get dressed." She brushed the crumbs from her hands and pulled a parcel out of her bag.

"What's this?" I peered inside. "Oh, no."

"When I struck the deal with Lydia to get you out of jail, she was adamant that you had to dress the part."

"But I hate black! And I don't know how to wear a cape," I said disgustedly, pawing through the stuff.

"She gave you a white shirt and tie to go with it." Catarina held up a frilly white thing.

"Great. That means I'll look like a penguin."

"Cheer up. I talked her out of rubber fangs." She handed me a small bottle from her bag. "Here, you can even splash on some of the cologne your aunt Alicia gave you for your high school graduation."

"I thought I threw this away. Aunt Alicia's cologne reminds me of embalming fluid."

"You did and it does. At least you won't have to pretend to turn yourself into a bat."

"That's good. The laws governing conservation of mass and energy being what they are, anybody who thinks that I can turn myself into a bat needs to lighten up on the incense." A horrible thought struck me. "What *do* I have to pretend to turn myself into?"

"A cat." She rummaged through her purse and handed me a ring.

"What's this, a star ranger secret decoder ring?"

"It's a miniature hologram projector. Apparently the Macdonalds have heard some of the stories about the cat hologram that Cheeves used to take over Genghis's flagship, and they're dead sure that it was one of us."

"If Lydia wanted magic tricks, she should have hired my ex-wife's accountant."

While I reluctantly climbed into my costume, Catarina switched to a black gown and silver jewelry, including her favorite piece, an enameled butterfly pin. Pausing to inspect my image in the mirror, I was forced to admit that the cape looked sharp.

Catarina whistled. "Not bad. There's hope for you yet."

"You're going to go to hell for that."

She shrugged. "Hope springs infernal."

I gave up. We marched out together dressed for the twentieth remake of *Bride of Dracula*. The Marine in the lobby almost dropped his rifle.

Outside the embassy it was just getting dark, which obviated our usual problems with sunburn. The Macdonalds have adopted most of the truly repellent aspects of Confederation civilization, including newspapers. I found a newsstand and was checking to see if anyone else had spotted Elvis's ghost shacking up with the shade of Dolly Parton when our two cops pulled up and did the Macdonald equivalent of a double take.

Catarina handed the driver the address for the reception, and after they showed us pictures of their kids, we burned synthetic rubber.

As we moved out of the slum district I spotted a pair of the golden arches which are the Confederation's major contribution to interstellar architecture. Public buildings and mud-brick hovels gave way to large and sturdy edifices built from stone and mortar, with narrow windows on the upper stories and picturesque little artificial moats.

"Trusting sorts, aren't they?" I commented. "Burglars here must use scaling ladders."

"Homeowner's insurance must be dirt cheap." Catarina rested her chin against the window. "I'd swear we just passed Rapunzel's hair."

"Please excuse," one of our cops interrupted, "we are about to arrived."

Catarina took the hint. "Ken, it's a nice night. I think we can walk from here." We spread some banknotes on the seat and got out so the cops could tail us the rest of the way.

The mansion the Friendship Society was using appeared indistinguishable from the others—apart from a few small touches to make humans feel at home, like the cement deer and plastic flamingos on the lawn and a phony satellite dish decked out in fake ivy. High up on the wall somebody had spray-painted the inscription SURRENDER DOROTHY.

"It looks like the Marines were here first," I whispered to Catarina. "I won't say anything about the decorations if you won't."

She winked. "Deer me. Of course not. Mum's the bird." She looked up at the massive iron door. "Do we ring the bell or fire siege cannon?"

Taking notice of our presence, the servants inside

raised the portcullis and ushered us into the hall, where a huge banner welcoming us in two languages had Catarina's name spelled right. As we entered, the president of the Friendship Society stood and made a speech in our honor, some of which I actually understood. Then the reception turned into a bunch of male Macdonalds in tartan ties looking bored and affected—my kind of party.

We split up and mingled. The crowd seemed to have a fair knowledge of Earth, and asked questions like, "Is tee Confederation planning to go to war wit' us?" and "What are tee Cubs' chances t'is season?" Someone pushed a scotch and water into my hand, and I tried a sip before I remembered that whiskey is basically distilled beer. Scots mature scotch in old sherry casks. Macdonalds apparently use old cement mixers.

After I emerged from the bathroom, a pair of Macdonalds steered me into a corner. The taller of the two, lean and saturnine with points to his ears, introduced himself as Warship-Captain Xhia and asked, "Is it true you are a vampire, Mr. MacKay?"

I nodded. "Yes, Miss Lindquist and I both suffer from McLendon's Syndrome."

The short one, whose name I didn't catch, jumped into the conversation. "How very interesting. What kind of coffin do you prefer?"

Xhia gave him a hip bump which shut him up temporarily. "You are a naval officer, Mr. MacKay."

"Just a reservist," I assured him hastily.

"Perhaps you would like to tour one of our warships. I would consider it an honor to arrange it for you."

Xhia had an unpleasant way of being pleasant. "It sounds like fun, but maybe not this trip. How about a rain check?"

"Another time," Xhia agreed cordially.

Shorty suddenly realized that it was his turn. "A rain check, is t'is similar to a reindeer?" He consulted his notes. "Have you ever had measles, and if so, how many?"

Xhia elbowed his compatriot aside. "Some of us, at least, are not unaware of your exploits, Mr. MacKay. Tell me, did you enjoy fighting tee Plixxi?"

Some things don't belong in polite conversation, assuming that was what I was engaged in. "I can take it or leave it."

Xhia craned his ears forward in earnest. "Life is struggle, Mr. MacKay, and battle its highest culmination. It is a spirit of struggle, a force which is infinitely refined into a myriad tiny impulses, which coalesces into a collective state of mind to form a whirlwind to uproot fortresses, palaces, empires, and confederations. Where, as in nature, t'ere is no law, no judge, conflict cannot be resolved by reason and all must accept a convention t'at victory will determine who is right. In tee presence of vast forces of history which mortal beings cannot comprehend or judge, mere reason must retreat and battle must enforce its sway. Only a being who is prepared to accept tee crimes necessary for success, who understands tee irrational forces, can comprehend t'at good and bad are mixed, life and death confounded, creation and destruction inseparable, and reality and illusion inextricably entangled. It is survival of tee fittest, and it is tee fittest who are inspired to grow and extend beyond all boundaries of imagination."

His eyes seemed to glow with the intensity of reflected light, which, because Macdonalds have a reflective tapetum in the back of the retina, was exactly what they were doing.

I said hurriedly, "Is there a water fountain here somewhere—"

Xhia lifted one lip to show me his teeth. "We understand one anot'er, Mr. MacKay. You are my twin, my opposite principle. Perhaps next time you engage in naval combat, we can ensure you have opposition of a higher caliber."

A footman tapped me on the shoulder and solemnly handed me a note that read, "Telephone call for you in the study," and I excused myself. On my way to the study I cut Catarina out of a crowd and showed it to her.

She glanced at the note. "It's probably Harry."

"How much is bail here, I wonder? Oh, well." I motioned to the impassive footman. "Lead on, Macduff."

He took me to a little room and gestured toward the phone. I stuffed money in his hand to get rid of him and switched the phone on.

Harry's smiling visage filled the screen. A small Macdonald woman was clinging tenaciously to his neck. "Hey, Ken! You wouldn't believe how much trouble I had finding a phone."

"Have you been arrested yet, and did you leave anyone tied up in the immediate vicinity?"

"Oh, no. Nothing like that! Things are going great," Harry assured me breezily.

"I don't hear any fire engines."

"Oh, no. You said Rosalee and I couldn't do that anymore. I even remembered what you said about borrowing armored fighting vehicles when the buses stop running."

"Where did you leave Wyma Jean, Rosalee, Minnie and Mickey; and who is that clinging to your neck?"

Harry waved a hand dismissively. "Oh, they're in a bar down the street. Or at least they were until the fight started. This here is Muffy. At least, that's what I call her—I can't make heads or tails out of this funny language. Remember you told us to make friends?" He used his free hand to squeeze her. "This is Ken, honey. Say hello to Ken."

She licked her eyebrows. " 'Ello."

"Muffy, is he sober?"

" 'Ello."

Harry nodded vigorously. "Isn't she cute, Ken? Can I keep her? Can I keep her?"

"Harry, it may have escaped your notice, but you already have a girlfriend."

"Oh, yeah. Right. That's a problem, isn't it?" Harry pondered this. "Well, Muffy wouldn't be a real girlfriend because she's a Macdonald, right?"

"Let's backtrack a moment—did you say something about a fight?"

"Oh, yeah. That. Did you know that Mickey's been practicing karate? At least it looks like karate. Anyway, the people around here cheat at pool—they use square tables, and they got all sorts of funny rules."

"Harry, let's stick to basics. Where did the fight start, how did it start, and how many casualties?"

Possibly misconstruing the question, Muffy made a passionate speech in her own language which would have sounded great on a piccolo. The dictionary caught part of it.

"Harry, does Muffy's father, the 'moo-yup,' know she's with you?" A "moo-yup" was apparently a high-ranking official.

Muffy's English may have been fragmentary, but she

made a vigorous thrusting gesture with the first two fingers of her left hand to convey what she thought her father could do about it.

"I don't think her father will mind," Harry said slowly, "and her husband neglects her, can you believe that?"

"Harry, listen to me—"

A loud commotion erupted in the background. "Oops, excuse me, Ken. We got to run. We'll call you back as soon as we get the chance!"

"Harry!" I said. The phone blanked out.

I spent a few minutes playing with it to see if I could get him back. Then I heard a little Macdonald voice behind me say, "Are you free, Mr. MacKay?"

"No, but I'm usually cheap. Who are you?"

"My name is Dr. Blok." It came out like "mbloqk." His English was stiff but understandable.

"Uh, pleased to meet you," I stammered.

Blok was an older Macdonald with green-gray age spots on his skin and a pronounced *aigrette*, a spiked fringe of reddish-orange bristles above the eyes. I compared him with the photograph Crenshaw had given us. He matched.

He tilted his head. "I like your human literature very much. My favorite poem is 'Tee Owl and tee Pussycat.' What precisely is an owl?"

"It's a bird. It flies around at night and eats rodents— er, mice. My favorite line from the poem is 'the cow jumped over the moon.' "

Blok twitched as if galvanized and clutched me by the arm. "Yes, tee poet juxtaposed tee little dog laughing and tee cow jumping," he said carefully. "It is an interesting effect."

I sighed. Crenshaw must stay awake nights thinking

up silly lines for agents to use to identify each other. "Pea green is my favorite color."

"I prefer blue myself." He carefully pulled out a notepad and scribbled on a sheet of paper, "Act normally. They are listening!"

I can't act very well, so I produced a voice scrambler. "Now we can talk."

"I presume you are here to take me off tee planet before tee Secret Police discover t'at I have been providing information to tee Confederation."

"Nice guess."

"I have not yet determined t'at it is completely appropriate for me to leave."

We had a problem. "Ah, why not?"

Blok slumped down on a lumpy divan. "As suspicion of me increases, I find myself beset by a moral dilemma, Mr. MacKay. Are you perhaps familiar with tee so-called 'Vampire Master Race T'eory'? My contacts in tee Special Secret Police have given me documents which cause me to believe it is true." He looked at me. "Your name figured prominently."

I squeezed my eyes shut.

"Our rulers—what is the word?" He snapped his wrist, which was apparently the Macdonald equivalent of a finger snap.

I passed my dictionary across, and he warbled a word into it. The dictionary obediently translated the word as "ephors."

"Tee ephors are greatly concerned as am I. While I believe t'at humans are peacefully intentioned—"

"You haven't met my crew."

"—who knows if vampires are peacefully intentioned and what evil lurks in a vampire's heart? What are tee motives of creatures who live eternally? Am I doing what is in tee best interests of my people? So I ponder, and miraculously, two vampires appear. But is t'is truly a miracle?"

"Never underestimate the power of coincidence," I said awkwardly, thinking that Lydia had truly outsmarted herself this time. Catarina, who is very devout in her own way, has convinced me that there really is a God with a truly divine sense of humor, and I think He's out to get me. "Also, let me assure you that some of the things you may have heard about vampires were greatly exaggerated."

Blok rose and began pacing the floor with his head down and his hands folded behind him. "My people need many t'ings: reduction of our military forces, channeling of our energies into the ways of peace, reform of our healt' care system—yet if vampires secretly rule tee Confederation, dare I to trust you?" He looked at me sternly. "I have observed tee human beings sent here, and it disturbs me, Mr. MacKay. I have not been able to dismiss from my mind tee horrendous fear t'at vampires may be secretly breeding humans to be stupid, vapid creatures."

"You mean like cocker spaniels?"

"You represent danger, Mr. MacKay, and you feast upon blood. Blood is power. Hunters drink blood from animals t'ey kill, to absorb courage and life force from t'at which t'ey have vanquished." Blok resumed pacing. "I ask myself what dread forces you may summon and muster."

Catarina has been teaching me deep breathing exercises to help me remain calm in situations like this, but they didn't seem to be working. "Look, let me make this simple. There is no Vampire Master Race. Vampires do not control the Confederation. And I don't drink blood."

"Tee risks are too great for me to accept your unsupported statement," Blok said mournfully. "However fair your words, it may be t'ey merely cloak tee evil you represent in a mask of illusion. I must have proof. Forgive me, but I must be absolutely certain what I am doing is correct." He snapped the voice scrambler off and bawled, "Guards!"

Three Special Secret Policemen appeared in the room a few seconds later.

Blok said something in Sklo'kotax and then repeated it in English, presumably for my benefit. "T'is human has attempted to bribe me to betray our planet."

The officer in charge stiffened. "Mr. MacKay, you are under arrest," he said in charmingly accented English while pointing his gun at my midriff. "Do not move or your intestines will gently fall like midsummer dew upon tee carpet."

Dr. Blok also pulled a gun. "Please do not resist. My gun is loaded with silver bullets."

Another Macdonald stepped in, dressed in a plain gray uniform. The guards who weren't busy pointing guns at me immediately abased themselves.

"Mr. MacKay, we meet again," he said drolly. It took me a minute or two to recognize my blind beggar from the space station.

He turned to Blok and said something in Sklo'kotax which caused Blok's gill openings to ripple. Blok left the room.

I tried to ignore the various weapons pointed in my direction. "Ah, hello there, Wipo."

He showed his teeth and hung his tongue in what was

intended to be an imitation of a smile. "I was quite
annoyed when you penetrated my remarkable disguise so
easily. Still, flinging money to me was a superb gesture
of disdain."

This was shaping up as one of those days when I
should have read my horoscope. "Does this mean that
you won't believe me when I tell you that I didn't try to
bribe Blok?"

"Oh, but I do believe you, Mr. MacKay. Tee good
doctor has become irrational on tee subject of vampires."

"Does that mean you're going to let me go?"

"In time, perhaps. But, you see, Dr. Blok's accusation
gives us a perfect excuse to detain and question you.
Quite a coup for me, actually."

Since the issue had come up, I asked, "This is a touchy
subject, but how will you know if I'm telling the truth?"

"Oh, we have our ways, Mr. MacKay. You may even
enjoy tee experience."

After he let me leave a note telling Catarina I'd met
Blok and not to wait up, his men drove me to Special
Secret Police headquarters, which turned out to be your
typical dull, featureless, underground fortress of steel and
concrete.

"Quite a place you have here," I commented. "It
reminds of the DMV back home."

"Bare concrete is so reassuring to tee eye," Wipo
quipped. "How do you like our sign, 'Abandon hope all
you who enter here'?"

"Yup, it's the DMV."

"I understand you play bridge."

"On occasion."

"An exquisite game. I often play when my duties
permit." In the dim light his eyes glowed. "Perhaps we

will have time to play a few hands. Do you know, I once had a partner who declared on weak red suits? I eventually had him shot, of course."

He led me downstairs to the lower dungeon level, where he pointed to a square hole in the floor and a ladder leading down. "Our VIP suite. Tee ladder is mounted on a cantilever to allow us to pull it up after you descend, and tee trapdoor has a one-way mirror to enable us to observe your movements."

I peered down the hole and saw a sleeping pallet in one corner, a sink and Turkish toilet in another, and dust bunnies everywhere. "I'd hate to see the two-star accommodations."

Wipo smiled. "In you go!"

In I went. Several hours later six or seven guards prodded me awake. "It is time. Take off your clothing. Come with us," one of them said.

"This is how people catch colds," I mumbled. "Can I keep my shorts?"

The guards looked at each other and apparently decided that was all right. They took me down the corridor to a small room, strapped me to a chair, and took up positions on either side.

While I waited for the whips and rubber hoses to appear, I snarled, "All right, coppers, you got me, but you'll never make me talk!"

Privately, I decided to give Catarina time to make it back to the ship before spilling my guts, and to faint a lot if the circumstances warranted.

A cheery voice behind me said, "How melodramatic!" A perky little female Macdonald with large oval eyes and a slightly silver cast to her skin leaned over my left shoulder. "Hello, Mr. MacKay. May I call you Ken?"

She was wearing a flimsy pink robe and had the kind of personality you associate with aerobics instructors, which aroused my suspicions. "I don't believe we've been introduced."

"My name is Xuexue," she trilled. "But you may call me 'Trixie.' "

For some reason, this did not sound promising. "Ah, excuse me for not getting up."

She held her hand to her mouth and tittered, "I quite understand." Then she turned to the officer in charge. "Please leave us."

The officer bowed, and he and the guards departed. Gracefully hopping up on my lap, she tapped me on the nose. "T'ey would just be in tee way."

"Now that they're gone, you wouldn't consider turning me loose as a gesture of universal galactic friendship?"

"No." She pushed a button on the control panel beside the chair, which stretched me out flat. Then she planted an elbow in the middle of my chest and leaned over to contemplate my predicament. "How are you feeling?"

"Like the cockroach at a chicken dance, although I can think of several people who would pay serious money to switch places with me right now. You wouldn't, by chance, have some extra clothes that one of the two of us could wear, would you?"

"Sorry."

"Your English is very good."

" 'Tee Spain, in main, stays plainly in tee rain.' "

"To what do I owe the pleasure of your company?"

"I am to obtain information from you." She stretched and switched elbows. "You see, I read minds."

I tried to look impressed. "I can't say that I've ever

met a mind reader before. I wouldn't think there would be much call for your specialty. Most of the folks I run into don't have a heck of a lot to read."

"Tee Special Secret Police have use for me, unfortunately. It makes me dangerous. And so I will be married off as secondary wife to some minor nobleman to preserve my genes and will spend my days and nights eating kumquats and growing fat." She tittered. "I was kidding about tee kumquats."

I got the impression that even by admittedly lax local standards, she was one sick puppy.

She tweaked my nose. "Naughty, naughty! Now you are t'inking I am crazy."

"Would you watch where you're putting your other hand—thank you!—and, ah, how does this mind-reading thing work?"

"Are you sure you want to know?" she asked coyly.

"Absolutely."

"It's something only females can do."

"That figures."

"We can only read men's minds."

"That also figures."

She stroked my brow. "Our lateral line can detect slight changes in bioelectrical fields. By interpreting t'ese changes and scenting pheromones, t'ose of us who possess tee gift can understand t'oughts."

"And some of you can do this with humans?"

"Just little me," she said proudly.

"Do you have to sit in my lap?"

Little Miss Mental Health and Hygiene giggled and crooned, "The bioelectrical currents are *so* weak. I have to be very, very close to detect t'em. Poor little vampire, don't you want to bite my neck?"

"To be truthful, no."

She sat up and clapped her hands together. "Well, we will just have to t'ink of somet'ing else fun to do!" She snapped the waistband on my underpants. "And what are t'ese cute little animals on your clot'ing?"

"Those are baby bunnies, and I would rather not discuss them." I crossed my eyes. "While I'm thinking of it, what do Wipo's boys have me tied up with?"

"It is called *kwisti*. It is made from a plant."

One of the real pleasures in being a vamp is the allergies, which included, as I was rapidly beginning to discover, *kwisti* fiber. It was causing me to break out in a body rash. I sneezed, and Trixie delicately wiped my nose.

"I guess the first question you'll want to ask is whether I'm a secret agent," I said, thinking the words "NO. NO. NO."

She tittered again. "Don't be silly. We already know t'at." She pulled a lever on the control panel beside the chair so that I could listen to a taped recording of Bobby Stemm's voice saying, "I just can't believe that the Powers That Be would send someone as inept as MacKay to spy on the greasers."

"We have his office beetled," she announced triumphantly.

"You mean bugged."

"Oh. Yes. Bugged. How cute." She tittered again, which was becoming monotonous. "Now let us see what our silly security people want to know from you. Here is a nice question: Are you working for Navy Intelligence?"

"No!"

"T'at means yes! T'is is so much fun. Next, does your

mission here have anyt'ing to do wit' warships? Anot'er yes! Of course it does! Oh, you are squirming so!"

"This stupid rope itches like crazy."

The next half-dozen questions on her list were about Earth's politics, which required yes or no answers. She ran through them impersonally and came up with one yes, one no, and a bunch of darned-if-I-knows.

"Here are some vampire questions! Do you drink blood?"

"No."

She gave me a startled look, but wrote it down anyway. "How long do vampires live?"

"That's a silly question. Even people who write life insurance sometimes miscalculate how long someone will live, and I'm making a mental note to add to my policy."

"Have you used names other t'an Ken MacKay?"

"No," I said hastily. Until I was five, my great-aunts used to call me things like "Binky." Apparently, my subconscious gave me away.

"Ha!" she said.

Her questions were beginning to get a little too close to sensitive subjects for comfort, and so was her left hand, so I tried thinking about mathematical tables.

"How many names have— Ah! Naughty, naughty! You're not concentrating!" She pinched me in a rather private place.

"Excuse me. Do you have to do that?"

"Aren't you getting your money's worth, sailor?" she coaxed slyly. "Come tell Auntie Trixie what you are t'inking."

I was thinking that if I managed to get out of this in one piece, Catarina was going to tease me about it unmercifully for months. Or years. Or longer. "Ah, how did a nice girl like you get mixed up in a racket like this?"

"Oh, but I'm a very naughty girl. It is kind of fun, really. Males have such dirty minds! Poor little vampire, would you like to take me home wit' you?"

To tell the truth, I was beginning to feel a little sorry for her. "Well, if you ever want to get out of here, we have a spare bunk down in Stores."

Something about my reaction surprised her. Her eyes slitted. "You just want me to read minds for you!"

"Uh, no." Unfortunately, I seem to have acquired a good dose of religion from Catarina, which manifests itself at inopportune moments. "Your technique is a little, ah, indecorous, and besides, most of the folks we dicker with have enough trouble not gyping themselves. Can you cook?"

"T'en you just want me for my body!"

I was beginning to figure out why mind-reading never caught on with human beings. It's extremely difficult to carry on intersexual communications if you have to stick to the whole truth and nothing but the truth. "Well, no. There's my partner Catarina to consider. One weird relationship I can deal with, but two would be pushing it."

"But you would still risk yourself to help me escape?"

"Well, yeah, I suppose, but you know, I'm beginning to think that this stuff about rescuing damsels in distress isn't all it's cracked up to be."

I was also seeing two of her and beginning to fade in and out of the conversation as my glands began pumping things into my system to deal with my allergic reaction to the stupid rope.

The last thing I heard her say was, "Poor little vamp."

I woke up in a double bed. Catarina was sitting at the far end. "Are you alive yet?"

I looked around the room, which had chartreuse wallpaper. "If this is heaven, I want my money back."

"Ah, you are awakened, Mr. MacKay." A little Oriental guy in a white coat was standing next to Catarina with his hands folded. "I am Dr. Ye, the embassy primary care physician. After conferring, Miss Lindquist and I have decided to have you fixed."

I blinked my eyes rapidly a few times. "Excuse me, but I thought that was something people did to unruly house pets."

"I meant restored to health." Ye turned on his heel and left.

I asked Catarina, "Why are you here, and where is here anyway?"

"The Special Secret Police have seized our ship. We're in the embassy. Your friend, Supreme Agent Wipo, shipped you here after I convinced him that you'd probably croak without better medical attention than he could provide." She gestured toward the little refrigerator in the corner. "He left a bottle of the local *vin ordinaire* to show that there's no hard feelings on his part, but you're out on loan, so to speak. The ambassador has promised to return you to Macdonald custody as soon as you're well enough to travel."

"I suddenly feel very, very sick. It may be months."

She coughed delicately. "Gwen has been in here three times to see you."

"Nothing like a miraculous recovery. Suddenly, I feel great." I ran my fingers over the welts on my arms. "What was the good doctor in a snit about?"

"You'll be up and about in another day, which touches on a problem he alluded to. Technically, you're not on the government payroll, and he isn't authorized to accept your health insurance."

"I ought to call Lydia and make her cough up enough funny money to cover it." I reflected for a second or two. "Of course, that might also be hazardous to my health."

"Bunkie and I worked out a deal. To ask a very intimate question, how do you feel about donating your body to science after you're finished using it?"

"Nothing like having a doctor who won't get paid off if I get well."

"Oh, nothing that crude. Currently, the betting line is two-to-one against your surviving more than a week, but I understand that Mickey managed to get about a thousand down at four-to-one." She handed me a tray with a fruit plate and several servings of chocolate mousse. "Here, eat something. Doctor's orders."

"Thanks," I said, opting for dessert first. "This isn't what the embassy dining room is serving, is it?"

"No, they're serving ethnic food tonight—meat loaf à la Des Moines, with green beans Dubuque and instant mashed potatoes. I'm told the ambassador has declared next week health food week, so we'd better lay in a stock of provisions."

I repressed yet another shudder. "How's our crew?" I asked between mouthfuls.

"Bunkie and Clyde came down when the Macdonalds took the *Scupper* into custody. I assigned Bunkie to keep an eye on Mickey and Minnie, who are like two cute little sticks of dynamite. Rosalee and Harry have both disappeared, leaving behind a swath of destruction. Harry left Wyma Jean with the impression that we dispatched him on a secret mission, so she's not real happy with us. I got your note. So why did Dr. Blok finger you?"

I quickly outlined our conversation. "So as near as I can tell, he's looking for proof that vampires have benign intentions. For the record, after meeting Blok, I think that Lydia ought to think about employing a better class of agent."

"I'm sure that she would agree," Catarina replied with a straight face. She shook her head. "How much did you tell Wipo?"

"Nothing about Blok. More than enough about other things. They know I'm an agent." I ran through Trixie's interrogation, omitting the low points. "If Blok knows about Trixie, his turning me in makes even less sense."

Catarina shut her eyes and pondered this. "Are you sure it was Bobby Stemm's voice you heard on Trixie's recording?"

"New England accent, weevily whine. Yeah, it was Bobby."

"And this Trixie—she can actually read your mind?"

"Like a book."

Catarina nodded solemnly. "I guess it made you see read when she made you an author you couldn't refuse."

I made small, growling noises in my throat.

"Think of it as a new chapter in your life. I meant to ask, were you wearing—"

"Yes. I happen to *like* bunnies."

"Here, I have something to show you." She passed across a thick stack of paper. "Take a look at these numbers."

"Sure." I scanned them briefly. "What are they?"

"Economic figures. Real data for a change. Credit here

is incredibly tight. What little there is the government is steering into heavy industry, but the output isn't reappearing in the civilian sector."

"That's great. What does it mean?"

"My guess is that it means that the Macdonalds are switching to a war economy and that their navy is going to be ready to challenge us sooner than we think. I've been looking at recent government appointments, and it looks like the war party is in the saddle. I'm guessing that a surprise attack on the Confederation is imminent."

"We have to get this information back to Lydia!" I said, hoping, of course, that she would say it was our duty to get it back as soon as possible.

"That's already been taken care of. Unfortunately, those numbers probably aren't enough to convince the analysts on Earth. We need Blok. My guess is that Trixie is one of his agents, and he turned you in so she could find out whether he could trust the vampires who he suspects of running the Confederation." She unwrapped a chocolate bar and split it with me while she mulled this over. "Did Trixie squeeze enough out of you?"

"I probably passed out a little too early in the proceedings."

"I'm the only other vamp they know of."

"From Trixie's comments, I gather that this mindreading stuff only works across genders. Do you mean I've got to go back and let Trixie pick my brain again?"

Catarina nodded, her mouth full.

"Why isn't it somebody else's turn to save the universe for a change? What was it that guy Nathan Hale said, 'I regret that I have but one life to give for my country.' "

"I think he emphasized different words."

"If Trixie picks my brain, they're going to know that we know they're planning to attack."

"It may spook them into attacking before they're ready. How does the saying go, 'Hasty strokes often go awry'?"

"Isn't that the third verse to 'Auld Lang Syne'?" I scratched my legs, which were still itching. "Darn it! And to top everything off, I have bites from whatever was crawling around that miserable hole they stuck me in. I thought this blood-sucking stuff was supposed to work the other way around."

"Your fluids probably poisoned whatever bit you." Catarina smiled lazily. "Just take things lice and easy."

I closed my eyes.

"Should I have said 'nice and fleasy'?" She leaned over and kissed me on the cheek. "First, get some rest. I'll look into what Bobby's been up to, and we'll play things by ear for a day or two."

A few minutes after she left, I heard a tentative rapping at my window. I tried to burrow underneath my pillow. A moment later the window came crashing down on the floor.

"Psst! Ken! Are you awake?"

"I am now," I groaned. "Harry, what are you doing out there?"

Harry climbed into the room over the wreckage of the window frame and dusted himself off. "I need to talk to you, Ken. You know, man-to-man, or man-to-vamp."

"You wouldn't happen to have an extra breathing mask on you?"

"Uh, right! Sure thing." He pulled one out of his pocket and handed it to me.

"I'm surprised we haven't heard any alarms. Normally,

about sixteen of them go on when you break into an embassy."

"Oh, I got Muffy to take care of it," Harry said proudly as he sat down on the end of the bed. "She's pretty good with that sort of thing." Muffy stuck her head up, chirruped, and disappeared.

"How's Wyma Jean?" I asked as my end of the bed tilted upward alarmingly.

Harry nodded assertively. "She's doing pretty well. She's been kind of peckish the last three or four days. I think she's worried about her pet snake."

I croaked, "Her pet *what*?"

"He's a Colombian boa. He's really cute. You should see him. We named him Frisky."

"I'll just bet you did." I swallowed hard. "I don't remember anybody asking me if they could bring a snake on board my ship."

"Well, after the cat split, we had to get her some kind of pet." Harry began moving his hands like a windmill. "And with the ship about to lift and with you in jail so we really couldn't talk to you about it, well—"

I reached out to slow down his left hand as it passed. "What does this snake eat?"

"Well, do you know that big bag marked 'linguine' in the back of the freezer that's full of frozen mice?"

I shut my eyes. "So you're telling me there's a pet snake aboard my ship."

"Well, we're pretty sure he's still there. I mean, he got loose, but it's not like he can walk off the ship or anything." After a moment of pregnant silence Harry leaned forward. "Could we talk about the snake later? I need help, Ken. I don't know who else to turn to."

I sighed. "Okay, Harry. Calm down. There's some

wine in the refrigerator. Why don't you pour yourself a glass and tell me about it."

"Yeah, that's a good idea." He took the bottle out. Not finding a corkscrew immediately handy, he absently used the side of the refrigerator to knock the neck off the bottle. He poured himself a glass, took a sip, and his face convulsed. "What is this stuff?"

"It's a local product." I took the bottle out of his hand and squinted at the label. "It says 'Genuine California White Zinfandel.' "

Harry dropped the glass and leaped away, forming a cross with his index fingers. "White Zin?" It came out like "White Death." "Do you know what kind of people drink White Zin?"

Although I knew Harry equated alcohol-free beer with hydrogen-free water, I didn't know he had wine fetishes. "Well, yes, but—"

"Ken, if people see me drinking White Zin, it's all over. They'll start thinking that I can't walk and chew gum at the same time."

"Harry, they already think that."

"I mean it's the end, Ken," Harry said hoarsely, shaking his head. "People catch me drinking this and I might as well buy a cat and register Democrat. You won't tell, will you? Promise me you won't tell!"

"I promise," I said soothingly. "Pour it down the sink and no one will ever know that zinfandel sullied your fair lips."

He poured the wine down the sink and glared at me. "Where did the Macdonalds get the idea of drinking this stuff?"

"Well, I guess the Contact boys taught them how to make it."

"God! What foul fiends in human form!" His eyes blazed. "Don't you see," he said eagerly, "it all fits. The fanaticism, the envy, the hatred the Macdonalds have for human beings—it's from drinking this! Ken, we can *save* these people!"

"I had no idea," I said. Then reality kicked in. "Wait a minute. No. No. No. Harry, you're overreacting. Are you seriously trying to tell me that the Macdonalds are upgrading themselves to become the scourge of the galaxy because they've been drinking cheap wine?"

Harry drew on his professional expertise. "White Zin makes for a *mean* drunk." He shook me by the arm to emphasize his point. "Have you ever heard of . . . *yuppies*?"

"Well, yes, but—"

"This is what they drink." He motioned across his chest. "Cross my heart and hope to die."

I coughed. "Maybe we can come back to this White Zin thing later. What did you want to talk to me about?"

"Well, it's about Muffy. I want to help her, Ken."

"Have you talked to Wyma Jean, your g-i-r-l-f-r-i-e-n-d, about this?"

"Well, no. She won't mind, will she?"

"Harry, I know Wyma Jean likes vegetable oil, but I don't think she's into threesomes."

Harry puffed his chest indignantly. "You don't understand. My relationship with Muffy is all business."

"Harry, I don't care if it's all business—whether you're paying Muffy or Muffy's paying you, Wyma Jean is still going to take a hacksaw to your genitals."

"It's not like that at all, Ken. Like, Muffy is a revolutionary, and I want to help her."

I sighed. "A revolutionary."

"Right!"

"And she wants to overthrow the government."

"Yeah."

I sighed again. "I liked it better when I thought you were screwing around with her."

"Well, that, too, but I want her revolution to succeed. That's why I need your help."

"Stop! Let's backtrack. I thought you said your relationship with Muffy was all business."

"Well, yeah. It's all business, but it's not *all* business," Harry responded, obviously perplexed by the question.

"All right. What is Muffy revolutionary about?"

"Well, I'm not exactly sure. Her English isn't so good. But I really want to help."

I buried my face in my hands. "All right. Exactly what do you want from me?"

"I'd like a leave of absence so I can help out, Ken."

"Done. The Macdonalds have impounded our ship, so we're going to have to delay our departure anyway. What else?"

"Uh, do you remember those blasting charges we keep for light salvage?"

"As I say, the Macdonalds have our ship, so you're welcome to take a few *if* you can figure out how."

"Thanks, Ken. You're a true friend." He pumped my hand up and down.

"Have you seen Rosalee?"

"Oh, she's around. Do you remember that big high-speed chase through the city yesterday?"

I buried my face in my hands again. "I don't want to hear about it."

There was a furtive tapping at what was left of the window.

"Oh, I've got to run. Muffy's waiting for me." Harry climbed through the window and waved. "Thanks, Ken. Thanks."

I opened my mouth and took a deep breath and found out that that was an exceedingly stupid thing to do even with a breathing mask on, so I called maintenance to come fix the window. The two guys who arrived came decked out in strings of garlic. Although I made it to the bathroom in time, it was a sobering reminder that there's still a lot of superstitious prejudice against vamps.

Catarina wasn't in her room, so I decided to wait in the embassy's Blue Parrot Lounge until they finished.

Because diplomats don't start drinking seriously until after teatime, the lounge was mostly empty. I found myself a corner booth, ordered up a lemon water, and leafed through a four-year-old magazine whose articles ranged from "32 Ways to a Better Butt" to "My Ten Worst Yeast Infections."

I was contemplating the many things seriously wrong with my life when I heard a female voice say, "Excuse me, but you look very familiar. Haven't we met somewhere?"

I frowned. Not only does that pickup line rank about fortieth on the all-time list, but it was one of my ex-wife's favorites. Of course, although the woman in question was now blonde in a hard, attractive way, she *was* my ex-wife. Out of all the gin joints in all of the towns on this world, she had to walk into mine. "Hi, Gwen."

"Oh, Ken! I almost didn't recognize you, you've gotten so pale." She sat down opposite me. "You need to take better care of yourself."

"Won't you sit down? You're looking—different."

"Isn't plastic surgery wonderful?" She leaned over,

touched her cheek against mine, and made a kissing noise. Then she pulled a tissue out of the satchel she carries as a purse and dabbed at my cheek. "Hold still." She took my jaw in her hand and tilted it from side to side to appraise her handiwork. "There! All better. I didn't get a Christmas card from you this year, but I'm sure that was just an oversight."

"Ah, right."

"Oh, Ken, you're so cute when you try to lie! But I'm shocked at the way you look! You need to get some sun."

"Vamps can't stand sun."

"Oh, that's right! I'd almost forgotten!" She pouted. "Seriously, Ken MacKay—I mean seriously—did you have to go and make yourself into a vampire?"

"Ah, nice dress you're wearing."

She laughed. "It's an original. It's my color, don't you think?" She winked. "I did some work for Alex Chris Fashion Designs, and they paid me in kind. I saved three hundred on my taxes."

I turned my head slightly so I wouldn't pick up glare from the sequins. "How's the advertising business these days?"

"Just fine, no thanks to you! Turning yourself into a vampire and then getting yourself in the news was a pretty loathsome trick, you have to admit. Why, you can't imagine the fast talking I had to do with the people at the country club." She smiled, grasped my hand playfully, and said in an earnest tone of voice, "But let's let bygones be bygones. How are you doing, Ken? How are you really doing?"

Over the last few years, I've come to realize that Gwen taught me many valuable lessons during the six months we were married. One was to ask questions like, "How is your last boyfriend, and are you a suspect?" While most people think of male-female relationships in terms of gladiators battling it out, I've always felt more like a Christian shaking hands with the lion just before they ring the bell.

"I've had *Rustam's Slipper* back in commission for about four months now. She's a good ship," I said cautiously.

"I've always understood how you felt about ships." She patted me on the arm. "It's a shame you can't bring that kind of feeling into your relationships with people, but I'm not bitter, I've come to accept it."

"Gwen, time out. One of the things I've always admired about you is your ability to lie like a cheap rug and make me feel guilty for catching you at it. Is there something else we could fight about?"

She laughed. "Oh, you charmer. I don't know why you feel you have to flatter me every time we meet."

"Uh, right." Advertising executives truly are a different breed. "How is your job here going?"

Her eyes glistened. "It's the opportunity of a lifetime. These people have a major-league image problem. I mean they're *amateurs* when it comes to molding public opinion!"

"But you can fix them up?"

"Piece of cake." She waved her hand negligently. "They have no idea here where to put their money to get exposure. Those tight uniforms and those cute little collars the boys wear—a couple of ads in the right magazines, and I could create a tourist industry overnight. And as for wanting to take over the universe, I mean why shouldn't they aspire to be on top of the heap? As I see it, all they need is a carefully run campaign that appeals to that have-not give-till-it-hurts instinct in people."

"I don't know. Their wanting to enslave humanity sounds like it would be tough to put across in a sixty-second spot."

"I think the public will buy into it if I work up the right theme and concept." She folded her hands. "It's a professional challenge—there has to be something about them I can play up. Macdonald babies are cute, aren't they?"

"I'm not really sure. As I understand it, the cartilage isn't set when they're born, so they come out like little gray slugs."

"Well, there's always the tried and true approach. I'll just have one of the agencies ship over some models in skimpy bathing suits for the shoot."

"Gwen! This isn't an election where you can put a two-hundred-dollar haircut on some slick hick and get him elected. There's a difference between selling soap and selling Hitler."

"Ken, that's the difference between an advertising professional and a lay person. You just don't have vision! Hitler—wasn't he the Hun with the cute mustache? Or am I thinking of Pancho Villa? Anyway, of course selling a politician is different from selling soap—your market demographics are nowhere near the same."

In the course of our many one-sided conversations, I had learned long ago that professional ethics for ad people largely consist of paying bar tabs regularly, so I dropped further discussion on the subject as unprofitable. "How are the people you're working for treating you?"

"No complaints. But they ask so many questions! They want to know about *everything*. It's such a relief to come back here to the embassy and talk to, well, you know, real people. Can you believe it—they even asked questions about you!"

"What did they want to know?" I asked in what was intended to be a casual manner.

"All kinds of things. They were fascinated by what I had to say. It must be this vampire kick you're on, you poor dear," she said, in what could have easily been mistaken for a sympathetic tone of voice. "Look at your hair—is it getting thin on top?" The remark, of course, gave her an excuse to run her fingers through it.

"Uh, no. It's not." Catarina appeared at the door, and I waved frantically to get her to come over. "Catarina, do you know Gwen?"

"We've met." Catarina looked at Gwen like she was a leftover that had been sitting in the refrigerator too long. "I have to warn you, this place is full of vultures—vultures everywhere."

"Why, ah, Ken, it was so good to talk to you." Gwen scrambled to her feet. "We'll have to get together for a drink soon."

As she departed, Catarina took her place. "I hope I didn't interrupt anything important."

I gestured. "The Macdonalds have been quizzing her about me. My only consolation is that whatever she told them was probably just inaccurate enough to confuse them. Fortunately, you arrived before she got around to nagging me about her lawsuit."

Catarina raised one eyebrow. "Dear me, under that cynical shell you're really a sentimentalist." Her voice turned professional. "I talked to Bobby about the tape. He tried to say you were imagining things until I found the bug in his office."

"You still don't sound happy."

"I'm not. I've asked Clyde to shadow him. Bobby is nervous about something. I wish I knew what it was."

"It might be Harry. He came by here an hour or so ago. His friend Muffy is a revolutionary of some sort, and he wants to help her out."

There was a pregnant silence while Catarina digested this. "Ambassador Meisenhelder is already annoyed because Rosalee got herself elected captain of the local Guild of Free Women and marched them out on strike for higher wages and better working conditions, including arch supports. He's going to absolutely adore hearing about Harry. I hope you don't feel any pressing need to burden him with the details."

She stopped speaking when she saw Minnie, Mickey, and Bunkie appear. They waved in unison and came our way.

Minnie appointed herself spokes-Rodent. "Friend Ken, in passing us, Miss Gwen said that you were up and about. We congratulate you on your speedy recovery. As Bucky says, 'Good health is a boon to friendship.' "

"Uh, right. What have you guys been doing?"

"Miss Bunkie took us to the market and let us purchase a few things with the pocket money Uncle Cheeves gave us. It was very instructive."

"That was thoughtful of Bunkie." I was a little surprised because Bunkie tends to be a bit of a tightwad. "Did you all have fun?"

"Oh, yes. Very much so," Mickey assured me.

"That's good. Well, I really appreciate your concern." The three of them nodded solemnly and wandered off.

Catarina looked at me and began polishing her sunglasses. "Ken, is it my imagination, or is Bunkie going Rodent on us?"

"Now that you mention it, they're all starting to walk the same way. Well, I need to think about turning myself back over to Wipo. Gwen is better than an intercom system. In about ten minutes everyone in the building will know I'm up and about."

"Wait a day. Build up some strength first. Maybe Blok will get in touch with us on his own," Catarina said, although I could tell that she didn't believe it.

We had a quiet dinner together, and I spent a day resting. After Dr. Ye gave me a quick physical and reluctantly concluded that I was going to live, Catarina sat down on the edge of the bed and laid a small package on the pillow beside me. "Happy birthday a few months early."

"You shouldn't have." I opened the package and looked inside. "I mean that sincerely. You shouldn't have."

"Plain white briefs. No little hearts or bunnies." She smiled. "We have the honor of the Confederation to uphold."

Hi, We're from the Secret Police, and We're Here to Help You

I got my police escort to give me a lift over to Special Secret Police Headquarters, and the gate guards directed me to Wipo's office. "Hello, Wipo." I looked around. "Nice place you have here. Did your brother-in-law decorate?"

Wipo unfolded his knobby hands. "Actually, I had my minions duplicate tee furnishings in Ambassador Meisenhelder's office."

"You know, I thought it looked familiar." I glanced at my watch. "Now that we've dispensed with pleasantries, why don't you have Trixie read my mind and I'll get out of here?"

Wipo's eyes glittered. "Despite your feeble attempt at deception, I am sure you are aware t'at Trixie disappeared yesterday. I have already deduced t'at you suborned her prior to your conveniently timed allergic reaction."

I winced. My mother told me that I'd have days like this. I wish I could space them out better.

Wipo rubbed his gill slits in short circular motions. "I have reviewed tee tape of your interrogation. Your skillfully feigned buffoonery does not fool me."

"Trust me, Wipo. Buffoonery is one thing I don't feign."

"It is clear t'at you exerted tee exact amount of effort necessary to extricate yourself without revealing tee mastery you and your fellow vampires exert over Terra's affairs. I must have information to assess tee danger t'at you vampires represent. I suppose I could torture you."

"Torture?" I grimaced. "Ah, what did you have in mind?"

"Perhaps a few hours of home movies."

Everyone has their breaking point. "What did you want to know?"

"Ah, your very willingness to respond illustrates my dilemma! How can I test tee veracity of your responses? Yes, I am afraid torturing you is an inherently unreliable way to obtain information."

I tried not to smile. "What a darn shame."

"So instead we will execute you."

"Ah, come again?"

"When Terra and Plixxi inevitably deliver protests, we will sorrowfully attribute your unfortunate demise to your delicate healt', a clever touch, would not you say?"

"Ah, excuse me." I coughed. "I must have been dozing off during part of this conversation. Why execute me?"

"Several years ago, we realized t'at tee Confederation was denying us access to many of Terra's books, including books about such topics as vampires."

I nodded. "I mean, this is all very fascinating, and I don't mean to be pushy, but on Earth you hardly ever get executed unless some computer company catches you with unregistered software—can, uh, we revisit the part about me being executed?"

"In due course. Initially, we focused our information-gathering on Terra's colonies, where our activities are not as closely monitored. We encountered difficulties."

This was understandable. Your average colonist only reads the back of cereal boxes. "Ah, I hate to belabor the point—"

Wipo reached into his desk and held up a sleazy novel in dramatic fashion. "Yet we have circumvented Terra's elaborate safeguards. And while much has been censored from tee forbidden books we have been able to acquire, we have learned far more t'an you ever expected us to, Mr. MacKay—or should I call you Mr. Bond? Mr. James Bond, secret agent 007."

My jaw dropped about twelve centimeters.

Wipo's gill slits flared. "Ah, you react! I am greatly obliged to you for confirming my suspicions." He picked up a small bastinado off the top of a filing cabinet and began fingering it.

"Wipo, I'm not quite sure how to break this to you, but you're making a very big mistake."

"Spare me your denials. To recapitulate our reasoning, in perusing various texts, we discovered t'at James Bond's career spans nearly seventy-five years, yet he does not age and is not subject to civil service rules. We were deeply puzzled until one scholar recognized t'at vampires also do not age. Obviously, James Bond is a vampire."

At least they hadn't gotten their hands on any vampire novels written by women in heavy makeup. I sucked in my breath. "Uh, Wipo, let me try this one step at a time. There is no James Bond. James Bond is a made-up character for stories. James Bond doesn't exist."

"Oh, I realize t'is."

Just as I started to relax, he added, "James Bond is, of

course, a persona you adopted and discarded as soon as his exploits became too notorious. But when we saw a movie about tee exploits of Ken MacKay, tee resemblance became obvious."

As programmers are fond of saying, garbage in, garbage out. I looked up at the ceiling. "Okay, Wipo, how does this squirrely idea of yours factor in to me getting executed?"

"One constant in James Bond narratives is t'at when your enemies capture you, instead of simply killing you, t'ey subject you to an elaborate death trap from which you invariably escape. T'is occurs far too frequently to be coincidental. A group of scholars finally recognized what was being censored out."

"Dear Lord," I murmured. "Why me?"

"It is manifest, Mr. Bond, t'at tee ingenious death traps in t'ese narratives were conceived to force you to reveal your vampirish nature and tee extent of your powers."

It occurred to me that if I could only figure out how to get out of this alive, I could make Alt Bauernhof the laughingstock of the known universe. "Why do you guys want to conquer the universe anyway? Think of the bureaucracy you'd need to run it."

"We have never quite understood tee squeamishness you Terrans manifest about taking ot'er beings' property, even when you really want it. 'Tee good old rule / Sufficet' t'em, tee simple plan / T at t'ey should take, who have tee power / And t'ey should keep who can,' " Wipo declaimed. He looked at me expectantly.

"Shakespeare?" I guessed.

"Wordsworth. From 'Rob Roy's Grave.' To better perform my duties, I have made myself an expert on your culture. Fitting lines, would not you say?"

"Uh, sure." Every second alien seems to know more English literature than I do.

Wipo drew himself up to his full height. "We will place you in your escape-proof cell to contemplate your fate. T'en you will be forced to establish your vampirish superiority beyond question, or perish."

"I want my lawyer."

Wipo decided he had enough vermin around the place and had me marched to my cell, where, to shorten an otherwise tedious story, the dust bunnies were larger and the food was atrocious.

Bright and early the next morning a gaggle of guards appeared to haul me away. I thought about slugging a couple and making a dash for it in the hope that the other twenty or so would shoot each other instead of me, but after they trussed me up and hung me over a pole, the moment did not appear opportune.

Wipo was waiting for me in his usual good spirits. "Ah, Mr. Bond! Good morning. Prepare to meet your doom."

"Can we knock it off with this 'Mr. Bond' stuff?"

"As you wish."

As his boys unhitched me from my pole, I noticed a very large metal door with a few dents in it, and a very rank odor. "I gather what I'm smelling isn't breakfast."

"Ah, such levity in tee face of doom! Come see for yourself." He escorted me over to the view slit. "T'is is tee arena, tee Vor'dur. Two go in. Only one comes out. As for your opponent, call him 'Big Boy.' "

Big Boy was wine-colored with a green belly, and uglier than Gwen's mother. He was lounging around the far end of the arena snacking on what looked like half a cow. I may not know the difference between

Yangchouanosaurus shangyouensis and *Allosaurus atrox*, but I do know a theropod dinosaur when I see one. Theropod dinosaurs have two big feet with very large claws, and a big head full of very large teeth. They also have long, stiff tails for balance and other characteristics of interest to paleontologists, but teeth and claws are what I focus on.

"If this is a hologram, it's not funny. In fact, even if this is *not* a hologram, it's not funny."

"It is a shadur, our planet's largest predator. It bears an uncanny resemblance to certain Terran predators which died out over sixty-five million of your years—"

"I know what it bears an uncanny resemblance to," I snapped.

Wipo made a curious little noise in his throat. He pulled out a little notebook and began writing something down, speaking aloud as he did so. My dictionary translated, "Subject appears familiar with Earth predators called dinosaurs. Query: Can vampires have far longer life spans than previously suspected?"

He looked at me. "You excite my curiosity, Mr. MacKay. Up until now, tee longest life span we have been able to identify for a vampire is t'at of one Nicholas of Myra, alias Santa Claus."

"Let's get back to the issue at hand. You're going to feed me to *that*?"

"Oh, no, Mr. MacKay. T'at would obviously be unfair. Merely feeding you to a shadur would not afford you an opportunity to display your sophisticated skills, nor would it give us a meaningful basis to assess your vampirish potential." Wipo reached into his pouch and produced an eight-centimeter pocketknife. "Your weapon."

"Thanks a whole heck of a lot." A nine-millimeter pistol would have been nicer. Then I could have at least plugged Wipo.

"Oh!" Wipo reached into his pouch and pulled out what looked like a metal Frisbee. "You may have a shield as well."

"Gee, thanks." I stared at my undersized sword and buckler with distaste.

Wipo folded his hands as the guards surrounded us. "Any last words, Mr. MacKay? A final request? A plea for leniency?"

"We're not up to that part yet. What happens if I whip old brontosaur-breath there?"

"I suppose we will have to find anot'er way to dispose of you."

"Not good enough." I folded my arms. "As my mother used to say, 'If at first you don't succeed, quit.' If I win, I go free. Otherwise, I don't perform."

"Are you attempting to bargain with me, Mr. MacKay?"

"Think about it. You want information from this little encounter. If I just stand around and become fast food, you don't learn anything. So what do you say?"

"Good-bye, Mr. MacKay."

"Well, it was worth a try."

The guards opened the door and pushed me into the Vor'dur at pike-point. They quickly slammed the door shut behind me.

I didn't have much time to sightsee, but the Vor'dur looked to be a hundred and fifty meters across, with a fif-teen meter ceiling and a flooring of crushed stone under-foot. The shadur seemed to take up most of it.

Close up, the animal appeared to be fifteen meters long

from the tip of its snout to the tip of its tail, which meant that it was probably about half that size. Its belly was stretched taut, which indicated that it hadn't been eating regularly, and its hairless skin was covered with knobby protuberances, suggesting poor personal hygiene. Its eyes were situated around the sides of its barrel-shaped head, which it turned first to one side and then to the other to get a good look at me.

The economy-size chewing equipment didn't leave much room for brains. On the other hand, I didn't have a great deal to lose by attempting to make polite conversation. "Ah, hello, there. Fancy running into you like this."

The thing put its head down and its tail up and headed in my direction at a dead run.

I took a backward step. "Uh, can we talk this over?"

A raking foreclaw slashed the air over my head.

I felt the wall against my back. "Uh, have you considered alternate career choices? I don't know what the zoos are paying, but I hear there's real money in kiddie shows."

A pair of maroon jaws descended. Dodging right, I put my right foot in a large pile of desiccated dung and fell flat on my face. Dazzlingly white teeth the size of bowie knives clicked shut a few centimeters over my head. Lacking binocular vision, the monster immediately straightened and looked around to see where dinner had gotten to.

Now, if life were perfect, I would have experienced a sudden surge of hysterical strength, grabbed Big Boy by his tail, and practiced the hammer throw. Instead I felt like a sack of manure could have outwrestled me two falls out of three.

The public address system came on. "An excellent

start, Mr. MacKay," Wipo quipped. "I would point out to you t'at a shadur's fangs are set in multiple rows and curve backward. A shadur's upper fangs are, of course, larger and sharper so t'at when its biting muscles contract, tee lower fangs hold flesh in position for tee saw edges of tee upper fangs to slash. A most ingenious system, would you not say?"

I was really beginning to dislike the guy.

As I scrambled to my knees, Big Boy eyed me the way a robin eyes a worm. Finding that I had misplaced my penknife, which was lying next to the claws on the animal's right foot, I flung my shield and bounced it off its nose.

It tilted its head the other way and looked at me with the other eye.

"Didn't your mother teach you not to play with your food?" I muttered. Determined to go down fighting, I followed up the shield with a handful of rock-solid shadur poop.

Its head cocked sideways, the shadur took this one in the eye. For the moment, it was even less happy than I was. Tilting its head toward the ceiling, it voiced a wild and terrible cry.

I took advantage of the situation to crawl between its legs and retrieve my penknife. Then I was struck by the sudden inspiration that the only place in the room where it couldn't reach me was on top of its back. After twenty-odd hours of starvation, the dumbest ideas seem plausible. Using the knobs on its hide for handholds, I climbed up.

I found out two things very quickly. The first was that the nodules on the shadur's hide were fine for climbing while the animal was standing still, but weren't easy to hang on to when it started moving. The second was the critter had a cartilaginous frame. Being boneless, it was effectively double-jointed.

As I found myself sliding down the shadur's back I tried jamming my knife in its hide to halt my slide. About a half second later I noticed that the animal had twisted its head around 180 degrees and was about to take a bite out of my midriff. I quickly lost interest in trying to hang on.

Several things happened very quickly. When my knife penetrated the skin, it creased the nerve cord, causing the shadur to twitch convulsively as it chomped down on the spot where I was before I went flying gracefully through the air like a rag doll. Distracted by pain and with its vision screwed up, the animal missed and bit into its own back.

I, of course, landed on my head. It hurt.

A few moments later Wipo opened the door and joined me to watch the beast in its death throes.

I used my free hand to find my spine, hoping for an out-of-body experience because the body I had wasn't working very well. As a vamp, I am, of course, allergic to aspirin, ibuprofen, and acetaminophen, so when I get a headache, it comes to stay and brings suitcases. "Excuse me for not getting up. You, ah, wouldn't happen to know a good chiropractor, would you?"

Wipo bobbed his head at me in obvious disbelief, then pulled out his notepad and began writing. My banged-up little dictionary translated, "Possible application of Cotdenis Theory of Economics to hunting of shadurs. Apparently if paid enough, shadurs will hunt themselves."

I sat up and tried twisting my neck back into place. "So, what's next? Do you feed me to giant sandworms or send me over Niagara Falls in a barrel?"

Wipo paused to consider this. "Hmmm, no. Not tonight. We would have to lay on a plane, and it would take too long. I must consult with our ephors."

He ordered the guards to dump me back in my cell, which is where I ended up after I washed up and signed a few autographs.

The cell was depressing. Lunch was some sort of fricassee, and I thought I recognized bits of Big Boy floating around in it. For some reason, my guards also sent down a bottle of mediocre whiskey and a carton of Bulgarian cigarettes on the end of a boat hook. As the day wore on my blood sugar began doing flip-flops.

I amused myself by reciting all I remembered of *Richard III*. That used up all of ten minutes, including long pauses. I switched to mumbling prayers of the "Dear God, if You get me out of this, I'll never, ever do whatever it was again" variety.

The praying, interestingly enough, really spooked the guards. I could hear them talking to each other and running around overhead. Figuring God would understand, I started praying louder.

As the hours passed and I started feeling loopy, I tried working my way through the Bible, improvising freely whenever memory failed, which was fairly frequently. I got up to Ecclesiastes and was trying to remember whether the chapter starts out "Vanity of vanities" or "Insanity of insanities"—both of which applied to my situation—when God finally came through. I heard a voice say, "Psst. Ken!"

"Oh, great." I rubbed my sore neck. "Now I'm hallucinating."

"You're not hallucinating. It's me."

"Even better. My hallucinations are arguing with me."

The ladder came floating down, and Catarina followed. "We're here to get you out, Ken."

"Great." I staggered to my feet and leaned against the wall for a moment. "You should have rung me up and told me you were going to drop in."

She let it slide. Catching me by the arm, she handed me a carton of Leopard Milk. "Here, drink this."

"Can we send out for Chinese?" I downed the Leopard Milk and swayed. "I don't think I'm thinking too well. You'll have to think for both of us."

She steered me toward the ladder. "I didn't realize the danger you were in until Trixie called me."

Trixie appeared at the trapdoor in a gas mask with a submachine gun in her hand. "Oh, poor Ken. You look terrible."

I put my foot through the ladder. "Fortunately, I look much better than I feel."

"Come on, Ken, it's better when you help," Catarina coaxed. When we reached the top, she handed me a squeeze bottle. "Here, drink this."

I downed it. "Tell Harry to stop trying to make beer in the sink."

"That was medicine." She unwrapped a chocolate bar and gave it to me. "You'll feel better in a minute."

"My neck is killing me." While I was trying to figure out which end of the chocolate bar to stick in my mouth, a second Macdonald appeared, also wearing a gas mask.

Catarina gently guided my hand. "Ken, this is Battalion Leader Tskhingamsa from Army Intelligence."

"Pleased to meet you, Mr. T. Excuse me for talking with my mouth full. Isn't Army Intelligence a contradiction in terms?"

Catarina tightened her grip. "Ken, please don't make any jokes." She turned me over to Trixie for a second. Pulling on the counterweight to haul the ladder up, she locked the trapdoor and carefully stuffed the keys into the pocket of one of my guards who was slumped against the wall snoring.

"Sleep gas," Tskhingamsa explained. "Very effective. Please come t'is way."

He led us down the hall to a broom closet. When Trixie opened the door, I saw narrow steps leading away from a false back and my head started to clear. I looked at Tskhingamsa. "I, uh, appreciate your helping me escape, but aren't you going to get in trouble for this?"

"I must help to prevent tee ephors from making irreversible mistakes," Tskhingamsa said stiffly as Catarina and Trixie helped me down the steps and he sealed up the back of the broom closet behind us.

Catarina smiled grimly. "The navy and the Special Secret Police back the war faction, while the army supports the peace faction."

Tskhingamsa added, "It is my sworn duty to protect our people from all foreign and domestic enemies, especially tee navy and tee Special Secret Police. If t'eir plannings are not disconcerted, t'ey will drag our people into a senseless war wit' tee Confederation, and wreck tee army's budget."

"You guys in Army Intelligence don't think I'm James Bond, do you?"

"Army Intelligence has grasped tee essential distinction between fiction books, which are artistic lies, and

nonfiction books, which are only partly artistic lies."
Tskhingamsa cocked his head the way Catarina does.
"However, we have noticed in tee category of autobi-
ographies, t'is distinction tends to blur."

I stopped to rest for a moment when we reached the
bottom of the staircase. Trixie cooed, "Poor Ken. What
did t'ey do to you?"

I'm always polite to women carrying submachine
guns, so I did my best to recount my combat with the
shadur in the Vor'dur. As I described the shadur's final
belly flop into the dirt in moderately graphic detail, I
noticed Catarina standing next to me, shaking her head.
"Am I making this too easy?"

She nodded. Then she intoned, "Over all of middle
earth, a great shadur has fallen."

The expression on my face probably resembled the
expression on the shadur's face when it hit ground.
"Catarina, dearest," I said as sweetly as I could manage.

She gave my arm a squeeze. "How about, 'In the sand
of Vor'dur, where the shadurs lie'?"

Although my eyes were focusing, my recovery was
definitely on hold, so I switched topics. "What have I
missed?"

"Things have been a little hectic. Wyma Jean tried to
commit suicide by overdosing herself with Korean food.
After we got her stomach pumped and let her sleep it off,
she ripped a fire ax off the wall and went looking for
Harry."

"Love makes such fools of people, and people are such
fools to begin with that it's compounding a felony," I
quoted.

"Also, Clyde got caught rifling the papers in Bobby's
office. Old Bobby foxed us with the kind of private secu-

rity system you can't afford on a lieutenant commander's salary. I had a bad four hours in Ambassador Meisenhelder's office trying to keep him from crucifying Clyde, who is still under house arrest."

Tskhingamsa interrupted, "Please, enough talk now. We must go into tee tunnel."

Trixie pushed aside a panel and disappeared. As I bent over to follow, everything looked pitch-black to me. "Uh, can we turn on the lights in here?"

The playful expression on Catarina's face told me more than I wanted to know.

"Regrettably, we Klo'klotixag see deeper into tee ultraviolet spectrum t'an humans do," Tskhingamsa said. "My deepest apologies."

"You must hold on to my belt very, very tightly," Trixie purred.

"And I'll have a hand in your pocket all the way," Catarina assured me. "Just remember not to try to stand up."

Four bruises later we emerged in a sewer pumping station. While Tskhingamsa went to get the car, Catarina reached into her belt pouch and fished out a chocolate bar. "You look like you could use this."

"Thanks." I bit into it.

As soon as Tskhingamsa was out of earshot, Catarina said quietly, "Trixie has been passing information to Dr. Blok for about two years. For all practical purposes, she was Blok's agent network, so she has serious reservations about staying behind if Blok goes with us. She set up a meeting, but Blok isn't sure how far to trust her or us."

I nodded. "Should I ask what our deal is with her?"

Catarina raised one eyebrow. "Dear me. Someone said something about a spare bunk in Stores."

"Catarina promised to show me how to fly a spaceship, which is much better t'an eating kumquats," Trixie said cheerfully. "And I will see lots of human colonial worlds."

You had to feel sorry for her. "How did we get set up with the battalion leader there?" I asked Catarina.

"He gave me a call and offered to exchange information." Catarina grinned. "The Macdonald intelligence agencies cut cards on us. Army Intelligence got me, and Wipo got you."

"Is t'is not fortunate?" Trixie simpered. "Ot'erwise, we would never have met."

"Tskhingamsa and I got together this morning for a cup of cocoa to discuss our mutual interests, which by then included you. He loaned us his tunnel, which the army uses to keep abreast of Special Secret Police matters."

Trixie giggled. "She told Battalion Leader Tskhingamsa t'at she would have to rescue you herself if he didn't help, and he would lose his source if she got caught. He was very put out."

I noticed a cut over Catarina's right eye. "Where did you get that?"

"Klo'klotixag Navy Intelligence drew a deuce in the big stakeout lottery. Apparently, they're a little peeved about it. Someone left a letter bomb for me, and they appear to be the likeliest suspects."

"So what's the embassy kitchen serving for dinner?" I asked, suddenly feeling very cold.

"Tee Special Secret Police will be watching for you. You cannot go back t'ere!" Trixie admonished.

Catarina nodded. "I've arranged a place for us to hide. I have food in the car to last us a couple of days. I promised Trixie I'd teach her how to cook."

"What about the rest of our crew?"

"Harry and Rosalee are still at large. I haven't had time to see what our three musketeers have been up to."

I glanced at my watch. "They're probably eating lunch right now."

"You could call t'em," Trixie volunteered. "Battalion Leader Tskhingamsa said telephone calls from here cannot be traced."

I shrugged. "Why not?" I picked up the phone and let it dial the embassy, explained what I needed to the electronic secretary, and let the secretary route the call through to the cafeteria. A minute later Minnie, Mickey, and Bunkie appeared on the screen.

"Friend Ken!" Mickey said. "We were exceedingly worried about you. As Bucky says, 'Prolonged silence from friends indicates trouble in the relationship.' "

"Uh, thanks. I've only got a minute, and I called to see what you three have been up to."

They looked at each other. Finally Bunkie spoke. "Well, we stopped by a factory to see how it operated, and then we went to the market."

"Why a factory?"

"We were considering buying it," Minnie explained.

"Buying a factory? What kind?"

"It was for light metals. The managers running it had no idea how to organize efficiently. It took us most of the morning to straighten matters out," Minnie said with a virtuous air.

"Don't tell me you spent all of your money on a factory."

"Oh, no," Mickey interjected. "We would never do that. What would Uncle Cheeves say? But we had to reinvest our profits in something."

Dear old Uncle Cheeves was Bucky's Prime Minister for Life. Cheeves was usually six steps ahead of anyone else, and anything he had a paw in was cause for concern. "What profits?" I asked, watching Catarina's ivory complexion suddenly turn a few shades lighter.

"From the market," Mickey said innocently.

I shut my eyes. "What . . . did . . . you . . . buy?"

Mickey's furry head pumped up and down. "Oh, the usual sorts of things. Some nice stocks. A few commodities. Friend Ken, are you certain you are all right? You really don't look very well."

"Oh, I'm fine, just—fine. How much pocket money did Uncle Cheeves give you?"

"Well, he made us convert it to gold because the inhabitants here apparently have some silly restrictions on bringing currency to their planet."

"How . . . much . . . gold?"

Mickey turned to Minnie, while Bunkie did her best to avoid meeting my eyes. "How much did we bring? Wasn't it five *quanats*?" Mickey used the calculator on his wristwatch to convert this into metric. "That is 94.13 kilograms!" he announced proudly.

Minnie nodded. "It seemed silly to us to use up most of our weight allowance on gold, but Uncle Cheeves insisted. Because of the war scare, we got a very good price."

"Bunkie?" I said very softly.

"Well, sir, Miss Lindquist told me to keep them out of trouble, so I thought I should do my best to make sure that they didn't lose their money. The markets here aren't regulated, so you have to be very careful what you buy and sell," Bunkie said, trying to look off into space.

"We gave Bunkie five percent of our profits," Minnie added.

I rubbed my temples. "Bunkie, what have you done?"

She consulted her notes. "Well, on Monday we effected a partial corner on mercury, let the price go up twelve percent and sold. Then we shifted into laser technology stocks—people here don't understand how to value options. That was a good long-term investment, so after they took off we only sold half of our holdings. On Tuesday—"

I saw Tskhingamsa approach. "Our transportation just arrived," I said, "so let's skip ahead. How much are the three of you worth?"

"Ownership or control?" Bunkie asked.

"Let's say control."

"Well, it's hard to be precise—"

"Ballpark figure."

Bunkie played with her calculator. She made a sickly smile. "Roughly a hundred and forty million in Confederation currency."

"We took Tuesday morning off to sightsee," Minnie explained.

"They don't know anything about employee incentives to increase productivity here," Mickey protested.

I shut my eyes. "Aren't you afraid of what the government is going to do when it finds out what you three have been up to?"

"Oh, no. We bought ourselves a few ephors. Uncle Cheeves was very specific about that," Mickey said solemnly.

"Friend Ken, may we have the rest of the day off?" Minnie asked. "We need to do some restructuring."

"Yes," I said in a very tiny voice.

As they trooped away I noticed that Trixie was a little pinkish around the gills. Clearly she wasn't used to dealing with Rodents.

Before I could hang up the phone, another face appeared on the screen. "MacKay," Bobby Stemm whispered hoarsely, "this is important. The Special Secret Police have informed us that you killed a shadur. Is this true?"

"Well, sort of, but—"

"Oh, my God, MacKay! Whatever possessed you?!"

"How about self-preservation."

"Don't you know that shadurs are an endangered species?"

"No, but at the time it didn't seem that important."

"Well, you've gone and done it now! Do you have the slightest idea how much trouble you're in? A delegation from the Peace Coalition for a Just Ecology arrived this morning to discuss preservation of the shadur with the Klo'klotixa government now that they've finished with their crusade to save the hepatitis-B virus, and they closeted themselves with the ambassador as soon as they heard."

"Wait a minute, Bobby," Catarina interjected. "What is the Peace Coalition for a Just Ecology?"

Bobby mopped his forehead. "The PCJE is a militant umbrella organization of animal rights activists. Their motto is 'Hug Trees, Not People.' The delegation has sworn a blood oath to vivisect you on sight."

"How serious are these folks?" I asked.

Stemm held up a "Save the Elephant" flyer, and I

skimmed it quickly. Instead of culling elephants to keep them from overpopulating their habitats, it recommended culling Africans.

Stemm explained, "A few members of the delegation know the ambassador from his activist days, and the ambassador is so furious with you for having to listen to them that he's ordered the Marines to turn you back if you try and enter the embassy."

I sighed. Conquest's Law holds that you can anticipate the behavior of an organization by assuming that it is controlled by a secret cabal of its enemies bent on discrediting it.

Tskhingamsa positioned himself where Bobby couldn't see him and motioned. "We must leave!"

Bidding Bobby a fond farewell, we hurried outside to where the car was waiting. Tskhingamsa climbed into the driver's seat while the rest of us piled in back and opaqued the glass.

"What do you think?" I asked Catarina as we headed south along the river.

She shrugged. "Slow week, isn't it?"

We drove over a bridge and went about a dozen blocks when Catarina suddenly pointed to a parking garage and Tskhingamsa pulled in. He stopped the car and turned around in his seat. "Are you certain you will be safe? I could perhaps hide you."

Catarina opened the door and looked to see if anyone was around. "I appreciate the offer, but I don't think it would be prudent for either of us." We got out, and Tskhingamsa sped off.

Trixie had discarded her submachine gun, which made me feel slightly more secure. "What next?" I asked as we stepped behind a pillar.

Catarina sat down and leaned her back against the pillar. "Our ride should be arriving any minute now."

Ten minutes later a wrinkled little Macdonald with pale pink eyes drove up in a beat-up copy of a Volkswagen and cautiously eased into a parking space.

Catarina nudged Trixie. "That looks like it now."

Trixie ran over and exchanged a few words. Then she waved both her arms, and Catarina and I moved to join her.

Catarina took charge of introductions, "Deacon Mjarlen, may I present Xuexue and Ken MacKay."

"Miss Catarina, I am delighted to make your charming acquaintance and t'at of your friends." Mjarlen made the sign of the cross. "May you be a half hour in heaven before tee Devil knows you're dead. Finest kind. Climb in."

Trixie and I exchanged baffled looks. Seeing me hesitate, Catarina opened the rear door and pushed me in while Trixie took the front seat.

"My venerable vehicle does not have opaque glass, so it would be prudent to pull tee curtains," Mjarlen said as he backed us out slowly and almost into the far wall.

I looked around for the seat belt while Catarina pulled the curtains. "Uh, are you a Christian?"

"Of course, Cat'olic. Finest kind. Rah rah, Notre Dame!" Guided at least as much by divine providence as Mjarlen, our vehicle lurched out into the street, bringing several oxcarts to a screeching halt.

"But—" I began.

"Human religions would be proscribed if tee government realized t'ey existed, but God has preserved us t'us far," Mjarlen explained smugly.

"How—" I began.

"Tee mailship arrived today, and Fat'er Yakub sent me a letter mentioning t'at you and Catarina were bret'ren and might need help as well as God's grace, you especially, Mr. MacKay."

"Call me Ken. But how—" I began.

"Did Fat'er Yakub not tell you? He came here as an et'nologist years and years and years ago. He stayed in my house. I cannot understand why he didn't mention it. Oh, I remember, your government would not have approved. But still, it was years and years ago, so t'ey could hardly hold it against him."

"But why—"

"Ah, Ken, it is an ancient tradition of tee Church to provide sanctuary to tee poor and oppressed."

If I was befuddled, Trixie was clueless. She turned around and leaned her chin on the headrest. "What is a church?" she asked in a small voice.

Mjarlen explained, trusting in God's grace a bit more than I would have done. "A church is a building used for Christian worship, but it also signifies tee body of believers in Christ's message and tee communion of saints."

"Oh," Trixie said in an especially small voice.

"We use my home as our church, and I will hide you t'ere, Ken. From what Fat'er Yakub said, no one would ever t'ink to look for you in a church."

I looked at Catarina and shrugged helplessly. "I might as well take my lumps and get it over with. Theology is not my strong suit, but somewhere along the line I got the impression that Christ taught His message and died on the cross to save mankind from its sins. How do you Macdonalds fit in?"

Catarina gave me that slightly superior look she reserves for occasions when I have *truly* distinguished myself.

"Ken, you must consider Christ's teachings." Mjarlen, who had obviously studied with Jesuits, extended one digit skyward to emphasize his point, and heaven responded by steering several vehicles around us after we drifted over the center line. "Jesus died to bring a message of salvation to intelligent beings. Tee headline did not read, 'Jewish boy does good in front of hometown crowd.' Tee message of love, fait', and morality in tee Bible was not directed merely to a handful of puny creatures on one planet, but to all sentient beings, excepting lawyers and Pharisees."

We careened around a rider on a large dun-colored beast. I hastily pulled the curtain tight and stared at Catarina. "Did you just see someone riding a cow?"

"*Duocornis macdonaldensis*, the Macdonald duocorn," Catarina corrected me. Then, to distract me from my cares, she proceeded to "udderly milk" the resemblance for the next five minutes without repeating herself. I can be pretty "gullibull." I tried flinging myself out of the vehicle, but the rear doors had child-proof locks.

Mjarlen's car, with minor assistance from Mjarlen, finally stopped in front of a small stone-faced bungalow. Mjarlen turned around and handed us three of the flowing, ankle-length cloaks worn by very poor Macdonalds and the children of the very wealthy. "I will take you in now."

"How many, er, beings do you have in your congregation?" I asked, stumbling over my hem.

"Nearly one gross of families," Mjarlen answered proudly as he rooted through his pouch for the key.

"Aren't the police suspicious of all the traffic in and out of here?" Catarina asked.

"Oh, no," Mjarlen assured her. "We just say we're playing bingo."

Most Macdonald homes have cellars to remind them of their ancestral caves and why they don't want to go back, and Mjarlen led us downstairs, where we pulled up some cushions and I told them about Wipo's James Bond theory.

"Perhaps if I write and explain to tee government t'at you are not James Bond at all, it will clear matters up," Mjarlen reflected.

I had a slight coughing fit. While it may be true that in the land of the blind, the one-eyed man is king, in the asylum of the witless, the merely half-witted are out of place.

"That might not be a very good idea," Catarina explained tactfully. "The government might not take your word for it. After all, you haven't known us very long."

"I suppose you are right. Still, *magna est veritas et praevalebit*, great is trut' and it will prevail."

"That's Latin, isn't it? Did Father Yakub teach you any other languages?" I asked.

"I know a smattering of all of tee languages of tee Bible—Latin, Greek, Hebrew, Aramaic, Gaelic," Mjarlen explained.

I blinked. "Gaelic?"

"Did not Fat'er Yakub tell you? Tee Galatians were shanty Irish who took a wrong turn somewhere around Macedonia. Like Fat'er Yakub himself, our Blessed Savior was just a little bit Irish on tee Virgin Mary's side." Mjarlen began humming the Notre Dame fight song.

With that to stop conversation, we heard the whistle for the front door, and Mjarlen went to answer it. He returned visibly shaken. "You must hide. Tee Special Secret Police are searching for you and for boxes of wood called coffins in every house in tee city. However, no one knows what wood is. But tee Special Secret Police are rut'less males habituated to violence, former convicts and postal workers. Daily, we ask God to relieve of tee terror t'ey represent."

He passed across a newspaper one of his parishioners had brought. Trixie read us the headline. "Terran Schooled in Mysteries Defies Special Secret Police, Kills Shadur, and Levitates out of Escape-Proof Cell."

Underneath was Harry's picture. I never get any respect.

Catarina smiled. "You have to admit you don't look very dangerous. The Special Secret Police may have been the tiniest bit embarrassed to give the newspaper your mug shot."

Using her dictionary to translate, she calmly read the article aloud. " 'Although the Special Secret Police have issued denials, several well-placed sources have confirmed MacKay's shadur-slaying and subsequent escape. Delegates from the human Peace Coalition for a Just Ecology expressed outrage over the cold-blooded killing and confirmed reports that MacKay is a vampire, a deathless, supernatural being which exists by drinking blood from living creatures. A Confederation spokesman declined comment. Further outrages are expected momentarily, and the Bureau of State Security urges citizens to remain calm, but to report any suspicious activity.' " She looked up. "We seem to have gotten their attention."

" 'Several well-placed sources,' " I scoffed. "Doesn't anybody know how to keep secrets?"

Mjarlen tugged at my sleeve. "Perhaps we may discuss t'is at greater leisure, but now you must hide. I have a priest's hole."

"A what?" I had lost the thread of the conversation and briefly considered lifting up some of the cushions to find it.

"During the sixteenth century, English Catholics built hiding places for priests into their houses," Catarina explained. "It's the sort of thing that Father Yakub would think of."

Mjarlen led us over to a corner of the cellar laid out in tiles made from some sort of hard plant fiber. Selecting one, he slid a thin, hooked tool into one of the joins and lifted up a block of flooring and subflooring. "Your hiding place."

"Right," I said, looking down. The cosy little pit was equipped with an alcove for books, track lighting, and a nice little chair. Unfortunately, what was a spacious hole for one Macdonald was decidedly cramped for the three of us. "I'm starting to get nervous about holes."

"In you go," Catarina said cheerfully, a phrase I was beginning to loathe. After we stuck Trixie in the chair and squeezed in around her, Mjarlen shut the lid.

"So what's our plan?" I asked, removing Trixie's elbow from my right eye, where it didn't belong.

"Lunch first. Then we hang loose. Trixie has the meeting with Dr. Blok set up for tonight. While we're waiting, I have a stack of mail that came in for you on the mailship."

"Was the mailship anyone I know?" Most mailships are operated by artificial-intelligence constructs, and some of them have extremely artificial personalities.

Catarina smiled. "One of your favorites. RVN 23. Swervin' Irvin." Irvin had a habit of erratically changing course and speed when approaching a gravity well, which had earned him his nickname and hopefully would shorten his career.

"Oh, joy." I skimmed through the sheaf of printouts she handed me. Half of it was from kooks, and the rest was from vamps who wanted to share their problems with another vamp and had seen my name in the papers. Vampires are not very well organized.

"Anything interesting?" Catarina asked sweetly.

"One correspondent writes, 'Dear Ken, I don't know who else to ask. I am a vamp. I am hopelessly in love with my best friend's wife. If I go for her neck when we are in bed together, do you think it will affect my relationship with my friend? Signed Lovestruck.' "

" 'Dear Lovestruck,' " Catarina suggested, " 'put a stake in it.' How are the lawsuits against us progressing?"

"*Schenectady Chamber of Commerce, et al.* is moving along at breakneck speed." I explained to Trixie, "When Prince Genghis's Rodent ships were massing over Schuyler's World and the police were off the streets, the citizens of Schenectady patriotically removed items from the stores that Prince Genghis's hordes might have been tempted to steal. Unfortunately, they were rather dilatory about returning them, and as a result the shop owners are suing everyone they can think of, including me."

Since I couldn't reach any of my pockets, I handed my

mail back to Catarina. "Well, that used up three minutes. What else can we do while we're waiting?"

"We could tell stories," Trixie suggested.

"I have one," Catarina volunteered before I could object. She proceeded to tell us a story about a pair of street entertainers who only spoke to each other in limericks. When one of the two failed to come up with an appropriate couplet to warn his partner of an oncoming road grader, the next day's headlines read, "A Hitch in Rhyme Paves Mime," thus reinforcing my belief that puns are not humor, but instead constitute a socially acceptable form of guerrilla warfare.

Moments later we heard the door whistle. "Okay," I whispered. "This is it."

Trixie raised her hand. "Miss Lindquist, I have to—"

"Hold out as long as you can, Trixie. And please, no talking until it's safe," Catarina said quietly.

Seconds later we heard loud footsteps directly overhead, only partly muffled by the layers of flooring. For a few seconds I stopped breathing.

Suddenly, the trapdoor opened. Mjarlen peered inside. "Sorry," he whispered, "it was tee meter reader. Tee Special Secret Police are on t'eir way."

"Right," I said, clutching my chest. Catarina smiled and took my hand. Trixie squirmed on her chair.

A few moments later we heard the door whistle again. This time we could make out three or four sets of footsteps tramping through the house. After an interminable wait, Mjarlen finally rapped the ancient all-clear signal.

"Some mysteries are difficult to fat'om," Trixie said, trying not to wriggle. " 'Shave and a haircut' I understand, but what is 'two bits'?"

Catarina winked at me. "Two small coins, which represent the price of putting up a good outward appearance."

Grimly, I prepared myself.

"Indeed," Catarina continued, "it is said, 'If the two bits, wear it.' "

Fortunately, Mjarlen opened the hatch a few seconds later. I boosted Trixie and Catarina out. While Trixie headed for the little girls' room at flank speed, got our food out of the trunk and threw lunch together, after which Mjarlen led us in a few choruses of the Notre Dame fight song and brought out a game called Bible Trivia that Father Yakub had left him. Fortunately, we weren't playing for money.

The Plot Inspissates

That evening, as Trixie drove us to the tavern where Blok was supposed to meet us, I complained to Catarina, "I'm not whining about the result, but don't you feel the tiniest bit guilty telling Mjarlen he had the abridged version of the Bible? St. Paul's letter to the Cretan drivers— 'Red means slow, green means go, and yellow means hit the gas'?"

"It was 'St. Paul's Letter to the New Yorkers' and the word I used was 'cretin,' not 'Cretan.' " She pulled her sunglasses down. "I had to talk him out of coming somehow. He's risking too much as it is."

"True. Did you get any mail from Father Yakub?"

"Just a quick note." She smiled. "He says that with all the Rodent immigrants, Schenectady is getting to look more like Plixxi every day. The mayor and city council are worried about the increase in literacy. It could cost them their jobs."

I changed the subject. "Trixie, you've been awfully quiet up there."

"I have been t'inking about what Mjarlen was saying. For example, what is heaven?"

I looked at Catarina, who pretended to be studying the watermarks on the roof of the car. "Heaven is a place where you are admitted into the full presence of God," I said slowly.

"It sounds dull."

I thought for a minute. "I don't know if this has anything to do with it, but the bonds of marriage are loosed up there."

"Oh. And what is hell?"

"Hell, as I understand it, is a place where there's no God, and bureaucracy works the way it's intended."

Catarina cleared her throat. "There's the tavern. Trixie, park the car around the corner," she directed. "If something goes wrong, we'll ditch it and let Mjarlen pick it up tomorrow."

Trixie eased us into a spot and then went inside to case the premises. She returned a few minutes later. "Dr. Blok has taken a room. T'ere is a back stairway we can use."

Muffled in our cloaks, Catarina and I followed her up to the tavern's second floor.

"Hide in here while I find him," Trixie said, pointing to the rest room.

We wedged the door shut. Catarina inspected the walls while I discovered the hard way that Macdonalds don't believe in toilet paper. "The boys here need to improve their aim," she commented.

"It's interesting to see how these double-headed things work in practice. How do you want to handle Blok?"

"Good cop, bad cop?"

"Can I be bad cop?"

"He knows you."

"Darn." I rinsed my hands again. A few seconds later we heard the familiar "shave and a haircut" knock on the door.

Catarina kicked away the wedge and opened it a crack. Trixie gestured for us to follow.

We entered Blok's room and bolted the door behind us. Blok was waiting for us, dressed in a shabby kilt and a porkpie hat, with his back to us. When he turned, Trixie bowed her head. He ignored her. "Well, Mr. MacKay, we meet again."

"Happy to see you, too."

He gestured at Catarina and said sharply, "Bade t'is female to depart. We must discuss matters male-to-male!"

"Trixie and I will just go into the bathroom and powder our noses while you men chat," Catarina said in a sweet voice that meant the powder she had in mind was gunpowder.

"No!" Blok pointed to Trixie. "Xuexue must stay! I must know if he is veracious!"

"I'm keeping my clothes on," I said, remembering the last time.

Trixie gave me a frightened look. She pointed at the four-legged stool in the room. "Please sit here."

Catarina gave me the thumbs-up and disappeared into the water closet. Perching myself on the stool with my knees flexed, I let Trixie slip behind me and rest her elbows on my shoulders. "The fate of the universe may depend on this," I whispered, "so don't tickle."

She nodded, baring her teeth slightly. Taking a cue from Blok, she said, "Please say somet'ing, Ken."

"Something. Hello, I'm Ken MacKay."

"He is being trut'ful. Please say somet'ing untrue."

"I'm sure Dr. Blok and I can work out our differences like reasonable beings."

She rested her chin on top of my head. "Now he is lying. You may begin speaking to him, honorable one."

Blok walked toward me with his hands folded behind his back. "Many disquieting portents have been observed since your arrival, Mr. MacKay. Tee stock market is unsettled, and my informants speak of mysterious activity by revolutionary movements." He stopped a few centimeters away. "I sense great peril in you. You have a fair seeming, yet t'at which seems fair can be most foul."

"Uh, care for a breath mint?" I said, pulling the package out of my pocket.

"Tee Special Secret Police have identified you as a deat'less and notorious vampire named James Bond!"

"A base canard."

"I do not understand. What does t'is have to do wit' ducks?"

"Never mind. Let's just say that I am not and never have been James Bond."

Blok studied Trixie's face intently, then resumed pacing. "Tee Special Secret Police have also identified a member of your crew named Harry as a notorious vampire named Tarzan."

"Wrong again, although speech analysis does indicate that he was raised by monkeys."

Blok stopped in front of me. "I sense a great troubling in you. Supreme Agent Wipo, t'at foolish, foolish being, little knew tee forces he was dabbling in. By t'reatening your destruction in tee Vor'dur, he forced you to call upon unseen powers."

"I can explain!"

Blok held up his hand. "Tee first law of power is t'at explanations must not be asked for. I will not do so. Yet, I have listened to tapes of your incantations. Before I dare aid you I must know if your fair seeming is but an illusion masking evil, and if tee ancient, awful, blighting forces you evoke to do your bidding are wholesome, or shadows darker t'an any night."

Blok was on a roll, and at a guess, I was about three somersaults behind. "Can we go over that part again?"

"You t'ink I do not understand t'ese matters." He gazed at me scornfully. "Into some beings is born tee desire to rule, and it eats into t'em as a fire. Such beings, besotted with control of energies beyond mortal comprehension, have long sought knowledge beyond the bounds set by prudence for such seeking. If you vampires have gone along such paths, t'ey may prove to be your undoing. Be not deceived—when such begins to stir which promises no safety in sky, land, or water, t'ose of us who would resist domination must seek allies where allies can be found!"

I whispered to Trixie, "Does he talk like this all the time?"

She nodded, playing with the hair on the back of my neck.

"Look, Doc. I'm just your average, garden-variety vamp."

"You slew tee shadur and expect me to believe t'is?"

"I'd have been in real trouble if Wipo had sicced a couple of CPAs on me."

"No! You are a channel for power, a doorway t'rough which nameless powers may enter our world, just as it is clear to me t'at vampires are tee secret hand controlling Terra, Mr. MacKay," Blok said stridently.

"Hey! I resent that!"

"Who governs, t'en? Your legislature and your chief executive? Pishposh! Your legislature is entirely composed of venal hacks, who build day-care centers for whales to atone for past oppression."

I shrugged. "The civil rights lobby and the tree-huggers are hurting for business."

"And your chief executive is a middle-aged alcoholic who plays tee xylophone on late night talk shows!" he hissed.

I shrugged. "Democratic government is government by the people and for the people, on the theory that the people ought to get the kind of government they want, good and hard."

As he was mulling this over, someone knocked sharply on the door and tried to force it.

"Catarina," I whispered, "if you're finished powdering, you may want to get out here."

"Powder corrupts, and absolute powder corrupts absolutely," Catarina stated as she emerged. "What is it?"

"It is tee police!" Trixie wailed.

Blok threw up his hands in agitation. "T'is is terrible! I cannot be seen wit' you! I will climb out tee window."

"We don't have a window," Catarina observed.

The police rattled the door and began pounding on it.

"Nice doors. Good dead bolt." I eyed Blok up and down. "How the heck did the cops know we were in here?"

"Ahh. Er," Blok responded.

Catarina nodded. Trixie walked over and leaned on his shoulder.

"T'ey were not supposed to be here for anot'er hour!" Blok moaned.

"There's just no honor among thieves anymore. Is the good doctor in or out?" Catarina asked as the police outside began slamming their shoulders against the door in a rhythmic fashion.

"Who knows?" I shrugged. "Good cop, bad cop?"

Her mouth smiled. "Bad cop. Dr. Blok, do you know what a pinhead is?"

"Yes, of course. I am completely fluent in your childishly simple language," Blok said dismissively as he walked in circles and wrung his hands in a very human fashion.

"Good. Are you in or out, pinhead?"

"I demand—"

Catarina stuck her hands on her hips. "Ken, we've been trying to civilize this planet for seventy-five years, and I say this bunch of warmongers is never going to catch on. We ought to vaporize the place."

Blok halted, stunned. "What do you mean?"

I tried to ignore the pounding on the door. "Ah, vaporize the place. Not with—the weapon!"

Catarina nodded implacably. "Yes. With—the weapon."

"But Catarina, that would sweep away the innocent with the guilty. Ah, line."

She held up five fingers with her left hand and made an O with her right.

"Oh, right. Suppose we could find fifty innocent people on this planet. Rather than wipe it out, couldn't we spare it for the sake of the innocent fifty?"

Catarina shrugged. "Okay. Fifty innocent people, and we'll let it ride."

The pounding stopped for a moment, and Trixie ran over to the door to listen.

The fish was on the hook. "Wait!" Blok waved his arms frantically. "T'ere is my sister's second husband. T'at only leaves forty-nine."

"Ah, suppose we find five less than fifty innocent people?"

A lightbulb figuratively began to glow over Trixie's head. "Bible trivia," she murmured.

"We did not mean it!" Blok protested. "We can be peaceful!"

"Okay, forty-five it is."

Trixie interrupted. "Tee police are about to use a bench to break tee door down."

I nodded. "Right. Let's speed this up. I hear forty-five innocent people, going once. Do I hear ten?"

Blok held his hand up. "Wait! I can find ten!"

"Catarina, how about if we cut these folks some slack?"

"If you insist." She stared at Blok. "Look, pinhead. Your species has one more chance. Are you in or out? If you're in, we'll get you out of here and you'll quit screwing around. If not . . ." She left her sentence unfinished.

"What do you say, Doc?" I coaxed. "As a special favor, we won't mention the thirty-two nonexistent agents you've been billing Admiral Crenshaw for."

"In," he sighed. "I place my fate in your hands."

The telephone rang. Catarina snatched up the receiver. Then she handed it to me. "It's for you."

It was Mickey. "Friend Ken, you won't believe how difficult it was to get hold of you."

We heard a massive thud, and the door shook.

"Dr. Blok is not tee only one about to be in," Trixie observed.

"Uh, Mickey, we're a little bit busy now—"

"I understand completely. However, we are in a bit of a quandary here, and we elected to solicit your sagacious advice. We sold considerable portions of our companies back to the employees—'bind not the mouths of the kine,' as Bunkie put it so eloquently—and now find ourselves in a disadvantageous corporate tax situation. Miss Gwen suggested that we might want to sponsor a television program—"

The pounding increased.

"Do you consider this a wise venture?"

"Sounds great. Need to run! Bye!" I slammed the phone down. "Any ideas?" I asked Catarina.

She took me by the arm and moved next to the door. "Ken, we have no choice. We have to use the death ray," she said in a loud voice.

I blinked at her. "The death what? Ouch! That was my foot you stepped on. Ah, yes. The death ray. Yes, we must use the death ray. We have no choice."

"Translate for them, Trixie—Blok, I don't want to hear a peep out of you," Catarina said quietly, handing them breathing masks from her belt pouch and uncorking what looked like a gas grenade.

Trixie burst into a freehand translation as Blok sensibly dove under the bed.

"But Ken, the death ray is so cruel a weapon to employ!" Catarina declaimed.

The ramming outside lost some of its rhythm.

"Ah, we will make it up to the widows and orphans someday, but the peace of the galaxy is at stake!" I responded, striking an appropriate pose. As Trixie translated, Catarina wedged a sputtering gas grenade against the bottom of the door.

The ramming stopped. I jerked Catarina out of the way as two or three Special Secret Policemen emptied the magazines of their submachine guns through the door. Then we heard a couple of cops drop, and footsteps as the remaining gendarmes pounded down the steps.

"Grab Blok!" Catarina directed, opening the door and scooping up a weapon and some spare clips.

I fished Blok out of his hole, and then Trixie and I followed Catarina down the steps, which ended in a small landing. "Maybe they're all gone," I said hopefully.

Catarina plucked the porkpie hat off Blok's head. Swinging open the door, she cautiously extended Blok's hat from the end of her submachine gun. A burst of gunfire knocked it away and riddled the back wall, breaking glass on the far side.

Blok gasped and hit the deck, muttering imprecations, while the people inside the tavern pounded on the wall and shouted. "Tee hat cost plenty," Trixie translated, "and tee tavern owner is telling us to knock it off."

With Blok clutching my left ankle, I found my movements hampered, so I leaned against the wall to scrape him off. "What now?"

"This requires thought," Catarina conceded. "About how many cops do we have out there, do you think?"

Another torrent of submachine gun fire came pouring through the open door and shot out the lighting.

"Five or six," I guessed as little pieces of tile and plaster bounced off my head.

Having led a dull life prior to meeting us, Trixie squealed, "T'is is so exciting!"

Catarina suddenly snapped her fingers. "Ken, give me all the local currency you're carrying."

I pulled a couple of wads out of my belt pouch and forked it over. Catarina combined it with what she was carrying. Another two or three quick bursts of submachine gun fire cut through the doorway. "Tee people inside are becoming very annoyed," Trixie informed us.

Some of the gunfire was beginning to come from inside the building, which suggested that the people inside were becoming very annoyed indeed.

Catarina reached down and pulled Blok to his feet. "Where are you parked?"

Blok swallowed like a frog downing dinner and described the location.

"Good." She leaned over to judge the arc of the streetlights and began pitching bank notes into the parking lot.

Two cops emptied magazines at the disturbance. "Do you really think this is going to work?" I asked. "On the planets we frequent, I can't actually recall running into an honest cop, but there's always a first time."

Catarina's teeth sparkled in the starlight. "These boys have been pretty nervous. How much ammo do you think they have left?"

"Point taken."

The breeze outside was fairly stiff. The submachine gun fire suddenly stopped as the money began drifting downwind. It collectively took the cops about three seconds to recognize and react, and then it was like a January White Sale.

As the patter of little gray feet disappeared, I covered Catarina from the doorway as she cautiously waved Trixie's scarf. Then she darted outside, flattened, and rolled behind a Dumpster. A few seconds later she waved us on.

We ran to Blok's car, which was parked about a block away. Catarina and I got in back and crouched down while Trixie sat in front with a borrowed submachine gun in case we ran into problems or Blok had second thoughts—the good doctor obviously thought that his car was about to ferry plutonium, and he wasn't very happy about it.

A noisy crowd was already beginning to gather in front of the tavern as we drove by. "Tee people are very displeased. Tee stairway backed on to tee wine rack," Trixie observed.

Catarina touched my cheek. "You don't look happy."

"I'm getting used to being shot at," I whispered back, "and that's frightening."

A new wave of police began arriving, and the crowd showed signs of hostility. A stray bottle took out the rear window on Catarina's side as Blok, oozing profusely, moved us smartly away from the scene. Suddenly he wailed, "Tee police are looking for all of us including me! It is on tee radio! Oh, no! All is lost!" Carping about the injustice of it all, he bounced the car off a pothole and I suddenly remembered that I was still in need of a good chiropractor.

I commented to Catarina, "Sometime soon, I'd like an opportunity to get in touch with my feelings."

"I take it you feel like killing Dr. Blok."

"There are too many mind-readers in this crowd."

Catarina reached over and began rubbing the sore spot. "Relax. Think gentle thoughts. Think of the look on Lydia's face when we hand her your expense account."

"What's our next move? I'd hate to get Mjarlen into trouble."

"Where is the last place they'd think of looking for us?"

"The embassy?"

She nodded.

"Correct me if I'm wrong, but the ambassador wants

to turn me in, and the PCJE wants to take a scalpel to my hide. Also, at a guess, between the Secret Police and the Marines manning the gates, getting in ranks as a two point six degree of difficulty."

She smiled and patted my cheek. "It's in the bag." She gave Blok directions, put her head on my knee, and fell asleep.

As we neared the compound I had Blok circle the block while I cautiously raised my head high enough to peer out. Special Secret Policemen, recognizable by their trench coats and general air of insouciance, were thick on the ground. As we turned a corner I spied a small and obviously nervous Macdonald female in a dark beret sitting on top of an oversized garment bag.

"Oh, heck," I murmured, "slow down."

"What is it?" Trixie asked.

"I recognize her," I sighed, "and the garment bag is a friend of mine."

Blok drifted to a stop, and I rolled down the window. "Psst. Muffy! Harry?"

Harry unzipped. "Ken! How the hell are you? Catarina said that you'd be by. Hey, stop it, honey! That tickles."

Muffy jumped down, clicked her heels together, and gave us a stirring exhortation in what was intended to be English.

Apparently, she had taught herself the language from one of those trendy little dictionaries which list words like "womyn" and "herstory." I caught the part about "the struggle to focus on processes and trajectories to cross gender-defined subject-boundaries in order to repudiate eviscerating gender-determined cultural oppression and avoid being trapped in a cultural-historical pre-processual paradigm," and I formed a mental image of the ghost of Noah Webster dropping his lunch in a small New England cemetery.

"Sure, whatever you say, honey." Harry, who obviously didn't realize that she was speaking English, waved his hand nonchalantly. "Right now, I've got to talk to Ken."

"Can the two of you get us inside?" I asked.

"No sweat. The cops are greased."

"Are they going to *stay* greased?"

Harry nodded vigorously. "I offered them some of Bunkie's dresses for their wives, and they got to get us in if they want to collect. They even gave us a group discount."

"What about the Marines?"

"Hey, they're good Joes, and those PCJE women are *ugly*."

Blok had been hanging on to my sleeve in an effort to gain my attention. "Do you know what she is?" he hissed with a horrified look on his face.

Harry's eyes narrowed. "Who's the pipsqueak, Ken?"

"Oh, yeah. Let me do introductions." I gestured. "Harry Halsey and Muffy, this is Dr. Blok and Trixie."

"Charmed, I am sure," Blok said stiffly.

"Harry is our, ah, supercargo. He used to own a bar on Schuyler's World, next to the morgue."

Harry corrected me. "It was Jake's funeral parlor, Ken. Their advertising jingle was, 'Coffins, all sizes and models—have we got the shape for the shape you're in!' Hey, did you ever check out their gift shop? They had personalized toe tags."

"Harry, Ken has told me so much about you," Trixie said, batting her eyes. Muffy gave her a look of absolute hostility.

I looked around nervously as Catarina began to stir. "I don't mean to rush everyone, but can we go in?"

We tipped the cops who waved us through, and after Muffy disabled the alarms, we entered the embassy through the window to my room. I kept expecting to see the embassy security detail waiting for us with a bill for damages.

Catarina took charge. "We might as well call it a night. Ken, why don't you and Harry keep an eye on Dr. Blok. I'll take Muffy and Trixie with me. We'll tackle Ambassador Meisenhelder in the morning after he's had his coffee."

Harry and I fixed the window, and then we rolled to see who got the bed. Unfortunately, we used Harry's dice, which meant that Blok got the sofa and I got what the littlest piggy got. After I switched off the lights and tried to fall asleep, I was awakened by a tug on my blanket.

"Mr. MacKay!" Blok gave my blanket another pull. "Are you asleep?"

"No." The problem with suffering fools gladly is that they don't suffer nearly as much as you do.

"You must know—t'is female who calls herself Muffy! She is a dangerous radical who wishes to upset tee ordering of society!"

"Thanks. See you in the morning."

He gave me a soulful look. "Oh, what will become of me!"

"Cheer up. Lydia will find you a new career."

"You t'ink so?"

"Sure. It will probably be the same one she offered me, which is painting those little yellow lines down the center of busy freeways."

"I feel better."

"Great. I'm glad one of us does. Good night."

I should mention that Harry snores.

Around six Catarina came by to collect us. Muffy had a basket of moderately active invertebrates to feed Blok and Trixie; the rest of us headed for the embassy dining room. I whispered to Catarina, "Did you tell Harry that Muffy is a radical feminist?"

She shook her head. "Ignorance is a delicate exotic fruit; touch it and the bloom is gone."

The embassy dining room was mostly empty when we arrived. Harry went for the sausage and powdered eggs. Catarina and I opted for cereal of dubious provenance—"Bran X," as Catarina dubbed it—and mugs of cocoa, chocolate being one of the four food groups.

A few tables over, a crew-cut woman from Feline Liberation Front noticed us. I saw her push aside her breakfast salad and grab a chubby guy from the Save the Gerbils Foundation so hard that he almost spilled his mineral water.

"Are your ears burning?" Catarina asked me.

"I'll handle this," Harry sniffed.

The woman marched over to our table, narrowing her closely spaced eyes. "I'm Wild. Felicia Wild of the PCJE. I'm looking for a man named Ken MacKay."

Harry stood. "Hey, babe, you're wasting your time. He's already got a girlfriend. My name's Harry."

One of the buttons Wild was wearing read "Friends Don't Let Friends Eat Meat." She stared at Harry's plate, where a greasy sausage was dripping on the end of the fork we made him use. "I'd rather fornicate with a goat than eat the meat of a slaughtered, defenseless animal."

I cringed.

Harry looked down at his plate and back again. "I didn't know I got a choice, today. Your place or mine?"

The woman's mouth and chest moved, but no sound came out. She had that stricken look you sometimes see on the faces of small animals crossing against traffic.

"I'll bring the oil," Harry offered.

The cat lady whimpered and ran.

Harry sat back down, speared his sausage, and munched on it enthusiastically. "You know, I bet I could really get a rise out of her if I came back tomorrow, but then I'd miss the bomb."

I almost choked on my cocoa. "What bomb?" Catarina asked in a very faint voice.

"What was it we were going to blow up? Oh, yeah, at the capitol building. You know, with the parliament inside?"

I whispered a quick prayer. "Uh, Harry, was it a— teeny-weeny little bomb, or a big bomb?"

"Oh, a *big* one." Harry used the sugar bowl to demonstrate. "A dust initiator. You remember when Prince Adolf was shooting missiles at the *Scupper* and you tried to touch off a cloud of fertilizer?"

"Well, yes. You only made me tell you the story forty-seven times."

"When I told all of Muffy's little friends about it, they got real excited."

I stared at Harry. "Oh, no."

To initiate a dust explosion, you mix powdered TNT with an incendiary—preferably three parts powdered ferric oxide to two parts powdered aluminum or magnesium—and use it to touch off a "surround," which is a fine powder or volatilized gasoline evenly distributed in the air. A kilo of explosive and forty kilos of surround is good for about thirteen hundred cubic meters of building, which makes it a nice way to get a big bang out of a limited amount of explosive.

"We pumped about half a ton of fertilizer into the building and used the air conditioners to swirl it around," Harry said complacently. "That was what we needed the demo charges from the ship for. Oh, yeah, Muffy wanted me to thank you, Ken. You know, we couldn't have done it without you."

Harry finished mopping up his eggs and pushed his plate away. He looked at us with concern. "Are you all right, Ken? You're looking kind of pale—I mean, even more pale than usual. In fact, you and Catarina are both looking paler than usual."

Catarina purred, "Ken, we need to talk."

"Harry," I interjected, "are you saying the guards just let you drive right up to the capitol and pour in a truckload of fertilizer?"

Harry looked perplexed. "Hey, they're civil servants. They were on their coffee break. Union rules."

"Didn't anybody ask why you were pumping a half ton of manure into the building?"

Harry lifted his hand to his forehead. "Not that I remember. Well, one guy said that pumping manure into the capitol was redundant, but I think he was making a joke."

"Harry," I said desperately, "I know you're trying to help Muffy with her revolution, but don't you think that this might annoy people?"

He scratched his head. "You know, I asked Muffy about that, and she said that they did a telephone survey, and sixty-six percent of the people surveyed volunteered to push the plunger."

Catarina shook her head sadly. "Harry, when is the explosion timed to go off?"

"Tomorrow morning. Muffy says that the legislature has a ceremonial opening session where the legislators put on fancy robes and fling coins to the crowd while the crowd flings back road apples. We timed it so that the building blows up right when they open the doors."

Catarina stared up at the ceiling. "You do know that commercial explosives have little colored bits of plastic mixed in with the inert material so that people can identify the batch and lot number from the residue."

Harry appeared to digest this bit of information. "Is this a problem?"

"Harry, she's saying that after the explosion, the Macdonalds are going to know that the demo charges came off our ship," I explained.

Harry's brow furrowed in deep concentration. "Well, okay, but is this a problem?"

"It means that we'll have an awful lot of explaining to do," Catarina said, looking at me. "By linking us to the blast, the Macdonalds could use it to squeeze concessions out of the Confederation which would allow them to build up their warfleet. Alternatively, if they think they're ready to start a war, they would be hard-pressed to find a better casus belli."

"Is that some kind of spaghetti dish?" Harry inquired.

I looked at Catarina. "I guess maybe we don't want to talk to the ambassador just now."

"Maybe not." She pulled the sunglasses off her face, stuck one of the earpieces in her mouth, and smiled, a real jet job. "Ken, it's a little late to ask, but why did you let Harry have demo charges?"

"I didn't actually think the Macdonalds would let him have them."

She began examining her fingernails. "Ken?"

"Yes, I know. It is inappropriate to use mass extermination to settle petty grievances. Are you mad at me?"

"That would be an understatement."

Harry looked at each of us in turn. "Is something wrong?"

Catarina sighed. "Harry, we're going to have pull out those demo charges and stop the explosion."

"Aw, darn!" Harry lightly tapped his fist against the table to express his feelings, leaving behind a small dent.

I winced. "Couldn't we just make an anonymous phone call and tell them about the bomb?"

"The only thing easier to trace than the residue from the charges would be the serial numbers. Harry, do you know where the charges are planted?"

"No, they said that I was too conspicuous to take along. Muffy knows." He scratched his head. "She said that they were going to booby-trap the charges to keep anyone from tampering with them. Is that a problem?"

"It's a problem," Catarina agreed. "Ken, do you know anything about defusing bombs?"

"I was about to ask you the same question."

She shrugged. "We'd better plan on leaving as soon as it gets dark. I'll see if there's an ordnance expert on the staff here who is willing to come along without making it a matter of official record. Harry, I need you to break the news to Muffy and get her to help."

"She had her heart set on this," Harry observed sadly.

Mentioning the word "heart" around Catarina is like waving a red cape, but she turned the corner of her mouth down with barely a glimmer of her usual enthusiasm. "I wish the two of you had nipped this in the blood, but I suppose into everyone's life, a little vein must fall."

"She's real upset," Harry noted somberly. "Oops! Don't look now."

Bobby Stemm advanced into the room like Frank Clanton walking into the O.K. Corral. He pointed one finger menacingly. "You!"

I looked around.

"MacKay! What are you doing here?!"

I shrugged. "There's this thing called breakfast."

"Where did you come from? How did you get in here?"

Catarina said in a stage whisper, "I'll explain doors if you'll tell him about the birds and the bees."

Accurately reading the expression on her face, Bobby stepped back a pace.

"Shall we continue this discussion in your office?" she said politely.

Leaving Harry behind to finish breakfast, we marched off to Bobby's office. As soon as we got inside, Catarina slammed the door shut. "Bobby, to put this in concrete terms, let me be the first to assure you that if the ambassador boots us and bollixes up our mission, Admiral Crenshaw is going to ensure that your next duty station is cold and lonely."

Bobby considered this. He began banging his head on his desk. "My career is already in ruins. Aren't the two of you satisfied?"

Catarina and I looked at each other. "No."

"It's not fair," he sobbed.

Catarina sniffed the air cautiously. "What's that I smell?"

Bobby sat bolt upright. "You can't smell anything in

here. It's impossible. I mean, there's nothing in here to smell. Nothing!" He looked at us and mopped his brow nervously. "Obviously, it's all a figment of your imagination. Would you like a cup of tea? That's it—I could pour you a nice cup of tea!"

Catarina smiled slowly. "You know, Bobby, somehow I think that for you, the 'pour tea' is over." She picked up his phone. "Hello, Trixie? Do you mind coming down to room 132?" She stopped smiling when she put the phone down.

Stemm started to stand up. "Now you wait just one minute here!"

Catarina leaned across his desk. "Bobby, Ken has had a very bad week, what with the shadur and everything. If you don't sit down and behave yourself, I'm going to turn him loose."

I saw his hand creep toward one of the drawers. Without thinking, I grabbed his wrist. Catarina studied his face, then walked around the desk and opened the drawer he had been reaching for. She pulled out a leather pouch and dumped it out on the desk. There was a pistol and four packs of cigarettes inside. "An addict. I might have known."

Bobby turned pale.

Trixie stuck her head in the door.

"Trixie, this is Lieutenant Commander Stemm. Would you please stand behind him? All right, Bobby, where did you get the cancer sticks?"

Stemm started to say, "I confiscated them as evidence—"

Trixie coughed and shook her head.

Catarina smiled. "Trixie reads minds, Bobby. Want to try again?"

Trixie rested her elbows on his shoulder. "You may call me Xuexue if you like."

"Not you," Bobby gasped.

"Would you like to tell us who told you about her?" Catarina asked. When Bobby stood mute, she exploded. "Last chance, Bobby. This is serious. If you don't come clean, I guarantee Lydia is going to fry you up one slice at a time. Want to try the truth for a change?"

Stemm nodded, tears welling up in his eyes.

"You're a smoker, aren't you?"

Stemm buried his head in his hands and began weeping. "Yes, it's true. I'm hooked."

"How long?"

"Two, three years now."

Trixie stroked his back sympathetically.

"I've tried to quit. Lord knows how many times I've tried. I just can't help myself."

Despite my dislike for Stemm, I felt a touch of compassion for him. I actually smoked part of a cigar once. Even though I didn't inhale, I could dimly grasp how nicotine craving could claw its way into a man's soul.

"I knew it would cost me my commission if it ever came out," Bobby sobbed, "but I just couldn't help myself."

Catarina grilled him remorselessly. "The Macdonalds found out you were a junkie, didn't they?"

"Yes, the Special Secret Police, somehow they knew. They threatened to expose me unless I agreed to cooperate," Bobby said brokenly. "They never trusted me completely."

I nodded sympathetically. "I wouldn't, either."

"Someone must have outed me," he sniveled.

"Who knew you were a smoker? Who was your connection?" Catarina asked, her voice hardening.

Stemm glanced around the room as if seeking a means of escape.

Catarina looked him straight in the eye. "Bobby, are you connected with SLO?"

"Me? SLO? Part of the Smokers' Liberation Organization? Ha-ha! What ever gave you that crazy idea?" Stemm said nervously.

Trixie sadly rang up strike three.

Catarina made no effort to hide the contempt in her voice. "A navy officer, tied to tobacco terrorists."

Before our eyes Bobby degenerated into a blubbering mass of self-pity, which was only a slight improvement on his usual personality. "You don't know what it's like! Saying to pushers in the park, 'Gimme two packs of filtertips.' Puffing away in a closet, waiting for that knock on the door. Having your own children sniffing at your clothing, ready to turn you in. It's living hell, I tell you," he sniffed, another helpless, disheveled, wild-eyed victim of nicotine madness, driven past the edge of despair.

I squeezed my eyes shut. Then I opened them. "Bobby, you don't have any children."

"Who recruited you, Bobby?" Catarina asked sharply.

"No! Don't ask me to betray my fellow buttheads! Ask me anything but that!"

"Bobby, you were set up." Catarina softened her voice. "SLO must have told the Special Secret Police about your habit to give them leverage over you."

I chimed in, "The Macdonalds are getting ready to attack, Bobby. If you keep blowing smoke in our eyes, civilization as we know it may go up the flue!"

"Ah, Ken . . ." Catarina looked up at the ceiling.

"Right. You do the puns."

"Bobby," she said, "if you have any vestige of honor left, as a navy officer, tell us!"

"Aren't we grasping at straws here?" I whispered.

For a few seconds Bobby sat immobile, staring down at the floor. "Yes, I knew in my heart that war was brewing." He whispered hoarsely, "The man who knows—what I am—is Gregorio Smith."

I whistled. "Wow! Gregorio Smith." I asked Catarina, "Who's Gregorio Smith?"

"When cigarettes were banned and the cigarette lobby went underground, he became consigliore for the Interstellar Tobacco Institute," she said quietly.

Trixie said, "I do not understand."

Catarina sighed, then began speaking. "Smith is a ruthless rogue lobbyist. When the tobacco ban went into effect on Earth, he formulated the plan for the cigarette industry to take over organized crime. The Mafia never had a chance." She looked at Stemm. "Why did you do it, Bobby? Betray yourself, the navy, the Confederation? Why didn't you pull out before you got in too deep?"

"I couldn't help myself," he sniffled. "A thought kept running through my mind like some giant, tolling bell that the deeper I got in, the more the movie rights would be worth."

I guess there was a certain skewed logic to it. The line between news and entertainment has gotten pretty blurry, especially since the TV stations started calling up psychopaths on slow news nights. I'm not sure I approve of the trend. I mean, when the news desk says to your average sicko, "We're paying bonus rates for interviews, have you committed any interesting crimes lately?" the response is likely to be, "Can you call back in half an hour?"

Catarina cleared her throat. "We need to talk to the ambassador." She handed the pistol to Trixie. "Keep him here and don't let him hurt himself."

She picked up the phone. "Rizvi, this is Commander Lindquist. I need to see the ambassador. No, it can't wait until his show is over. We need to see him now!" She hung up the phone. "Come on, Ken."

The ambassador received us wearing a dressing gown and a hair net. He heard Catarina out while his cats committed indignities on the furniture.

"This is a very serious matter," he exclaimed, pacing back and forth. One of the ends of the belt holding his robe together dangled, and two of the cats following him around kept batting at it.

"Yes, sir. I strongly recommend placing Stemm in close confinement immediately."

"No, no, no. I meant your questioning him without advising him of his legal rights. Officially, I can't take action based on his responses. I mean, officially, he never said anything, right?"

"Sir, I disagree. There is also the matter of the cigarettes found in his desk."

"Well, they could have been anyone's cigarettes, and it was an illegal search and seizure, was it?"

"Sir, he's a smoker."

Meisenhelder wagged his finger. "I really think that you're being too hard on him. I mean, each of us is a product of his or her environment, and none of us are really responsible for our actions, are we? It's very important to keep perspective about things like this. I mean, Lieutenant Commander Stemm can't really help being a smoker, can he?"

"I am sure we could debate this at some length, Mr. Ambassador." Catarina flashed him the smile she generally reserves for people she'd like to machine gun. "Truthfully, I'm more concerned about the war that's about to erupt."

"Oh, that." Meisenhelder waved his hand dismissively. "The Klo'klotixa government has signed a solemn treaty outlawing the use of war. If they broke that treaty, it would—it would mean nothing less than war! Yesterday, I made some discreet inquiries, and I was personally assured of Alt Bauernhof's continued peaceful intentions by no less a personage than the chairman of the council of ephors. No, I do think that you're mistaken about them. At this junction, we need to address the real problem, which is Mr. MacKay."

"Look, I'm sorry about the shadur, but they were trying to execute me."

Meisenhelder gave me what was intended to be a formidable glare. "Now, come now, Mr. MacKay. You simply cannot believe that. The government here abolished capital punishment six months ago at my express urging."

"Oh, I'm sorry. I must have been mistaken," I said with what was intended to be heavy sarcasm.

"Well, I am glad you understand that now, but the damage is done. Lieutenant Commander Stemm has provided me with the more disreputable portions of your personnel file, and I am quite shocked."

I shook my head. "I don't care what it says. I turned in both those library books on time."

Meisenhelder looked away. "Well, be that as it may, the incident with the shadur was unforgivable, completely unforgivable. I don't know how we're going to smooth matters over with the Peace Coalition for a Just Ecology. Why, the newspapers may even take the matter up!"

I gathered that from the ambassador's point of view, anything that wasn't broke didn't require fixing, and anything that didn't make the newspapers wasn't broke. Catarina lightly rested the heel of her shoe on my toe.

"Mr. Ambassador, I'm sure you see how Lieutenant Commander Stemm's difficulties complicate matters." She patted my thigh. "If, for example, your staff were to misconstrue your instructions and allow Mr. MacKay to fall into the hands of the Special Secret Police, the press would naturally assume that this was done to prevent Mr. MacKay from implicating other members of your staff as SLO agents."

"Do you really think that they would do that? Oh, bother. This is so confusing!" Meisenhelder sat down and held his head in his hands.

Seeing him hesitate, Catarina went for the jugular. "Inasmuch as vampires have been a persecuted minority for centuries, the press might even intimate that you are biased against vampires."

I swear I saw the hair on the back of Meisenhelder's neck rise up when Catarina said "persecuted minority."

"I'm sure you're familiar with the sad facts," Catarina continued smoothly. "Merely for being vampires, people like Ken have been shunned, lynched, denied employment. I know that Ken won't appreciate my telling you this, but the Interstellar Society for the Advancement of Vampires has begun documenting abuses." She lowered her voice. "They might call you a bigot."

Meisenhelder covered his mouth with his hand. "Not that!"

"I really think that it would be best for all concerned if you could get the Klo'klotixa government to release *Rustam's Slipper* and allow us to depart," Catarina concluded.

"I suppose it wouldn't hurt to try. Oh, bother! The head of the maintenance staff came in here a few minutes ago with a protest from the employees union. The union is worried about infection, and there is a rumor someone started that you two have been sacrificing kittens to the Devil—I can't think how that got around. The upshot is that unless I enforce my order and have you out of here within twenty-four hours, the union intends to declare a strike, which places me in an impossible position. Oh, bother!"

As we left I commented, "I'm just afraid that I'm going to be standing next to you when God drops a bolt of lightning. The Interstellar Society for the Advancement of Vampires?"

"Best I could do on short notice."

I shook my head. "Either he's an idiot, or I am."

"I'd like to think there's some merit in both positions." She patted me on the shoulder. "Given the Confederation's policy toward this planet, only an idiot would have accepted the ambassador's job here. Come on, we can worry about Bobby after we deal with the bomb."

"I'm just wondering how serious the bunny-lovers are about poking me with sharp objects."

Catarina caught my arm. "Is that Harry's voice I'm hearing?"

I heard it, too. Around the corner ahead of us, Harry was saying, "Oh, yeah. You remember the little guy sitting next to me? That was Ken."

"Where is he now?" someone else asked in a thick voice.

I looked at Catarina. "That sounds like the Wild woman. She's been drinking."

Catarina held a finger to her lips.

Harry responded. "I think he went in to see the ambassador. Are you sure you want to carry around a knife like that? You really could trip and hurt yourself. Well, if I see him, I'll tell him you're looking for him."

"Honest, and helpful, too—all that in one man," Catarina commented. Apart from Meisenhelder's office, there were only a limited number of places to hide. She pointed to a door. "Quick! In there."

I went in and backed out almost as quickly. It was an occupied women's rest room.

"I think I'd rather die out here," I said sheepishly.

"Right." She snapped her fingers. "Your hologram projector."

"There's too much light here. It'll look phony as hell," I said, pulling it out.

She jumped up and put her fist through the light panel overhead, landing gracefully. She lifted her hand up to wipe away some of the blood. "Ouch. That hurt."

I kissed it hurriedly and flipped the projector on. As my cat persona materialized, Catarina slipped behind me.

Wild turned the corner with a commando dagger between her teeth and a stocking wrapped around her fists like a garotte. The look of shock on her face when she saw a huge black cat staring at her was priceless.

"Felicia, I have come for you," I said in the deepest voice I could manage.

Wild dropped to her knees and extended her arms. "Master!" The knife fell from her teeth and clanked on the floor.

"No one must know that you have seen me."

Wild hiccuped. "Yes, Master."

Catarina whispered in my ear, "Tell her she has to assist Ken MacKay."

"You must assist Ken MacKay, Felicia."

"But—"

"You must not question, you must obey. You and your comrades must not act in haste. All will become clear." I added in a suitably dramatic pause. "I will come for you then. Now go!"

As she disappeared I turned off my hologram and looked at Catarina. "Do you think she's really going to follow through when she sobers up?"

Catarina shrugged. She picked up Wild's commando knife and used one of the gemstones on her butterfly pin to scratch a kittycat happy face on the blade.

Moments later we collared Harry and watched him break the bad news to Muffy, who broke a few things herself to evidence her displeasure. After I explained how things stood, I left Harry to persuade her. He showed up at my room about an hour later, looking haggard, and locked the door behind him. "Well, I talked her into it. She called her friends, and they agreed."

I put down the paperback I was reading. "Great. How did you do that?"

"Well, did you know that Macdonalds can adjust their body temperature a couple of degrees?" He used his hands to demonstrate. "You take an electric blanket and a pitcher of ice water—"

"That's fine, Harry, I don't think I need to hear the details," I said hastily. "Any problems?"

"Well," he admitted, "we're going to have some trouble when we check out. The furniture here is made out of this really cheap plastic, so—"

"That's fine, Harry, I don't need to hear the details. Is Muffy willing to come along and show us where the charges are planted?"

He shook his head. "That was kind of a sticking point."

We were interrupted by a knock at the door.

Harry slapped his forehead. "Oh, hell. That's the other problem. Hide me, quick!"

"What do you mean, 'hide you'?"

The doorknob jiggled.

"How about in the closet?" he whispered.

I waved. "Bye."

As Harry shut the closet door behind himself, I opened the door and found Wyma Jean standing in the corridor with a fire ax in her hand. "Excuse me?"

"Oh. Hi, Ken." She looked at the ax in her hands.

"Here. Give me that." I took the ax and set it against the wall. "Come on in. I think we should talk."

She hung her head. "Uh, sure, Ken."

I sat her in a chair and carefully locked the door in case anyone else wandered by. "You want to tell me what's going on?"

She shook her head emphatically.

I folded my arms and stared at her. "Try me."

She sighed and buried her face in her hands. "I just get so mad!"

"Harry?"

"Yeah. I gave that sleazy slug the best months of my life!"

I heard a muffled gasp from the closet. "That's not true!"

Wyma Jean instantly sat bolt upright.

I hammered the back end of the fire ax on the bedpost to restore decorum. I pointed to Wyma Jean. "You stay." Shouldering the ax, I walked over to the closet and kicked the door. "Come on out, Harry."

He did so cautiously.

"All right, we're going to do this navy style. Listen up, both of you. You may not have caught on yet, but we're in a lot of trouble. A lot of people here want to see us dead. Do the two of you understand?"

The two of them nodded contritely.

"We have to keep a bomb in the capitol building from going off, and then we've got to get off this planet. You two owe me for not telling me about the snake. If you don't make up and stop feuding with each other, you're off my ship. Is this clear?"

"Yes, sir," they said, looking at each other.

I lifted the ax to examine the blade. "Well? Harry?"

"All right, I'm sorry."

"Wyma Jean?"

"It was just a little snake!"

"Wyma Jean?"

She put her chin down and pouted. "Well, all right. I forgive him."

I counted to three. "And you also have to be polite to Muffy."

"That little tramp?"

I nodded. "We need her help."

After a long silence she finally said, "Well, all right."

"Harry, now it's your turn again. You've always said that you bleed navy blue."

Harry sat up and began to look worried. "Yes sir, captain!"

"And you know what it cost us to keep the navy from kicking you out of the reserves when they found out you lied about your record."

"Yes, sir." Harry began to sweat as the little wheels turned in his head.

I eyed him dispassionately. "The mission we're on is vital to the navy, and you've already come close to screwing it up. So from here on out, consider yourself on active service."

"Yes, sir." Harry stood and saluted.

I returned his salute. "And in order to ensure the success of this mission, I am ordering you to refrain from fooling around with any of the local women, including Muffy, until and unless I tell you it's okay."

The look of horror on Harry's face was counter-balanced by the look of malicious glee on Wyma Jean's.

"Now both of you get out of here."

Wyma Jean was out the door first. As Harry followed I stopped him. "Harry?"

"Yes, sir?"

"Ask Muffy again if she'll go with us. Make sure she understands that if I'm not happy, she's not happy."

To get any mission accomplished, there is the right

way, the wrong way, and the navy way. With the navy way, the less you have to explain to higher authority, the better off you are.

I went to check on Clyde, who was still under house arrest, with Marines checking on him twice a shift, which was a nuisance because we could have used him to help with the bomb. I found him lounging about in a purple dashiki that could have easily been mistaken for a scrub rag.

Clyde put down the harmonica he was holding and uncoiled from the bed. "I'm really glad you made it back, sir."

"How much did it cost you?" I asked out of curiosity.

"Twenty bucks. I thought you were a goner for sure." He shrugged. "Sorry I got caught tapping Bobby's office."

"Not your fault. You've heard about Dr. Blok. I need you to keep an eye on him for us tonight."

"Yes, sir!"

"Teach him how to play poker. He can afford it. How are things going?"

"I've been writing some poetry and teaching myself how to play harmonica. I know two songs—do you want to hear them?"

"Which songs?"

"One is 'Lonesome Road.' The other isn't."

"I'll pass."

"How about listening to some of my poetry?" Before I could object, he commenced, " 'Sun-brown Ophelia / With her Russian last name, eyes dancing / On grass, under a tree.' What do you think?"

"It reminds me a lot of Robert Frost." Not the poet, the kid who played half a season in left field for Kansas City and received his unconditional release. Hands of stone and a bat of balsa. "Why poetry?"

Clyde folded his hands. "Well, it's like, women come up to me and hear the alarm going off on my biological clock."

"So what do you plan on doing about it? Fast-acting poison or the ol' .45 slug between the eyes?"

"Well, actually I just wanted to gripe a little," Clyde admitted sheepishly. "There was this blonde in the lounge—"

"If her name was Gwen, you're better off with the poison." I slapped him on the shoulder. "Look, I would take it as a personal favor if you could stay sane at least until next Thursday."

Clyde blinked. "Bad week?"

"And getting worse." I consulted my watch. "I'd like to stay, but Catarina and I need to go over our plans for tonight."

Clyde flipped his harmonica across the room with a sudden motion. It hit the wall and bounced. "Commander Lindquist told me about the bomb. I really wish I were going with you."

"I wish you were, too, but the first time you're not here for bed check, all hell breaks loose."

"Do you think you and Commander Lindquist can pull this off?"

I sighed. "See if you can get double or nothing on your twenty bucks."

Clyde shook his head. Then he grabbed my hand and shook it firmly. "Break a leg, sir. I've got one more poem if you'd like to hear it."

"Well, you know, Clyde—"

"I wrote it for the woman who brought me into this universe."

"Clyde, that's a really nice gesture."

"I call it 'Ode to an Obstetrician.' "

"Good-bye, Clyde."

Spring Cleaning at the Legislature

I headed back to my room and locked myself in until Catarina arrived with Trixie and planted herself at the end of the bed.

I moved over to make room. "So what's our plan?"

"I talked Calvin Lorenzo, the embassy bomb disposal technician, into helping. He should be here shortly."

"What about costumes? Do we have enough cloaks?"

"We cannot wear t'ose," Trixie interjected. "Tee police do not like poor people hanging around public buildings. It gives tee wrong impression."

"Costumes are arranged," Catarina said.

"How about transportation? We can't very well ask the Secret Police for a lift."

Catarina pointed out the window to a long-suffering Battalion Leader Tskhingamsa who was dozing in his car across the street. "Tskhingamsa volunteered to lend us his car."

"He wouldn't happen to know anything about pulling charges, would he?" I asked hopefully.

She shook her head. "He doesn't want to know what we're up to. He figures it's political dynamite."

"An apt simile." We heard a knock on the door. "That should be Harry." I opened it, and Harry and Blok

146

entered, followed by Muffy and a female Macdonald with a blanket-wrapped infant in her arms. Blok was wearing a very pained expression.

Catarina raised her eyebrows. I coughed politely. "Uh, Harry, what's your new friend doing here?"

Harry looked perplexed. "You said we needed someone who knew where the charges were."

"And where did the baby come from?"

"Gee, Ken." Harry scratched his head. "I thought you knew where babies came from."

"Let's break this down. First question, what's her name?"

Harry slapped his forehead, epitomizing sensitivity. "I knew there was something I should have asked."

I shut my eyes and turned to Trixie. "Please find out if she speaks English and ask her about the baby."

Trixie conferred. She reported, "Her name is Belkasim. She understands English, but does not speak it very well. As for tee child, have you ever tried to get a babysitter on short notice?"

Catarina shook her head.

"Hold on, I have an idea." I walked across the hall and knocked on Wyma Jean's door. "Wyma Jean? Are you in there?" She opened her door. "I need you to babysit for a few hours."

Catching a glimpse of Wyma Jean through the open doors, Belkasim stiffened and reflexively curled her arms about her little wriggler.

Wyma Jean smiled at Harry. "Oh, how cute. Is it yours?"

I coughed politely.

She shrugged. "Uh, sure, Ken. How much trouble can a cute little baby be?"

No one cleared up her misconception. After Trixie explained matters, Belkasim handed the baby over. Wyma Jean's smile disappeared when Belkasim ran to Harry's room and came back dragging a diaper bag the size of a steamer trunk.

Macdonalds do not lactate. Instead they regurgitate partially digested food for their babies, a process that sounds almost as disgusting as it is in practice. Belkasim pointed out feeding bottles and explained, with help from Trixie and a lot of pantomime, that her little nipper was good for a bottle every half hour.

"What we need to talk about next," I said after we reassembled, "is getting off this planet."

Blok produced a cloth and mopped his face nervously. "I cannot get you on board your ship. It is swarming wit' Special Secret Policemen. All is lost. Tee only ship I am aut'orized to board is our newest battle cruiser which is being built." He consulted my electronic dictionary for a translation. "It is called tee *Hunting Snark*." Like most things the government buys, my dictionary was purchased from the lowest bidder.

I looked at Catarina. Maybe this mind-reading stuff starts to rub off after a while. "No. Don't even think about it."

Harry looked bewildered. Taking pity on him, Trixie whispered in his ear. He immediately began jumping up and down. "If we steal a battle cruiser, can we keep it, can we keep it? Huh? Huh?"

"Maybe we could borrow it to swap for our ship later on," Catarina said, grinning.

"Maybe we have other options. Anybody got any ideas?" I asked desperately. Borrowing a battle cruiser seemed a little ostentatious.

Muffy stood up. "Tee battle cruiser, built from money wrung from tee ranks of tee economically disadvantaged, is a symbol of male hierarchical dictatorship and slavish adherence to linear, left-brain modes of t'ought!" I noticed her English was improving. "By seizing it in tee name of revolution, we will strike a blow for esteem-impoverished females everywhere!"

"To tee barricades!" Belkasim announced shrilly.

It reminded me of a logically underenhanced production of *Les Miserables*. "Any other ideas?" I asked.

Catarina shrugged. "If we're going to steal a ship, we might as well go first-class."

"We don't have the *Hunting Snark*'s command code, and I don't know how to hot-wire one of these things. Did the academy offer a course in Grand Theft Spaceship when you were going through?"

"I programmed tee command code," Blok admitted.

"We'll still have to figure how to get past security at the spaceport, steal a shuttle, and then get past security at the space station," Catarina said, ever practical. "Why don't we deal with one harebrained scheme at a time?"

"Good idea," I said.

A few minutes later our ordnance expert, Calvin Lorenzo, appeared dragging a satchel and an electronic easel, and Catarina made introductions. Calvin was a short guy with a beaky nose, very short hair, and ears that left his head at a ninety-degree angle. "I hear you need me." He set up his easel and turned it on. "I took the map of the building's interior you gave me and turned it into a diagram for easy reference."

I squinted at it. "I assume Catarina briefed you on the situation."

"Yes, and it appears to me that the first thing we need

is a plan." He erased the diagram. "Let me show you this chart."

"Fine." I studied it. "What is it?"

"It shows the above-average success rate of ventures with above-average leadership contrasted with the below-average success rate of ventures without proper leadership. There you have it—the first thing we need is the right leader. Let me show you another chart here."

Harry stirred. Harry may not be summa cum laude, but having shipped with us, he knows fertilizer. "Ken?" he rumbled.

"I don't think we need to see any more charts," I said tactfully. "Calvin, are you saying you want to be in charge?"

"Only if the people here want me," he stated piously.

"Fine. May I suggest a solution?"

"I'm all ears."

"Let's put it to a vote." I looked around the room. "All in favor of Lorenzo here running the operation, raise your hands."

Calvin cautiously raised his hand.

"Now, all in favor of Catarina and me running the operation, raise your hands."

Five hands went up. Belkasim, who looked somewhat bewildered, declined to cast a ballot. "Would you want a recount?" I asked politely.

Harry folded his arms.

"The people have spoken," Calvin concluded.

"Calvin, please put the diagram of the building back up. Trixie, I'd like you to translate for Muffy and Belkasim." I gestured. "There's a car waiting for us out-side. At 1900 we'll meet in the embassy garage and head out. Harry, can you arrange things with the Marine guards and the cops outside?"

"Sure, Ken."

"The car holds six, so the people going will be me, Catarina, Calvin, Muffy, Belkasim, and Trixie. Harry, I'm going to need you to stay behind."

"Aw, Ken! I want to go. Why can't I go?" Harry pouted.

"There isn't enough room in the car, and I need you here in case something goes wrong. Tell the ambassador about the bomb if you don't hear from us by 0500."

"Aw, Ken!"

"I promise I'll take you on the next suicide mission."

"Well, all right."

"Trixie, you'll drive." I pointed to the diagram. "Assuming the place isn't crawling with cops, we'll park across the street and try one of the back entrances. Muffy, can you and Belkasim mark where the charges are located on Calvin's diagram? Good. Here's what we do. I'll guard the door while Calvin goes inside to disarm the charges. You two will wait outside with Catarina in case we have trouble locating any of them. When we have all of the charges disarmed, we'll load them in the trunk, pitch them in the river, and come back here and get some sleep."

Harry raised his hand. "What about the fertilizer?"

"I doubt that anyone will notice an extra ton of manure in a statehouse," Catarina said, "but if they do, it's just too bad."

Calvin was shaking his head emphatically.

"Calvin?" I asked.

"As I see it, our biggest problem is determining how those charges are gimmicked before we try to disarm them," he observed forcefully. "Everything else depends on that."

"Good point. Muffy, do you and Belkasim know?"

Muffy and Belkasim didn't know.

Calvin pondered this. "Well, the simplest way to booby-trap one of those charges would be to run a hairfine wire to a spring attached to the detonator." He called up a sketch on his easel. "You just run that wire across a door knee-high, and the little noise you hear going into the room is actually a giant sucking sound from a southerly direction."

Muffy and Belkasim looked at each other. "No wires."

"Well, we'll take along an ultraviolet light, just in case," Calvin commented. "Now, another thing popular among the home explosives crowd is a tiny cup of mercury mounted inside the charge so that when you lift it, the mercury will spill and complete an electrical connection to trip the detonator, but this is tricky and best left to professionals."

No little cups of mercury.

Calvin appeared moderately disgruntled. "Well, the next best way to booby-trap a charge is to attach a motion sensor."

Harry gave him a quizzical look. "If you attached a motion sensor to a bomb, wouldn't you blow yourself up trying to leave the room?"

"If you were goofy enough not to have the motion sensor set on a timer, I suppose it would, but most people would just set the timer so that the motion sensor doesn't begin to operate until after they leave." Calvin rummaged through his satchel. "Let's see if I've got one here." He pulled one out.

Muffy and Belkasim both pointed and chattered away

in Sklo'kotax. "T'at is what was used," Trixie translated. "One motion sensor for each."

That meant ten motion sensors to be disarmed, and presumably the areas they covered overlapped. Calvin began sketching in arcs for the motion sensors.

"It looks like we can still go in the back door without setting anything off," I commented. "How do we neutralize them?"

"Easiest thing is a taser gun." Calvin reached into his satchel and pulled one out. "It shoots out a stream of electrical particles that will trip the cutouts on the sensors." He pointed to the diagram. "We can drill a few holes in the walls to get clear shots. Of course, we have to be careful not to hit the charges. If we hit one, half the city will be happy to tell us about it." Calvin looked at me. "It's going to take two of us in there."

Harry raised his hand. "Can I go? Can I go?"

"No." I looked at Catarina. "I'm not much of a pistol shot, but I'm a wizard with a drill."

She smiled and held out a coin. "I'll flip you for it."

I took the coin from her. "I'll flip. You cheat."

I tossed, and she lost. "All right, Calvin, what's the drill on disarming these things?"

Calvin held up both his hands. "Now, Ken, ordnance is not nuclear science. We don't know exactly what it's like in there, so there's no sense fiddling with the details. When the time comes, we'll just do the right thing."

"Uh, Calvin, I don't think you understand. Those of us who do not play with high explosives on a regular basis would feel much more comfortable if you outline what you expect we'll encounter when we get inside. That is *the plan*. Once we understand *the plan*, then we can all critique it to make it better."

"That's where you're wrong. Don't you see, Ken? That's where leadership comes in." Calvin threw his chest out and smiled to show that he really didn't hold my abject stupidity against me. "It isn't the critic who counts. The credit goes to the man down there in the arena, with dirt and sweat and blood on his face. That man strives valiantly and comes up short, but he knows, in the end, the triumph of high achievement; and if he fails, at least he fails while daring greatly. One percent planning and ninety-nine percent execution, that's the key to success!"

I ran my fingers through my hair to see if any of it was falling out. "Calvin, stay with me here—the idea behind planning is to anticipate things that can go wrong."

He looked at me with those shiny little eyes and said in a sympathetic voice, "Now, there's your trouble, Ken. If you go through life worrying about the bad things that can happen, pretty soon you convince yourself that it's best not to do anything at all."

We were interrupted by a knock on the door. "I didn't know we were expecting anyone else," I said in a deceptively calm voice.

"That's not Wyma Jean," Harry observed, from deep and bitter experience.

I looked around the room. "Harry, why don't you answer it while the rest of us disappear."

Whoever was outside knocked again. Calvin scooped up his satchel and disappeared into the closet with his charts, and we had an interesting moment figuring out how many Macdonalds could fit in there with him. Catarina and I crouched behind the bed, and I gestured to Harry to see who it was.

When he opened the door, Mickey, Minnie, and

Bunkie walked in. Minnie was towing a large, gaily colored shopping bag mounted on wheels, and she and Mickey bowed. "Mr. Harry, how pleasant it is to see you! We are looking for friend Ken and friend Catarina. Would you perhaps know where we could find them?"

Harry pointed.

"Friend Catarina and friend Ken, why are you hiding behind the bed?" Minnie asked. She and Mickey looked at each other and nodded their pointed little heads. "If it is a game, may we play, too?"

I looked at Catarina. "When we heard you at the door, we thought that people were coming to take us away. Either the Marines, or people dressed in white."

"No, it was us," Minnie observed. "Friend Ken, may we impose our company upon you?"

"Well, to be completely truthful, we're a little busy right now. Can this wait?"

Bunkie cleared her throat. "Sir, this should only take a moment and it is time-sensitive, otherwise we would not have interrupted."

Mickey produced a lengthy document from under his arm. "Friend Ken, would you be adverse to co-signing a loan for us? In place of Uncle Cheeves."

"How big a loan?"

"What is it? One hundred forty-seven million?" Mickey said airily.

I looked at Catarina. "This is a trick question, isn't it?"

"What do you need a hundred forty-seven million for?" Catarina asked.

"Computer projections indicate that this is an excellent time for us to diversify, and it would take at least two weeks for us to set up a stock offering," Bunkie said stiffly.

"Things here are dreadfully bureaucratic!" Minnie expostulated.

"The law doesn't recognize limited partnerships, and it would hurt Uncles Cheeves's feelings if we took in general partners—he worries about us so," Mickey explained. "So a small loan is the only possible solution."

I glanced at the document he was holding. Bunkie deftly grasped it and turned it right side up. Catarina studied it over my shoulder. I sighed. "Just run me through the high points, Bunkie."

"Well, sir," she said deferentially, "the loan falls due in a little over four months. The agreement provides for four essentially nominal interest payments and for repayment of the principal in gold at current rates. In effect, the investors here are so convinced that the value of gold will increase that they are willing to provide us the money interest-free."

"We tried to write in a clause allowing them to request repayment in currency in case gold loses value, but they declined." Mickey twitched his whiskers. "I really do not understand their attitude."

I sat down on the edge of the bed. "Looks great, guys. Now why do I need to sign?"

"Some of the investment bankers became concerned when they found out that we were minors," Minnie explained. "It is so unfair."

Bunkie looked away. "They, umm, feel that the government may try to restrict future importation of gold from Plixxi, and, umm, feel that your signature gives them a certain degree of assurance that we will fulfill our end of the contract."

"I wonder if smuggling pays better than espionage." I turned to Catarina. "What do you think?"

She smiled. "I think it's a great idea."

I blinked my eyes rapidly to make sure the system was functioning. "Excuse me, could you repeat that? For a minute there I thought you said that it was a great idea."

"Ken, if things go sour, the worst that could happen is that your creditors would seize *Rustam's Slipper*, which the government isn't going to return anyway."

"Well, yes." I mulled this over. Up until now I had managed to cherish the touching illusion that as soon as the unpleasantness with Wipo was settled, I could go back to being a ship captain. "Well, what's the absolute worst that could happen?"

"They do have debtor's prisons here," Bunkie said uneasily.

"If I get caught, the agency running the debtor's prison is going to have to stand in line to get me."

"I would mention," Catarina added, "that because we've become the Special Secret Police pension fund, we are running a little short on cash."

"You need cash?" Minnie looked in her shopping bag. "I'm afraid we didn't stop. Would a few hundred thousand tide you over until morning?"

"Thanks, Minnie. That would do just fine." I looked at Bunkie. "Bunkie, is this legitimate?"

"Yes, sir."

"Oh, well." I signed the thing.

Minnie and Mickey both bowed. "Thank you, friend Ken. We greatly appreciate your confidence in us," Mickey added. "As Bucky says, 'Trust is the superglue of friendship.' "

I watched them file out the door. "I wonder why Wipo hasn't tried to pick them up?"

Catarina shook her head. "No one could suspect those

three of being spies. Also, by now they can buy and sell Wipo out of petty cash."

There was another knock on the door. "This place is busier than a subway station. Harry, can you get that?" It turned out to be Rosalee. I searched for the proper euphemism. "Hello, Rosalee. How is the, ah, entertainment business?"

"I've been dirtside so long I'm starting to itch, but the whores in this burg are suffering," she complained, dropping herself in a chair. "Somebody needs to do something about this planet. I know the males around here can't do much with their little weed whackers, but they ought to learn to use what they've got."

"Maybe hookers here ought to push for professional status, like lawyers. They could emphasize the therapy angle—maybe offer courses."

"You know, Ken, you may be on to something there." She looked at me. "Excuse me, I need to find a phone."

"I have an awfully big mouth," I commented to Catarina as the door slammed shut. "We'd better polish up a scheme to get off this planet, because when the Macdonalds do catch up with us, they're going to want to shoot us on sight." A muffled thump emanated from the closet. "Did we forget something?"

Harry ran over, jerked the closet door open, and a stack of bodies spilled out. Calvin emerged from the bottom of the pile sporting a black eye and appearing none too pleased about it.

"Elbow?" Catarina inquired cheerfully.

"Easel," he admitted.

"All right, everybody." I glanced around the room. "Catarina has native dress for all of us to wear. If nobody has anything else to add, I'll see you all in the garage next to the elevator at 1900 hours."

"Wait! Hold your horses, Ken!" Calvin reached back into his satchel. "We're not done yet."

"But we will be," Trixie observed sadly.

Calvin pulled out a handful of pocket radios. "Now it stands to reason that we're going to need proper communications and proper communications security. Ken, what would you like for your call sign?"

Catarina started grinning, but I was drawing a blank. "Call sign?"

"Sure. Each tactical element gets a call sign. Since you're the strike force leader, your number would be 'Six.' "

I thought for a moment. "How about 'Blue'? I can be 'Blue Six.' "

"Blue Six! Ken, you've got to get with the program here! When somebody listening in hears a call sign, they've got to know the kind of people they're dealing with! 'Blue Six' sounds like a cheap food additive. You need something strong, a name like—like gunslinger! That's it! You'll be 'Gunslinger Six,' and I'll be 'Gunslinger Five.' "

Harry jumped up and down. "It's not fair. I want to be a gunslinger, too."

I shrugged. "All right, you can be 'Gunslinger Two.' "

Trixie was providing a running translation, and before Calvin could object, Belkasim broke in to insist that Wyma Jean have a radio.

"What should her call sign be?" Muffy asked.

Catarina's eyes twinkled. "How about 'Wild Woman'?"

Muffy and Belkasim conferred briefly. Apparently

they wanted to be "Wild Woman," too. With considerable ill grace, Calvin acceded to their demand. Then Catarina and I tossed everyone out so we could get some rest.

I pulled Harry aside as he was about to leave. "Harry, one thing's been bothering me. How you keep getting all the female Macdonalds past the Marines at the gates."

Harry began studying the tops of his shoes. "Uh . . ."

Catarina sprawled out on the bed and closed her eyes. "Harry, just pretend we didn't believe your first explanation and skip ahead to your second."

Harry took a deep breath. "Well, I gave them a few souvenirs. You know, from the Rats. Like, uh, some Rodent uniforms and a couple of battle flags."

I gazed up at him in amazement. "Why, Harry. I'm touched that you would do that to help out. Those souvenirs are some of your most treasured possessions. Wait a minute, you don't own any Rodent battle flags. In fact, Rodents don't have battle flags."

"Well, no," he admitted.

Catarina groaned and rolled over. "You haven't been palming phony souvenirs off on the Marines, have you?"

Harry's conscience got the better of him. "Ken?"

"Yes?"

"When the embassy bills us for bedsheets—go ahead and take it out of my share."

After the door closed behind him, I asked Catarina, "What do you think?"

"If everything goes right we'll have the charges and be out in fifteen minutes." She shrugged. "We can bring along a package of marshmallows in case everything doesn't go right. Are you sure you want to help Calvin disarm charges?"

"I feel responsible."

"You are responsible." She reached into her belt purse. "Here, want to split a chocolate bar? You look like you could use one."

"You're right about that." I accepted half of it from her and began gnawing on it thoughtfully. "You know, we really have to figure out how to get off this planet. When the Marines figure out that Harry has been passing out bogus Rodent war souvenirs, it'll be unanimous—every being on the planet with a gun will be trying for a piece of us."

"Excellent point."

"Besides, the laundry here insists on starching my underwear, so I'm running out of clean clothes." I finished off my chocolate and looked around the room for more. There was a knock at our door. "Now, who could that be?"

It was Trixie. She looked at us nervously. "I must show you somet'ing. You must come quickly."

She led us to Wyma Jean's room where the video was on. Trixie told her, "Please turn tee channel back."

Wyma Jean lifted her head off the sofa. "Do we have to? Soaprah's on."

"Just for a minute, Wyma Jean," I coaxed.

Catarina suddenly stiffened. "Ken," she said in a low voice, "I think we're in real, deep, deep trouble."

As we watched, a cute little animated animal that looked suspiciously like a Rodent poked its head out of what was obviously a beaver lodge with a beaver dam in the background.

"It is a new show called 'Tee Adventures of Bucky Beaver.' Tee narrator said t'is week's adventure is

'Bucky Beaver Meets Bun Rabbit,' " Trixie explained. "Tee narrator sounds exactly like Mjarlen."

We sat through the animated part of the adventure in stony silence. At the end, Mjarlen appeared to explain the story's moral overtones, including the symbolic significance of the penny that Bun Rabbit picked up, the phrase "And all the day you'll have good luck," and the applicability of the seventh commandment.

"Well, maybe it won't have much of an impact," I said with a greater degree of cheer than I felt.

Catarina silently pointed to Trixie. "It was such a beautiful story," Trixie sniffled, wiping her eyes.

"Can we put Soaprah back on now?" Wyma Jean demanded.

We went back to Catarina's room and laid down to get some rest. As I say, ours is a strange relationship. I studied her face as she napped. Her flowing hair was of white gold; her forehead the Elysian fields; her eyebrows two celestial arches; her eyes a pair of glorious suns; her cheeks two beds of roses; her neck alabaster; her hands of polished ivory; her bosom whiter than new-fallen snow—all the usual. Some of the Catholic religious orders know a lot more about vamps than they let on, and before Catarina had me to look after, she had seriously contemplated joining one of them. Of course, every time I suggest moving a step forward or sideways in our relationship, she starts dropping hints about the advantages of a contemplative life.

"Are you awake?" I asked.

She opened one eye. "No."

"I just wanted to apologize for telling Harry he could have the charges. It was a pretty dumb thing to do." I cocked my head. "Is that somebody out in the hall?"

She patted me on the arm and turned over. "Go to sleep."

"Are you sure nobody knows we're here? Rizvi struck me as a pretty sharp guy for a career bureaucrat, and the ambassador did leave orders to have us kicked out on sight." I heard a rattling noise and sat up. "What's that?"

"It's probably just a cartload of chocolate chip cookies," Catarina said sleepily, curling up next to me. "Take two and call me in the evening. As you say, Rizvi is a pretty sharp guy, for a bureaucrat."

Around 1850 hours Catarina and I dressed up as Elvis impersonators and headed down to the garage. As we were climbing into the elevator, a tall Marine captain took me by the guitar. "Mr. MacKay? I'm Captain Kuzmaul, head of the embassy security detachment. May I speak with you?"

Kuzmaul was tall and athletic-looking, and under the circumstances, he was easily the last person I wanted to see. However, the door wouldn't close with his arm in the way, so I smiled at him. "I'm in a bit of a hurry."

"This will only take a minute."

My arm didn't seem to be going anywhere of its own volition, so I smiled at Catarina. "I'll meet you in the garage in a minute."

Catarina looked at me with concern. "Do you need directions?"

"Not if they begin with 'Fourth floor and seven years ago.'"

What she meant was, "Did I need help?" to which the proper answer was, "Yes, but only my psychiatrist knows for sure."

I followed Kuzmaul down the hall to his office, where

I gingerly planted my posterior in an armchair. Kuzmaul locked the door. "Ah, Captain MacKay—"

"Please, call me Ken."

"A few matters have come to my attention."

"I'm sure I have an excellent, and possibly even believable explanation for everything."

"I'm not quite sure how to broach this subject with you. It seems that one of your crew members—a Mr. Harry Halsey—sold some of my men artifacts allegedly taken from Prince Genghis's Rodent warfleet." He paused. "There seems to be a question as to their authenticity. For example, one of the battle flags examined had 'Property of the Confederation Foreign Office' inscribed on the reverse side in the lower right-hand corner."

Truth is the first casualty in war, and it looked like I was the second. I shrugged. "Considering the source, I'd say that every souvenir your boys purchased is phonier than a three-term congressman."

Kuzmaul ran his fingers through his sandy hair. "This is very difficult for me."

"Placing me under arrest? I don't know. It seems like everyone else has."

"Oh, no sir." He looked down at the desk. "I meant that, well, Mr. Halsey is navy. It's just that, well, Marines have been selling fake war trophies to swabbies since the dawn of time, and if it ever got out my men bought fake war trophies from a swabbie, well—the Corps would never be the same, sir."

He looked me straight in the eye. "I've burned the stuff and sworn my men to secrecy."

I nodded. "Right. I'll handle my end. It never happened."

He shook my hand solemnly. "Thank you, sir."

He walked over and unlocked the door. "The boys all asked me to wish you luck on making it out of here."

"That's really nice of them. Tell them we'll give it our best shot."

"I'm glad to hear that, sir. Some of them may have bet a little more money than they should have." He reached into his jacket and pulled out an envelope. "I was asked to give you this. Once again, best of luck, sir."

"Thanks."

Catarina was waiting for me with Muffy, Trixie, and Belkasim. Trixie was wearing a submachine gun, crossed bandoleers, and an Interstellar Rifle Association hat. "How did it go with Kuzmaul?" Catarina asked.

"He wants us to forget those phony souvenirs of Harry's ever existed. He also gave me this." I opened the envelope and began reading. "I'm being audited."

Catarina folded her arms. "I told you that you couldn't accelerate depreciation on a missile launcher."

I tossed my audit notice into a corner and looked around. "Where's Calvin?" My radio beeped and I held it up to my ear. "Hello."

"Gunslinger Six, is that you? This is Wild Woman Six. You're supposed to answer with your call sign!"

"Uh, sure. What's up, Wyma Jean?"

I heard her say, "Oh, my God! Not again." There was a brief silence. Then she said in a subdued voice, "Ken, this isn't working. I figured out why the diaper bag is so big."

"Sorry. You'll just have to do the best you can until we get back."

"You know, Ken, I've been thinking."

"What's wrong? Er, ah, what have you been thinking about?"

"I want to be a dancer."

"Sure, and I want to be solvent."

"I'm serious, Ken!"

I thought I had at least as much of a chance of becoming solvent as she had of becoming a dancer, but I tried to inject some slight degree of sympathy into my voice. "What kind? Ballet? Tap? Belly?"

"Ken! I'm serious!"

"Sorry." I tried to imagine Wyma Jean doing *Swan Lake* but it kept coming out as *Pelican Wallow*. "Can you hold that thought for a moment?" I cupped my hand over the receiver and motioned to Catarina. "She wants to be a dancer. Does our health insurance cover psychiatric care?"

"You'll want to ask her what steps she plans to take to achieve her goal, but that looks like Calvin, so could we continue this discussion another time?"

Wyma Jean was saying, "Oh, my God! There he goes again. Where does the little slug hide it all? Ken, you got to get his mother up here quick with a shovel!"

"Uh, Wyma Jean, we've got to get moving here. Why don't you think about this dance thing for a day or so, and then we'll talk."

"Ken!!!!!"

"Gunslinger Six out." I turned off my radio and looked at Catarina. "When we bill Admiral Crenshaw, do we put this down as 'day care' or 'hazardous waste'?"

Calvin walked up and dropped his satchel. "I'm here. Why aren't we ready to go? We're already four minutes behind schedule."

We trooped out to where the car was waiting. Tskhingamsa tossed Catarina the car keys and disappeared. Muffy, Trixie, and Belkasim piled into the front of the vehicle. Catarina, Calvin, and I scrunched down in back.

Calvin grumbled, "You would think these people would appreciate what we're about to do for them. We're risking our necks to save their capitol and all of their elected representatives."

Catarina grinned.

"Calvin," I said earnestly, "think what you're saying."

Trixie stopped the car in the parking lot for the pet hotel. The capitol loomed over us, its massive dome showing the influence of human statuary styles. On top, beneath a very large dollar sign, a Legislator straddled a hog-tied Truth surrounded by gargoyles representing various special interests.

Calvin and I got out, brushed our hair, and walked across the street. When we reached the door, Calvin pushed down on the lever. "It's locked!" he announced in a high-pitched nasal voice.

Plans rarely survive contact with the people assigned to carry them out.

"Any ideas?" I inquired.

"We could blow it open. Of course, that's likely to detonate the charges inside. Now, I personally wouldn't do it that way, but you keep telling me that you're the boss, and—"

"Thanks, Calvin." I touched my radio. "Uh, Gunslinger Six to Gunslinger Four, we got a problem. The door's locked. Ask Muffy how she got in before."

"She says she used the key," Catarina reported back.

"Did she bring it?"

"No," Catarina said cheerfully.

"We're already seven minutes behind schedule," Calvin pointed out helpfully.

"Do you have any constructive ideas on how to get inside without setting off the charges?" I asked him.

"If I had planned this operation, obviously I would have considered the possibility of the door being locked and taken appropriate precautions," Calvin explained as he took out a small drill and bored a hole in the door to insert an optical relay and scope out the interior. "Now, I'm not running this show—as you keep telling me, you're in charge—but it's obvious to me that we have here a locked door with no key, so the solution is to pick the lock."

"Good idea," I said. "Can you?"

"What do I look like to you? A burglar? I am an ordnance disposal expert, and proud of it! Everybody knows there's no locked doors in ordnance disposal."

Swelled heads yes, locked doors no. I saw Catarina approach and fought down my first impulse, which was to embrace her, and my second, which involved Calvin. "Can you pick the lock?"

"But of course," she said, producing a tool designed for that purpose.

"She can cook, too," I explained to Calvin as Catarina worked on the lock. She gently pushed the door open.

Three cars full of cops pulled up. A dozen police piled out and began milling around the parking lot.

Catarina pulled the door shut. "Maybe we should defer this for a few minutes. Up on the roof?"

We grabbed Calvin and climbed a ladder conveniently positioned as a fire escape. From there we surveyed our predicament. Another three cop cars were pulled around in front, conveniently blocking our egress. I pointed. "That's Wipo. I recognize the hat. What's he doing here?" I looked at Calvin. "You didn't tell anybody where we were going, did you?"

"Not unless you count Lieutenant Commander Stemm—you all right, Ken? You look a little weak around the liver."

"No, I'm fine. I always groan when I feel this good." I asked Catarina, "What do you think?"

She smiled in the darkness. "I think we have a problem."

Feeling unusually conspicuous in silver spandex, I carefully ran my hand over the ledge where we were sitting. "Do they have pigeons here?"

"No," Catarina said judiciously.

"Good. That means that I'm sitting in something else."

"Things could be worse," Catarina observed as we watched the Special Secret Police sniff around the building.

"Excuse me? Here we are, trapped by people who intend to kill us, on top of a building that's going to blow up in six hours, and you say things could be worse. How could things possibly be worse?"

Just then I felt a raindrop hit the end of my nose. "That was intended to be a rhetorical question."

"We've got to get off of our bully pulpits and do something!" Calvin volunteered.

Catarina handed me her guitar and reached into her belt purse for some change. "You call it. Heads, we stay up here until we go out in small pieces. Tails, we go down there and eat lead."

"Maybe we could hold off on making a decision for an hour or so," I suggested.

Catarina brightened. "While we're waiting, we could tell ghost stories. I know some good ones about poltergeists who scrawl graffiti on subway trains, and other things that go bump when they write."

I took the coin from her and tossed it. "Tails it is," I lied.

She patted me on the arm. "Here's the plan. I create a diversion. You and Calvin slip inside and disarm the charges."

I shook my head. "Let's flip for the honor. That way if I win, I don't have to finish doing my taxes."

She looked down her nose at me. "Why do you always wait until the last minute to file?"

"Hey! I get an automatic thirty-day extension for being off-planet. Besides, there are several possible endings to this mission, not all of which necessitate my filing taxes this year."

"Would you believe I had to fill out a 4562 and an 8829 this year?" Calvin said gloomily. "*And* a schedule H."

Catarina took the coin from me. "Call it."

"Heads," I said.

"*And* I made a mistake figuring my capital gains, which means I've got to fork over an extra three hundred that I hadn't counted on," Calvin continued.

Catarina caught the coin neatly and slapped it on her wrist. "Tails it is." She held it out for me to see.

"Two out of three?" I suggested.

Catarina ignored me, and we both ignored Calvin. "I think I can crawl to the car without being noticed. Hopefully, the crowd will follow me. Give me the cash you're carrying." She began transferring it from my belt pouch to hers. "If I'm spotted, I'll try the money-scattering trick."

"Lydia is going to flip when she sees this on our expense account."

"We can always write it off on next year's taxes as an unreimbursed business expense." With that she was gone. We watched as she stealthily crept along a hedge that looked like embalmed sauerkraut until she reached the street.

"Not much of a diversion," Calvin sniffed.

He was closer to the edge than I was, and I considered creating my own diversion. A moment later Catarina reached the car without being spotted. She turned around, put her fingers to her mouth and whistled loudly. Instantly, every cop wandering around the building turned to see what was up. She held up her arm and waved. "Yoo hoo, over here!" She climbed inside, and Trixie put pedal to the plastic.

The effect on the cops was galvanic. They all piled back into their cars and sped off in hot pursuit.

"You know, Ken, I don't mean to sound critical, but this is almost as disorganized as if you had a bunch of politicians running it," Calvin grumped as we climbed down. I tried thinking pleasant thoughts.

The cops hadn't gotten around to locking the door on us, so we were in, a fact I immediately had cause to regret. Despite the breathing mask I was wearing, which was designed to filter out particulate matter and a number of unhealthy gases, the interior smelled like dead whale, which is one of those lively but penetrating odors that stick with your clothing and the lining of your respiratory apparatus. I had no doubt that I would be reminded of the moment for hours, if not years, to come.

The wig and Elvis mask weren't helping me very much so I ditched them. As fertilizer flakes drifted and eddied around the dome in the glare of our lights, I sighed and said, "I can't help feeling that there's something very symbolic about all of this."

"You know, Ken," Calvin observed, "your problem is that you talk so gosh-darned much that no one else can hardly get a word in edgewise. You know, when I was your age, I learned that the most important thing that a human being can learn is to be able to suffer in silence, which reminds me of a little story—"

"Oh, look," I said, "there's one of the charges."

We fried the motion sensor.

"So far, so good," I commented.

Calvin sat down with a pair of wire cutters and began working on the charge. Suddenly, he stopped. He waved the wire cutters for emphasis. "You know, Ken, I've been giving this some thought."

"Eh?"

"What is the right thing to do here? I mean, don't you see—these Macdonalds just aren't very nice people, and we're going to have to settle with the goomers sooner or later."

"Later is nice."

"I mean, they're spoiling for a fight, and the longer the dang-blasted Confederation bureaucrats wait to give them one, the tougher they're going to be."

"Come again?"

"Ken, the Confederation is just bumbling along here. The problem is a failure of leadership. These guys are trying to push past us, and all we do is sit around and whine about it. It's just goofy. We've stopped being tough and resilient. All we want to do is feel good for the moment and let the future take care of itself. What we need to do is hunker down and concentrate on some blocking and tackling—you see what I'm saying?"

"Can we talk about this after we disarm the charges here?"

"But don't you see, Ken, when you see a snake, you kill it—you don't hire a consultant and form a committee on snakes. If we just make things happen here, when the little people back home see what's going on, they'll force the bureaucrats to do the right thing!" His eyes misted over. "Don't you see that the future of the Confederation is in our hands?"

"Calvin, are you sure this is the right time and place to discuss this?"

Calvin folded his arms. "Ken, there is always no better time and place to start than the present."

I stared up at the ceiling. Calvin was clearly one of those people who would rather be right than president and didn't have to worry too much one way or the other. "If I'm understanding you correctly, you're saying we should let the bomb go off and wait for the war to start. Did it possibly occur to you that this might be the tiniest bit illegal, immoral, and fattening?"

"Ken, you got to quit hanging 'round those ivory tower guys. Roll up your sleeves and get under the hood on this thing!"

"But—"

"Get down here in the real world, where the rubber meets the road!"

"But—"

"Ken, let me try and explain this to you one more time, nice and simple." He pulled a piece of paper out of his pocket. "Now, see this diagram here—"

"Uh, Calvin—"

"Are you going to let me finish a sentence here? I have no patience with people who won't let me get a single word out. There aren't many hunters left, but everybody wants the meat. Now, as I was saying—"

"Calvin, can I—"

"Ken, can I just finish *one* sentence without interruption? I know what you're trying to do, and it won't work. It's like trying to slip sunrise past a rooster. You remember I don't need to be here, and if you keep badgering me like this, I'll be out of here in a New York minute. Let me tell you a little story."

The story had a great deal to do with goats and chickens, but not a whole lot to do with demolition charges, and "little" was obviously an elastic term. Sincerity being an overrated virtue, I picked up both of the taser guns. "Do these things work?" I aimed one and pulled the trigger.

"Ouch! That was my foot, you big dummy!"

"That was the general idea."

Whatever his other faults, Calvin was not stupid. "You wouldn't do that! It's inhuman!"

I fired another bolt of electricity that landed about an inch from his right shoe. "I'm not human—I'm a vamp. And I am having a really rotten week, so let's get with the program. If you help me pull the charges, you're a hero. If you don't, you're a lightning rod. Which would you prefer, Column A or Column B?"

Column A, it was. Using Belkasim's diagram, we drilled some holes, shot out the motion sensors, and removed the charges carefully to avoid creating sparks which might potentially complicate and/or shorten my existence. It took us ten or fifteen minutes, and Calvin, who apparently did have a rudimentary sense of self-preservation, was unnaturally quiet throughout.

As we stacked the last charge neatly by the door, I said, "Good job, Calvin."

"Don't imagine you can get back in my good graces just like that!" he snapped.

I opened the door. "Uh, Calvin—"

"There is no more forgiving man on the face of this planet, but if you think that I'm going to forget for one minute—"

I tugged at his sleeve. "Uh, Calvin—"

"And don't try and change the subject!" He turned his head to see what I was looking at and shut up.

I grinned weakly. "Hello, Wipo."

"We meet again, Mr. MacKay. Or may I say, Mr. Bond." Wipo was holding something that looked like a stovepipe with a steroid problem. "Place your hands in tee air and do not move. I am holding a zapor gun pointed at your heart."

"My least vulnerable part." I tilted my head. "Don't you mean vapor gun?"

"No." Wipo aimed the thing at my midsection. "It is a product of our technology. If I pull tee trigger, it will excite every nerve ending in your body with hideous pain."

It sounded too much like being married, so reluctantly I raised my hands. "You wouldn't happen to know a good bail bondsman, would you? Normally, I keep a card on me, but—"

"Come wit' me to tee car." Wipo wrinkled his nose. Then he wrinkled it again. "Perhaps, on second t'ought, we should hose you down first."

Plots Inspissate Better with Cornstarch

After Wipo's boys gave me a quick rinse and dry, we drove four blocks to Special Secret Police Headquarters. Along the way I figured out that, unlike their underlings, Macdonald bigwigs ride in cars with *big* fuzzy dice. When we arrived, large persons with sharp spears escorted me back down to my cell.

There were a few changes in the old hole. There was now fresh hardware on the wall—ringbolts and such—as well as a little table with a vase of white roses on top to give the place a homey atmosphere. A little guy with a hangdog expression came by to check my inseam and shuddered when he saw my taste in clothing. He took measurements and returned with form-fitting shackles for my waist, ankles, thighs, upper arms, and wrists.

Wipo dropped by a few hours later to assess progress and found me whistling "The Lonely Bull" to cope with what was turning out to be yet another set of Class 3 rapids in the river of life.

"Ah, Mr. Bond, hanging around, I see."

I remembered reading somewhere that Cro-Magnons used to scrawl that joke on cave walls. "I hope you're not planning on giving up your day job for the comedy circuit."

"You wound me, Mr. Bond."

"Call me MacKay. That thought *has* crossed my mind."

"Ah, such levity in tee face of horrible execution!"

"Touching on what is rapidly becoming a very sore point, I hear you guys abolished capital punishment."

Wipo clicked his tongue a few times. "Well, Mr. MacKay, modern penology embraces tee notion t'at every criminal has a sublimated deat' wish, so we merely view it as assisted suicide for our criminals in denial."

"How quaint. Modern liberalism in action."

"In your case, to be assured of your utter destruction, we have decided to lock you into a tiny spacecraft and fire you into tee sun."

I stared up at the ceiling, which needed repainting. "Mind telling me how you came up with this charming idea?"

"Actually, one of your commentators described it as, 'A recurring plot device affected by bored and perpetually clueless writers,' but we have not been able to uncover tee meaning of t'is statement."

"I don't mean to quibble, but isn't this a rather expensive way to get rid of me?"

Wipo smirked. "One of our movie studios has offered to pick up tee tab. We will call tee picture, 'Twilight of tee Vampire,' and as technical consultant, I will receive seven percent of tee Terran and Martian syndication rights. Moreover, as it is necessary for mailship RVN 23 to have an unfortunate accident to prevent you from blabbing our nefarious plot all over tee galaxy, combining tee two operations by stuffing you into tee mailship and shooting you into tee fiery heart of a star would appear to be an excellent way to reduce costs."

RVN 23 was Swervin' Irvin. I shivered at the thought of spending my final hours in his company. "Aren't you at least going to pump me for information before turning me into a Roman candle?"

"Why? Your accomplice has already confessed to unspeakable crimes." Wipo gestured to one of my guards, who brought down a wireless closed-circuit television that showed Calvin strapped to a chair with a red welt across his forehead.

I said tersely, "You didn't have to rough him up like that to get him to talk."

"Actually, we had to rough him up to get him to shut up." Wipo gestured for the guard to haul the TV away. "As furt'er evidence of your obvious guilt, we have uncovered tee missile launcher you cunningly concealed underneat' tee grain aboard your ship. Someone, er, accidentally pushed tee wrong button."

"Oh, great," I groaned. "Now I've got a new hole in the hull and a hold full of wheat toasties!"

"In a few short moments tee problem will cease to concern you, Mr. MacKay. Pardon me while I savor tee experience."

"The pinnacle of a postal career, huh?" I said, hoping to extend the conversation for a few hours, months, or years.

A subtle change came over Wipo. "Ah, once again, you surprise me, Mr. MacKay." He began pacing the room. "Having copied tee best features of tee Confederation's postal system, our postal service is brutal, tense, and violent, dedicated to converting individuals into mere machines. Only tee strongest survive, to become stronger, like steel tempered in a forge. I had to become hard—or break." He stared at me. "Having been forced as a vampire to maintain tee pretense t'at you serve mere humans, surely you comprehend how demeaning it was for me to have no one to release my frustrations upon, except customers? My tortured soul rebelled against such tyranny!"

"Uh, do you find you like secret police work better?"

"Tee hours are good, and I can play wit' guns on government time." He began pacing again. "You realize t'at you upset a wonderful plan. It took years of preparation to lure tee underground into discrediting t'emselves by accepting alien assistance to bomb tee very symbol of puling democracy, and you had to go and spoil it all."

"Uh, sorry." I shifted my weight and tried rubbing my back against the wall. The worst thing about being hung in chains is that when you itch, you can't scratch. "What have you got against democracy, anyway?"

Wipo glowered. "Democracy enshrines tee right of demagogues of tee lowest caliber to pander to tee base and selfish instincts of tee most ignoble elements in society, inevitably submerging superior beings in a tidal wave of tastelessness and stupidity and imperiling tee very existence of civilization and culture."

"Give it time. They used to say the same thing about TV."

Wipo stared at me for a moment without speaking. "Certain individuals wish to gloat over you prior to your demise." He gestured to the guards.

A Rodent, a human, and an elderly Macdonald came down the steps. The Rodent had a poniard hanging from a jeweled belt and what can best be described as a lean and hungry look. I squinted at him. "Excuse me, but you look familiar."

"It is the family resemblance, I am sure." Twirling his

vibrissae, he crossed over to the table and plucked a rose from the vase. "You may call me Mordred. You killed several of my demi-brothers and robbed me of the throne which rightfully should have been mine."

"Ah, pleased to meet you," I said feebly.

"You don't say?" Mordred began munching on the rose and stopped. "Oh, I beg your pardon. I am forgetting my manners. Would you care for one? They're quite tasty."

"Uh, no thanks, I'm on a diet. Who's your friend with the floppy eyebrows?"

The human had a long, bony jaw and the kind of impassive, ageless face you see anchoring the late night news. His eyes were yellow-gray. His chin was a jutting vee under the more flexible vee of his mouth. His nostrils curved to make another, smaller vee. The vee motif was repeated in his thick eyebrows, in the twin creases above his nose, in a small blonde goatee, and in his hair, which grew down to a point on his forehead. He looked rather pleasantly like a blonde Satan.

He smiled slowly and his cold, cold, horizontal eyes caught my attention—they looked like they had been dead for a long, long time. "Call me Smith," he said in a pleasant voice. "Gregorio Smith."

"The sotweed factor. That means the tobacco industry is behind this little conspiracy to overthrow truth and justice in the universe."

"Why not? We've done everything else."

I shook my head, which was one of the few things I could move, and looked at Wipo. "So you decided to let organized crime get its hooks into Alt Bauernhof."

"We are always looking for ways to improve tee efficiency of our government," Wipo explained smugly.

I asked Smith, "So why are you trying to help these two take over the universe? Lust for power? Revenge on a society that cast you out?"

He shrugged. "The money is good, and the Institute has a great pension plan."

"For peddling death?"

"I like to think of it as the South's revenge on pissant Yankeedom. But you've got to admit that the criticism we get is unfair. Tobacco is really the last all-natural product around."

"Ever try making it into a pill and selling it in health food stores?"

"Oh, yeah—health food nuts will buy anything—but the FDA was down on us like ugly on a hound dog."

"Beneath that warm, caring exterior you're utterly heartless, aren't you, Gregorio?"

Smith grinned, sharing a private joke. "I could show you my voter registration card to prove it."

I stared at the older Macdonald in the feather headdress. "Well, that's two out of three. So who are you, Chicken Man?"

Wipo bowed with a flourish. "May I present tee chairperson of our board of ephors. You may call him Lord Fowl."

"Impudent creature!" The befeathered Fowl looked me up and down. "Tee loat'some disease you are infested wit' is emblematic of tee spiritual degeneracy of tee Confederation."

"Yeah, yeah, and your mother wears army boots. So what is this wonderful plot the three of you have cooked up?"

Mordred waved his hand airily. "May I tell him?"

"Suit yourself," Fowl replied.

Mordred polished off another flower and licked his fingers. "Despite your unspeakable meddling, everything is finally coming up roses—cute turn of phrase, that. Shortly after you become a crispy critter, my darling demi-brother, Bucky, will have a rude surprise when a Klo'klotixag warfleet returns me to !Plixxi*, where I will reclaim my rightful inheritance and rally my loyal supporters to assist my Klo'klotixag shock troops in chopping my numerous enemies into chutney."

"I seem to recall that the last time Bucky did the handshake circuit, your loyal supporters faded into the woodwork."

"Ah, but this time will be different! At first, everyone on my planet welcomed my demi-brother with open arms, but can you imagine how infernally dull life is on !Plixxi* these days—no political skulduggery, no corruption on a grand scale, no lusty wenches pulling each other's fur out in the palace halls? By now my loyal subjects-to-be are eagerly awaiting my return."

Smith smiled coldly. "As we see it, Cheeves is the brains behind Bucky's throne and you're the muscle."

"I didn't like the way you said that."

"Once we polish you off, Cheeves will take a tour of the harbor with an old refrigerator, and Bucky, as they say, becomes history."

"I hope you realize that you'll never get away with this," I interjected at what seemed to be a timely moment.

The four of them guffawed. "After I expose tee Confederation's role in tee plot to bomb our capitol building, I will grudgingly accept tee Confederation's cringingly abject apologies," Fowl declared. "Tee Confederation will not dare to interfere when we move on Plixxi."

Mordred's whiskers twitched. "After Fowl's invincible legions assist me in deposing that goody-two-shoes sibling of mine—I think I'll use him to upholster a footstool—we revert back to the plan you messed up before. We base a few warships on !Plixxi* to force the Confederation Navy to divide its strength, and then the Macdonald Navy launches a surprise all-out assault while everybody's watching the Super Bowl."

I shook my head as fast as it would go. "The Super Bowl Sunday punch, that's got to be the oldest trick in the book! Well, maybe not the oldest trick—telling people that your opponent is going to raise taxes and cut social security benefits is the oldest trick—but you know what I mean."

"A time-honored trick, but an effective one," Smith gloated. "Then we move on to really interesting things, like discounting the dangers of secondhand smoke."

"Yeah. Right. Sure."

"Hey! We got scientific studies that *prove* our case! Who're you going to believe, us or the government?"

I conceded the point. "Earth hasn't grown tobacco for twenty years. What makes you think you can rebuild your empire?"

Smith's yellow eyes glowed with an unholy light. "On Earth, I have an army of tobacco farmers on government subsidies poised to begin planting at my command."

I gave up on Smith and turned my attention back to Mordred. "From the letters I've been getting, it doesn't sound like being Poobah is a bowl of brussels sprouts. Are you sure you want the job?"

"It is a matter of principle. Can you imagine how demoralizing it was to be defeated in a succession war by Bucky? I don't believe the little wimp even fornicates. I was depressed for months." Mordred blinked a few times. "To this day I don't know where we went wrong with him. As a child he seemed so normal. If only our dear, deceased father were alive to see our family name dragged so low."

"Ah, well," I said, "I suppose that every family has its white sheep."

"White sheep?" Mordred's nose quivered. "I don't believe I understand."

"It's a metaphor," I said limply, hanging limply.

"What is a metaphor?" Mordred asked.

I pondered my response. Catarina once told me that it was a good place for grazing cattle.

"A metaphor is a poetic device whereby humans allege similarities between unlike objects," Smith interjected smoothly. "It may interest you to learn, Mr. MacKay, that in order to avoid a repetition of events on Plixxi, I have persuaded Lord Fowl to ban 'The Bucky Beaver Show' before that particular cancer has a chance to spread."

"We have had a few scattered reports of rioting and individuals flaunting Bucky Beaver T-shirts," Wipo exclaimed, "but because of tee timely warning, my government was able to foil your plot to infect my people wit' tee foul execration of morality." He paused. "Why are you looking from side to side like t'at?"

"I'm looking for cows."

"What do you mean, looking for cows?"

"The manure in here is getting pretty deep."

Smith patted me on the cheek. "Where I grew up, we used to perform surgery on persons who made comments like that—on body parts that guys are attached to, you know?"

I gathered that he was talking about making it possible for me to host Tupperware parties.

"Come up with a better threat," I sneered. "My ex-wife used to use that one."

"Threatening him is fun, but it's almost prime time," Mordred observed. "What is that line in the play that Piglet uses, 'To be or not to be'?"

"That's *Hamlet*," I said, clenching my teeth.

"Whatever. In your case you are not to be. Although when I saw the play, it seemed as though Hamlet went to an awful lot of trouble just to usurp his uncle's throne and marry his mother." Mordred tugged at his whiskers. "Perhaps some of the finer nuances escaped me."

"It is time to leave you," Fowl said, "but understand t'at by implicating yourself in tee bombing attempt, you have served us, whom you revile and despise. You have given us tee staff by which we will break tee Confederation and turn your former victories against you, falsified by your arrogance and selfishness. And so die a deat' wit'out meaning, bereft even of tee bare dignity of solitude, betrayed by folly and broken dreams. Your existence will end in desolation wit'out comprehension and blame wit'out pity."

I coughed. "Excuse me, aren't we drifting into the realm of fantasy here."

Mordred tilted his head. "Good night then, sweet count. In your final seconds, console yourself with the thought that I shall not turn coward again. I shall conquer !Plixxi* or perish!"

I made one final effort. "Okay, let me get this straight—Mordred here doesn't want to be a coward, Smith is heartless, and Fowl, I can guess your problem.

Well, I want to be in Kansas. Now, I've got this wizard friend—"

Mordred's nose quivered. "Oh, I see what you're getting at! But you know, I've always believed that *The Wizard of Oz* represents the American political process between 1870 and 2011. The Tin Woodsman is the Republican Party, the Scarecrow is a Democrat, and the Cowardly Lion is the perennial third-party challenge; while Dorothy and Toto, with their touching belief in fiscal legerdemain, symbolize the voting public. Now—"

Wipo, Fowl, and Smith were already on their way up the ladder with their ears stopped up. I sighed deeply. "Can we get on with executing me?"

"Well, ta-ta, then!" Mordred's beady eyes glistened. "We'll be watching. Be sure and have a good fry!"

Wipo's guards hauled me off wrapped in chains, and we took an uncomfortable ride up to the space station, where they welded me into my seat in the mailship and stuck my guitar in beside me, although, as usual, there was a clown who had to play an air guitar riff with it when he thought the cameras weren't looking. As Wipo gratuitously pointed out, the controls had been removed so that even if I figured out how to get loose, I couldn't change course. As added insurance, they'd replaced the oxygen circulation system with a large chia pet. All they left me, apart from a TV camera so that the folks back on Klo'klotixa got their money's worth, was a viewscreen so that I could watch my own demise, and Swervin' Irvin's personality center for company.

Irvin, of course, was a babbling idiot. "This is interference with the public mail!" he fulminated as several Macdonalds in pocket protectors finished bolting me down and slammed the hatch shut. "When I tell the

Postal Service about this, they'll cut off TV service to these bozos for fifty years!"

I felt the acceleration as the mailship broke free of the station. "Irvin, I don't know how to break this to you, but we're about to die."

Irvin considered this. "What do you mean by 'die'?" he asked about twenty minutes later.

"Discorporate." It occurred to me that this might not help Irvin. "Cease to exist. Have our tapes erased." The sun began growing in my viewscreen.

"You mean, like, not be anymore? Ever again?"

"Right. Die."

"You mean, like, no more TV or music videos—ever?"

"Only if you've led a blameless life."

Irvin paused to consider this. "Ken?"

"What?"

"What happens to people when they die?"

"Well, generally, they put your body in a cemetery, except in parts of New Jersey where landfills are still popular."

"But I don't have a body! What's going to happen to me?"

Politely ignoring the question, I tried to summon up a surge of McLendon-induced hysterical strength to break myself free and come up with something resembling a plan for what to do next. Unfortunately, it seemed to be my week for rolling boxcars. As time passed, the solar orb in the viewscreen grew steadily larger.

"Ken?" Irvin whispered plaintively.

"What!"

"What's a soul?"

This is how I always wanted to go out, spending my last remaining minutes explaining eschatology to an artificial personality. "Look, Irvin, we're on TV. There are about fifty million Macdonalds watching us, so try and conduct yourself accordingly."

This was a mistake. Like any other television-trained personality, Irvin automatically whispered shyly, "Hi, Mom!"

Twenty minutes later Alt Bauernhof's primary completely filled the viewscreen, and all I had for my efforts was a cramp in my right leg. It really was shaping up as one of those weeks.

"Ken?"

"What?"

"Do you want to watch a movie?"

"No!"

"That's good. Being disconnected like this, I couldn't turn one on anyway, but my audio circuits are still hooked up." He paused. "You know, Ken, I've been thinking— life is like a merry-go-round: sometimes you're up, sometimes you're down, and periodically everything stops and you have to fork over some money."

"Sure." Just what I needed—homespun philosophy from a bucket of bolts. "Did Wipo leave anything else hooked up?"

"Nope," Irvin sniffed. "I feel so helpless."

I tried clicking my heels together three times and whispering, "There's no place like home, there's no place like home," but it didn't work.

A horrible sound filled every cranny of the tiny mailship. I tried to turn my head. "What's that noise?!"

"What noise?" Irvin asked.

"Can't you hear it? That hideous whining noise!"

"It's *Classics of Koto*," Irvin said defensively. "It's my favorite tape. It includes all-time favorites like 'Rokudan,' 'Chidori,' and, of course, 'Haru-No-Kyoku.' It calms my nerves."

"You don't have nerves, Irvin. You're a hunk of tin." It was the wrong thing to say. "Aw, come on, Irvin, don't cry! I didn't mean it."

"I can't help it," he bawled. "We're about to be burned, seared, and disintegrated into our component atoms, and—and—you don't like my music!"

To add to the psychological torment, Wipo and his pals hadn't bothered letting me go to the bathroom before we left.

A moment or two later Irvin stopped whimpering. "Ken!" he said excitedly. "There's a spaceship matching speeds with us. Who could it be?"

"We're saved—it's Catarina." I thought for a moment. "Either that, or those kids who sell stuff door-to-door to earn scholarships."

"We're saved?"

"Only if it's Catarina, unless you brought money."

"Hey, they're using cutting torches on my outer panels to disconnect the drive! Tell them to stop, Ken!"

"Consider the alternatives."

"Oh," Irvin said sheepishly. A moment later he said, "They're taking us aboard."

The hatch popped open and Catarina's head appeared.

"Boy, am I glad to see you," I exclaimed. "Another minute or two and I'd need fresh underwear." My second-favorite movie is *It's a Wonderful Life*, and I figure my guardian angel is Clarence's idiot brother.

She smiled. "After we saw the previews, I figured we had to hurry."

Rosalee and Clyde started cutting me free. Rosalee was grinning from ear to ear, although Clyde appeared to have placed money on the wrong side of the proposition and was experiencing mixed emotions. "I see you found yourself a ship," I commented.

Catarina nodded. "The *Hunting Snark*. Blok came through on getting us clearance, and we were able to catch the security detail with their pants down and jimmy the Club off the control panel. You'll like her. She's only about seventy percent completed, but she's a sweet ship."

I noticed Muffy and Belkasim. They were both wearing rabbit ears made out of blue satin with some sort of wire stiffener. "What are they doing here?"

"How do you think we got the security detail's pants down? The radical feminists were a little disappointed when the bombing of the capitol didn't come off, so we had to do something to make it up to them."

"Our government is differently principled, as well as kindness-impaired and morally out of tee mainstream, making it our duty to strike a blow for sisterhood," Muffy assured me.

"What about the *ears*?" I hissed.

"They decided that as a liberation army, they needed some sort of uniform. Unfortunately, they chose Harry as a technical consultant, and Harry indulged in what one can best describe as wish-fulfillment." She shook her head. "Officers wear blue ears, enlisted personnel wear pink."

"One of these days the law of averages is going to mug Harry in an alley somewhere. Although my best move is to thank you profusely and shut up, I confess that I started getting a trifle worried when you waited until the last minute to show up to rescue me."

"We just made sure you earned the maximum number of frequent flier miles. How did you keep yourself amused waiting?"

"Well, Irvin here has led a sheltered existence, so I occupied myself explaining the facts of life." I saw the little gleam appear in her eyes, so I said, "Oh, go ahead."

She bent over and whispered, "I guess we just broke up Alt Bauernhof's first bull and oyster roast."

After they cut me loose and we got the mailship safely stowed, I made a quick pit stop and went forward to the bridge to see how Catarina was making out. She was right about one thing, the ship was something special. I couldn't believe the size of the fuzzy dice in the control room.

I took over navigation, allowing Catarina to shift to the command seat, and let Bunkie show me how to call up the status log. Rosalee, Wyma Jean, and Blok were attending to propulsion, which left Clyde, Minnie, and Mickey to deal with major deficiencies in life support systems. A crowd of Muffy's friends were swarming over the ship redecorating. "Looks pretty bad," I commented.

Catarina smiled. "Aside from the troubles inherent in a not-quite-finished ship, we're being chased by six frigates. We have about two hours' head start on them."

"That's not much."

"I could mention all the time we lost trying to match speeds with someone."

Bunkie piped up, "We're receiving a Priority One transmission in clear."

"May I?" I asked Catarina. She nodded. I told Bunkie, "Let her rip," and Bunkie landed Mailboat Bobby's glowering visage on the viewscreen.

Stemm nervously mopped his brow. "So it's the Bonnie and Clyde of the spaceways. MacKay, do you know what a flap you've caused down here? You've got to bring that spaceship back immediately!"

"Bets?"

"This is no time for jokes. The ambassador orders you to bring that ship back!"

"And what do the Macdonalds propose to do to us if we bring their ship back?"

There was a pregnant silence while Bobby bent to confer. "Ambassador Meisenhelder wants me to assure you that you will have adequate legal representation."

"Have you explained to the ambassador just how much of a threat to the Confederation this ship will be if the Macdonalds manage to complete it?"

"Well, no, but that's hardly relevant—"

"Bobby, wouldn't you consider dying? Just think how lovely you'd look stuffed."

"Be serious, MacKay!"

"Actually, Bobby, I am. If this spaceship caper doesn't pan out, tormenting you is the only thing that would give my life meaning. MacKay out." I turned to Catarina. "Gee, that was fun." I noticed that the bridge was beginning to fill up with people that Catarina had presumably assigned to working parties.

"They're calling us back," Bunkie reported.

This time it was a chubby girl with Day-Glo hair. She was wearing a red vinyl one-piece and matching patent leather boots. "Mr. MacKay, I have a call for you from Ambassador Meisenhelder." She rearranged the gum in her mouth. "Will you accept the charges?"

"What if I just say no?" I inquired.

She was back a few seconds later. "The ambassador will speak with you now."

We faded into Ambassador Meisenhelder's beaming countenance. He adjusted his toupee. "Mr. MacKay, you have to return the ship to this planet immediately. Consider this an order."

Catarina winked.

"I'm sorry, Mr. Ambassador, that's just not in the cards."

Meisenhelder appeared perplexed. "But I just gave you an order."

I glanced at the piece of paper Bunkie shoved into my hand. "Sorry, sir. We passed out of your jurisdiction about two light-minutes back."

"Pretty please?"

I shook my head. "Sorry, sir."

"Oh, dear." The ambassador pushed his hair back with a worried expression on his face. "I just know that there's going to be trouble with the Klo'klotixa government over this."

"You give them hell, sir."

"I suppose that I should mention that your ex-wife has disappeared. Is she up there with you?"

I looked around. "Dear God, I hope not!"

"Captain Kuzmaul tells me that apart from your crew, she's the only Terran unaccounted for. Well, if you hear from her, please ask her to return to the embassy for her own safety. Since the theft of the *Hunting Snark* was announced, there's been a sudden outpouring of anti-Terran sentiment. I'm not sure that it's safe for her to be walking the streets."

"Don't worry, Mr. Ambassador. Gwen can walk the

streets with the best of them." I blanked the screen and paused. "Did I just say what I think I just said?"

"Yes, sir, you did." Bunkie shook her head. "We're receiving another communication in clear."

I shrugged. "Probably the Macdonalds, this time. Okay."

Bunkie flicked it on.

"Ah, Mr. MacKay, we meet again," the lean Macdonald on the screen whispered silkily.

I tried to place him. "Ah, do I know you?"

His pointed ears twitched. "The Friendship Society party?"

"Oh, yeah—now I remember. You're Captain Xhia. Look, I'm really sorry, you know how it is with people you meet at these things, and for the last couple of days it's just been one thing after another. You offered to give me a tour, right? Listen, I'd really love to, but something's come up—"

"Know you t'at tee warship you so audaciously stole was to be tee flagship of a fleet destined to sweep your Confederation Navy from tee heavens and allow my species to achieve its proper racial destiny." Xhia's eyes gleamed with the by-now-familiar luminous light. "It would not be fitting for us to allow an ugly species like yours to dominate the galaxy!"

"Yeah? Who are you calling ugly, short and squatty?"

"Ken," Catarina interjected, "you're babbling."

"Uh, right."

Xhia smiled evilly. "I knew tee seeds of great sins were wit'in you, Ken MacKay. Love t'ose who t'row golden words in advance of t'eir deeds and always perform more t'an t'ey promise," he intoned, "for t'ey will t'eir own downfall. Love t'ose whose souls are overfull so t'at t'ey forget t'emselves and all t'ings are in t'em and all t'ings become t'eir downfall."

"Excuse me for one second." I dampened the sound and turned to Catarina. "What have we got to defend ourselves?"

"You, me, our crew, Blok, Trixie, and nineteen of Muffy's radical feminists including four infants. No weapons are mounted on the ship yet, so we're virtually unarmed."

"Do we have a contingency plan?"

"Harry suggested taping the infants crying and broadcasting it to the ships chasing us to demoralize the crews, but I vetoed the idea."

I resumed voice communication with Xhia. "You were saying?"

"I command a squadron which will erase tee stain you have placed upon our species' blazon by removing you from tee universe!"

"Well, it certainly was nice talking with you," I said as his image disappeared.

Harry said fiercely, "Let the greasers come! We're not scared!"

Dr. Blok threw up his hands. "We're doomed," he moaned.

I closed my eyes. "I really wish you hadn't said that."

Harry and Rosalee grinned at each other, threw up their hands, and chanted, "We're doomed!" Then they went back to try it out on everyone else on board.

"Maybe they'll tire of it in a few hours," Catarina said hopefully. "What did you find out before you got launched?"

"Wipo's co-conspirators are Mordred, an ephor named Fowl, and lobbyist Gregorio Smith. It's the usual vast interstellar conspiracy to legalize tobacco. They're going to conquer Plixxi, base there, and hit the fleet on a Super Bowl Sunday. I told them it was the oldest trick in the book."

"Dear me." The corner of her mouth turned down. "I thought that the oldest trick in the book was the ninety-three-year-old guy they picked up waving a fifty on Fourteenth and K."

"Poor Captain Ken, you do appear bedraggled," Minnie exclaimed. "I wish that we had chocolate to offer to you as we commence this trip."

"As Bucky says, 'A journey without chocolate is like an evening without sunshine,' " Mickey concluded.

"Catarina," I coughed, "my guess is that everything is working out exactly the way Admiral Crenshaw planned. And I don't think she's a very nice person."

"If Xhia doesn't catch up with us before we reach our black hole, we can head for Brasilia Nuevo and place ourselves under the guns of the fleet. The Macdonalds aren't ready to start a war to stop us."

"Well, Xhia doesn't seem to be gaining on us, so we're in good shape so far." Just then our speed began dropping off. "Blok! What's wrong with this ship?"

"We may have a screw loose," Blok conceded. Catarina is an expert on dealing with loose screws, so she and Blok ran back to engineering while I detailed Wyma Jean to keep Harry from trying to help.

"It looks like they're beginning to gain ground on us," I explained to everyone, checking my instruments, "but we still have a pretty good lead on them."

About three seconds later we went from low thrust to no thrust. Blok reappeared, wringing his hands in 180-degree circles.

"What's wrong?" I asked.

"We have a slight problem," he said tactfully.

"The good doctor went to work on the main drive coupling. It blew, and none of the backups are installed yet," Catarina said with asperity.

"It was a calculated risk," Blok explained.

"How long will it take to get fixed?" I asked, not really wanting to hear the answer.

"Oh, two or t'ree days," Blok explained nervously.

"Make that two or three hours," Catarina snapped and signed off.

I wasn't too worried because the ship must have cost the Macdonalds billions and they knew that the Confederation would probably give it back, so I couldn't see them shooting holes in it just to get us. Two hours and nine minutes later Xhia's flotilla caught up to us. The first missile impacted four minutes after that.

The ship shuddered. Catarina called me up on the intercom. "Was that cannon fire or the pounding of my heart?"

"You know, we keep going into battle in unarmed ships. I'm beginning to think that God is trying to tell us something. Any ideas?"

"To be truthful, I'm wondering whether I shouldn't have given the convent a try."

Bunches of people miraculously began reappearing on the bridge. I looked at Harry. "Harry, I want you to take the feminists to the lifeboats in case we have to abandon ship. As they say, women and children first."

Harry looked at Wyma Jean mournfully. "Well, it looks like this is it for us, honey-bunny. I just want to say I'm really sorry about everything."

Wyma Jean gave him a cold stare. "Go peddle it somewhere else, buddy."

Harry left the bridge. As soon as the door closed behind him Wyma Jean jumped in the air and pumped her fist. "Yes!!! Got him!"

"Wyma Jean, why don't you go help him?"

"Uh, yes sir."

I turned my attention back to Catarina. "How are things working out with Blok?"

"I'd trade him for a wet sponge. Call up Xhia. Buy us twenty minutes."

Another small missile hit and blew out a slice of deck three. Harry appeared again. "We don't have any lifeboats."

I looked at Bunkie. "You heard the woman."

Bunkie was already in motion. A few seconds later Xhia's image reappeared on the screen.

"Ah, Captain MacKay! Tee hour of your demise rapidly approaches. Behold! What is tee greatest t'ing you can experience? It is tee hour of tee great contempt, an hour in which even happiness becomes loathsome to you, and your reason and virtue as well, for beings are polluted rivers. One must be a sea to receive a polluted river and not be defiled. It is not sin, but moderation t'at cries to heaven! Your very meanness in sinning cries out to heaven! Where is tee lightning to lick you wit' its tongue? Where is tee madness by which you are cleansed?"

I glanced at the clock thinking that it was going to be a long twenty minutes, but Xhia decided to cut our discussion short. "Love t'ose who are like heavy drops falling singly from tee dark cloud hanging overhead: t'ey prophesy tee coming of tee lightning and as prophets t'ey perish." He turned to his weapons officer. "Prepare to launch anot'er salvo."

"Wait! This is a very expensive ship! Aren't you even going to ask us to surrender?"

"And permit you to defy me?"

"You could at least ask. It's only polite."

"Very well," Xhia said, stiffening. "I have been instructed to attempt to retrieve tee vessel you stole undamaged if practicable. So, if you do not surrender immediately, I will harm tee being named Gwen."

"Look, do you have to use an ugly word like 'stole'? I mean, we really just wanted to borrow the ship for a while." I paused. "Did you just say 'Gwen'?"

"What callous beings they are to play upon friend Ken's sympathies in this unwholesome manner," Mickey observed.

Rosalee chuckled. "What a bunch of pencil-necked morons to imagine he has any."

"Rosalee, you're not helping."

"Oh. Sorry, Ken."

I told Xhia in a harsh voice, "I want to see her, Xhia. Put her on."

"As you wish." He disappeared.

My left hand was dangling down by my side, and Bunkie gave it a quick squeeze. "Be brave, sir!"

"Ask if you can watch when they torture her!" Rosalee crowed.

Harry had been thinking all this time. He tugged at my sleeve. "Ken, are you sure you want to talk to her? She might not be too happy when you tell her that you're not going to throw your life away for her." He shook his head. "Women are funny that way."

"Harry," I whispered back, "what's our goal?"

He looked at me, puzzled. "To kill time until Blok can get the drive working?"

"Trust me. This will work."

A few seconds later Gwen's image appeared on the screen. "Ken, hello! We were just discussing you here."

"Hi, Gwen." I tried to think of something to say. "You, ah, look different."

She touched her hair and pouted. "Are you saying you don't like it?"

"No, no, you look fine. In fact, I dislike you less as a redhead. Excuse me, that just slipped out. What are you doing on board that ship?"

She winked at me. "Ken, in my business, what the client wants, the client gets—you know that. But things haven't been easy for you. They told me about the shadur. Oh, you poor, poor dear! You must have been absolutely petrified. I know how you are around house pets."

"Ah, right." I gratefully accepted a handkerchief from Bunkie and mopped my forehead. "Did anyone explain the situation?"

She looked at me out of the corner of her eye. "They told me that you've been a bad, bad boy. And they want to cancel my contract as a result. I'm really not very happy with you, you know. But I'm sure the two of us can straighten this little misunderstanding out."

"I mean, did they mention to you what I've done?"

"They said something about a battle cruiser they want back and an Operation Circe that you're fouling up." Gwen tilted her head to be sure I could see her profile.

"Circe?" Mickey asked.

"She was a sorceress in Greek mythology," Bunkie explained. "In the *Odyssey* she lured some sailors from

Ulysses's ship onto her island and turned them into swine."

"She must have been a very powerful sorceress to turn men into swine," Minnie said, impressed.

Wyma Jean smiled a worldly smile. "Honey, I can work the same trick with a six-pack and a short skirt." She leaned forward. "Believe me—underneath those tight jeans they wear, they're *all* little porkers."

"Can we cut the chatter back there?" I murmured. I tried to concentrate on Gwen. "Ah, Gwen, did the Macdonalds say what would happen to you if I didn't cooperate?"

"My contract gets cancelled, after which I'm broke." Her eyes glittered. "Isn't that the most horrible thing you've ever heard?"

"Uh, did they mention anything about, say, pulling out your fingernails with pliers?"

"Oh, they joked about it a little, but it isn't as though I have time to grow real nails." She pulled one off and held it up to show me. "But let's cut to the chase here. Ken, do you have any idea just how much money I stand to lose if you keep behaving in your usual pigheaded, childish way? Knowing how much this means to me, I know you won't let me down, now *will* you?"

"Uh, right." I looked at Bunkie, who moved over where Gwen couldn't see her and held up a sign that said, DR. BLOK SAYS ONLY TWENTY MORE MINUTES. "Uh, Gwen, seen any good movies lately?"

"Ken, I'd love to chitchat, but this is big money we're talking here, a major client and interstellar exposure," Gwen said in a disarming tone of voice. She gave me the hair flip that meant she was going in for the kill. "Letting everyone know that Macdonalds are really warm and fuzzy people is a major, major ad campaign, the kind of campaign that can make an entire career. Ken, this thing is as big as diet pet food. No, it's bigger than that—as big as *organic* diet pet food. But they're blaming me for your failure to get with the program here."

"Ah, sure."

"Now I know we couldn't make a go of it, and that's almost as much my fault as it is yours, but I still remember those dreams we had." She batted her baby blue contacts at me. "Do you remember that little horse farm we always talked about?"

I gave her a funny look. "What little horse farm?"

"And the string of polo ponies? The little fantasies we used to talk about?" Her voice became a little huskier. "You can still make that happen for me, Ken."

I was clearly out of my depth here. The only fantasy of Gwen's I knew of involved being naked in a shopping mall with a major credit card.

Bunkie held up another sign, which read, DR. BLOK SAYS WE'RE READY TO GO FOR IT.

"How about it, Ken?" Gwen said sweetly. "Then we can sit back and talk about all the good times we had together."

I drew a blank on that, too.

By this time the bridge was full of unauthorized visitors. Minnie turned to Mickey. "Oh, dear! What a dreadful dilemma."

"Don't listen to her, Ken!" Harry shouted.

Rosalee waved a ten-spot over her head. "I got ten bucks that says he caves!"

Gwen gave me another hair flip and blew me a kiss for good measure. Her image disappeared and Xhia's replaced it. "Enough talk."

I glared at him. "You didn't tell her what you have planned for her—torture, mutilation."

He shrugged. "Why be unpleasant?"

"Can I have some time to talk things over with my crew?"

"You may have five minutes." The screen blanked.

"I have Commander Lindquist standing by," Bunkie said.

"Well, everybody, we have five minutes to think of something," I told my crew, trying to put the best face on things.

"Circe wasn't mentioned when we studied Greek mythic archetypes," Mickey commented. "However, it would appear that Miss Wyma Jean is the quintessential Aphrodite, while Mr. Harry would appear to personify Mars."

"Friend Catarina is, of course, Minerva, the Goddess of Wisdom," Minnie added. "We are still looking for an appropriate correlation for you, friend Ken."

I punched the intercom. "Catarina?"

"We're ready to try full thrust." Her voice sounded tired. "No guarantees. How are things at your end?"

"If we don't give up in about two minutes, Xhia intends to torture Gwen and blow us out of space." I glanced at the tactical display to study the cordon of warships surrounding us. "Their dispositions are a little sloppy, so if we try to scoot, there's a chance we'll make it."

I heard her chuckle. "Do what you have to do, Ken."

Xhia's face reappeared on the viewscreen. "Well, time's up!"

"Hey!" I pointed to the time display. "Your watch is fast."

Xhia shrugged. "So sue me. Do you surrender yourself to certain deat' or do I have tee pleasure of ridding tee universe of your presence?"

"I've got a better idea," I said before the peanut gallery in back of me had time to give me advice. "Why don't we settle this, just the two of us, one-on-one."

Xhia appeared interested. "What are you suggesting?"

"A duel, just you and me." I turned to Bunkie. "Is there a good place to fight a duel on board this ship?"

"There's the ship's auditorium," Bunkie said, a mixture of compassion and disbelief in her eyes.

I turned my attention back to Xhia. "A duel in the ship's auditorium, then. If you win, my crew surrenders this ship to you intact, and you go home a hero. If I win, you give me Gwen intact and let us pass through the jump point unmolested with, say, an hour's lead. That way, you still have a reasonable chance of blowing me out of space later."

He stroked his gill slits. "Your proposition intrigues me."

"Good. Now, how do I know that you and the fleet will follow through on the bargain if I win?"

He stiffened. "You have my word of honor as a gentleman."

"Yeah, but all kidding aside, how do I know that you'll follow through?"

"I suppose I could move my fleet off as a token gesture."

"So what do you say?" I ignored a sudden burst of chittering behind me as Muffy and her friends conferred.

"I accept your terms." Xhia smiled. "And as tee challenged party, I have tee choice of weapons. I choose light-sabers!"

Mentally, I counted to ten. "Why not heavy sabers?"

"No, no, no. *Light*-sabers. *Laser* swords. T'ey slice, t'ey dice, and t'ey obviate tee need to carry sterno on camping trips."

"Peachy," I said. "You wouldn't happen to have an extra one on you, would you?"

"As it happens, I do. A matched pair, in fact." Xhia's grin widened. "I am, after all, planetary champion. I will meet you at your airlock in fifteen of your minutes."

His image disappeared. I swiveled around in my seat. "What do you all think?"

"You really screwed up, big time," Rosalee observed candidly.

"No question about it, major league dumb," Wyma Jean said.

"Yeah," Harry added.

"Among you humans, there is a long-standing literary tradition of engaging in sword fights aboard spaceships," Mickey said judiciously. "It did not occur to me that this tradition was grounded in fact. But as Bucky says, 'We are all silly putty in the hands of God.'"

"Uncle Bucky will be most interested when we tell him how this turns out," Minnie added.

"Right," I said, moderately deflated and likely to become more so if Xhia really was planetary champion.

"I'll have Commander Lindquist meet you in the auditorium, sir." Bunkie's voice carried a trace of pity. "And I just want to say how much I've enjoyed serving under you."

I looked at Muffy and Trixie. "Do either of you know anything about light-sabers?"

Muffy nodded hesitantly.

"Okay, let's go." I gave Rosalee control of the board,

and Muffy and Trixie showed me how to get to the auditorium.

When we arrived, Catarina was waiting in a greasy set of coveralls. "Hello, Ken. Bunkie told me about your little brainstorm."

"You know anything about fencing?"

"I was pretty good with a foil at the academy."

"Good. How much can you teach me in ten minutes?"

"Not a lot."

"Is this the dumbest idea I've ever come up with?"

She reflected. "It's good enough for the top ten list."

"What part of it strikes you as unusually stupid?"

"Asking for Gwen. Being obnoxious requires talent. She has it."

"I couldn't just abandon her to a hideous fate. Well, maybe I could have. Are you upset?"

"Me? Upset? Now, why should I be upset?"

"You're upset."

"Did Gwen say anything about dropping one or more of her lawsuits against you in return for this?"

"Well, the subject didn't exactly come up." I coughed. "You know this business about getting religion and being nice to people really is a pain in the tail sometimes."

She smiled. "It is, at that. Did you actually stop and consider what it'll be like having Gwen aboard ship?"

I shuddered.

"I thought so." She looked at Muffy and Trixie, who were huddled together looking worried. "Can you tell us about fighting with a light-saber?"

"Yes," Trixie said. "Don't."

"Will you be fighting saber alone or saber and mirror shield?" Muffy asked.

"What's the difference?"

"A beam of light cannot parry anot'er beam of light, so saber-alone fight lasts approximately—" She conferred with Trixie for the proper time conversion. "—four seconds on average."

"How do my reflexes compare to Xhia's, do you think?" I asked Catarina.

"When is the last time you won a game of racquetball?"

I nodded. "Right. Let's go with the shield."

"How much do you know about fencing?" Catarina asked. "Never mind, we'll find out." She handed me a long stick. With Catarina to instruct me in the rudiments of sword-fighting and Muffy to explain the peculiarities of fighting with a light-saber, we quickly established that I was what is known in fencing circles as a slow learner.

"All right," Catarina said, brushing her hair out of her eyes impatiently, "let's try it one more time, from the top."

Minnie and Mickey applauded politely.

Rosalee interrupted over the intercom. "Skiff approaching. It looks to be our buddy, Xhia."

"What do you think?" I asked, leaning on my stick, breathing hard.

Muffy hid her face in her hands. "You might stand a chance if he had severe rheumatoid arthritis," Catarina said. "As it stands, our only chance is for me to take Xhia on in your place."

I shook my head. "You're a woman. Xhia would never agree to let you substitute for me. Besides, what would we tell him?"

Catarina thought for a moment. "We could say you

tripped coming down a ladder and broke your arm. Under the circumstances, he'd have to agree to a substitute."

Bunkie nodded. "It's a good story, sir. Nobody who knows you would have any trouble believing it."

"But Catarina," I protested, "I can't let you do that for me."

"Ken, this is no time to get chivalrous on me," Catarina said crossly, "and we don't have time to argue."

"But, I mean, I can't—er, I won't—"

"Are you trying to say it's all right if you get sliced up, but it's not all right if I get sliced up?"

"Well, yeah." I started to say something really mushy and never quite got it out before I noticed Catarina muttering a quick prayer—for herself, not me, which was a very bad sign. A few seconds later I asked, "What I am doing on the floor?"

Catarina bent over and rubbed my cheek. "At the academy I took judo in addition to foil. Think of this as our first argument."

I tested my left wrist. Bunkie produced an elastic bandage from the first aid cabinet and began wrapping me up.

"Is it broken?" Catarina inquired.

"It may just be sprained. Do you have to be such a stickler for authenticity?"

"Never hurts."

"Speak for yourself." I looked at her thoughtfully. "I hope you're not going to use this as a precedent for settling future arguments."

She kissed me on the nose. "Promise."

"Are you going to win this fight?"

"No, but hold the gestures of affection and really stupid comments anyway."

"Got it."

While Bunkie finished checking me out, Muffy and Catarina experimented with technique. A minute later Rosalee reported that Xhia's skiff was docking, and Bunkie went to the airlock to meet him.

Catarina looked at me. "Ken—"

"Yeah, I know. The next time I feel like doing something for Gwen, send her a nice Christmas present instead."

She grinned and blew a kiss at me. "It was the honorable thing to do."

Escorted by Bunkie, Xhia appeared wearing black— black cape, black boots, black tunic, and black coal-scuttle helmet—which contrasted well with my silver-sequined bodysuit. Behind him was an honor guard of fourteen, Gwen, a couple of camera crews, and a few hangers-on.

"Xhia! Nice to see you." I held up my arm. "Unfortunately, I had a minor accident, so there's been a slight change in plan. Excuse me for a second. You, there— please get that camera out of my face *right now*! Thank you. I'm back. Ah, instead of turning me into chopped meat, you get to go up against my partner, Commander Lindquist, instead."

"What farce is t'is?" Xhia opened the faceplate on his helmet and scowled. "A warrior born, fighting against a woman?"

Catarina smiled for the cameras. "What's wrong?" she asked with a mischievous glint in her eyes. "Think you'll have trouble hacking it?"

Xhia gestured violently. "A woman has to obey and find a dept' for her surface, for her nature is surface, a changeable, stormy film upon shallow waters. But a warrior's nature is deep, his torrent roars in subterranean caves: a woman senses his power but does not comprehend it. For t'is reason, a woman hates a warrior as iron speaks to a magnet, 'I hate you most because you attract me but are not strong enough to draw me to you.' "

At this point Muffy stepped forward with a blistering barrage of comments in Sklo'kotax.

"She just told him to go soak his head," Trixie reported.

Xhia stiffened. "One can be silent and sit still only when one is armed. You say t'at a good cause hallows any war, but I say t'at a good war hallows any cause! Yet a warrior may have enemies whom he hates, but not enemies whom he despises. You must be proud of your enemy: t'en tee success of your enemy will be your success, too!"

Catarina grinned lazily while these remarks were being translated for broadcast back on Alt Bauernhof. "But I'm a vamp, and that should count for something. If you can't defeat a vamp who happens to be a woman, well, tsk tsk tsk."

"Pardon me," the translator interrupted, "but what is tee best definition of 'tsk'?"

"Xhia, let me put it to you this way," Catarina said, ignoring the translator. "We've got an audience. The show must go on! Light-sabers with shields?"

Xhia nodded abruptly, a curiously human gesture. "Tee being consummating his life dies triumphantly surrounded by warriors full of hope and making solemn vows; t'at is tee best demise, but tee second best is to die in battle and squander a great soul." He motioned, and a little robotic wastebasket wheeled up and spit out two light-sabers and two shields. "I believe it is customary for you to choose a weapon first."

Muffy picked out a saber and shield for Catarina, and then we broke for commercials. A professional to her fingertips, Gwen immediately gathered the technical staff around her to work on their camera angles. I was touched, and wondered how I could have ever grown up this stupid.

"I t'ink it is a natural talent," Trixie said, reading my mind.

When we came back live, one of the honor guard stepped forward, blew something that looked like a pregnant tuba, and shouted, "Let tee battle begin!" A petite female Macdonald carried a sign around that my beat-up dictionary translated as "Round One."

Xhia and Catarina flicked on their light-sabers and circled each other warily while a Macdonald in a loud polyester suit did color commentary. Then Xhia moved in fast, and he was very, very good, which meant that my original estimate that I would have lasted at least ten seconds was hopelessly optimistic. Catarina was fast, but not fast enough.

She gave ground steadily. Xhia talked steadily as he forced her back toward the wall. "A warrior does not like fruit which is too sweet. T'erefore, a warrior likes women, for even tee sweetest woman is still bitter."

"I don't mean to criticize," she said gently, probing at him. "But has anyone ever told you that you talk too much?"

For an answer, he made a sudden slash at her left leg. She managed to get her shield down to block it, but not completely. I could see the pain on her face, and her coveralls smoldered where the light-saber had touched them.

"What good is long life to a warrior?" He hit her with a sudden flurry of blows, the beam of light from his saber bending against her shield and miraculously springing erect. It was all very Freudian, and I could see why light-saber fighting was so popular on Alt Bauernhof.

"What is any being but a heap of festering diseases reaching out into tee universe t'rough tee spirit, a knot of savage serpents devoid of inner peace which seek out prey alone?" He launched a vicious head cut at her. "Knowing t'is, what warrior wants to be spared?"

Catarina remained silent, retreating steadily and occasionally chopping at Xhia as she tried to find an opening.

"Yes, I find you wort'y," Xhia said, his eyes smiling behind the black metal of his helmet. "Yet tee unwort'y will hold t'is against you and never forgive, for tee higher you climb, tee smaller you appear in envious eyes; and we who fly highest are hated most of all. Life is a fountain of delight, but where rabble also drinks, all wells are poisoned. Flame is unwilling to burn where t'ey have put t'eir damp hearts. Fruit trees grow wit'ered and bend where t'ey gaze. For tee rabble were born to be yoked. T'ey fling away t'eir true wort' when t'ey cast aside t'eir bondage! But you are free, and for what are you free? Can you furnish yourself wit' your own good and evil and hang up your own will above yourself as a law? Can you be judge of yourself and avenger of your own law? It is like being a star tossed into empty space and tee icy breat' of solitude. And so it is fated t'at for you life must end!"

So saying, he leaped forward, and even my untutored eye saw Catarina's mistake; she was holding her shield too low, wide open for a downward stroke.

"Catarina, no!" I shouted just as Xhia's light-saber

came over his head and began descending, only to intersect with a fire sprinkler that Catarina had thoughtfully stationed herself a meter or so behind.

When the retardant chemicals connected with Xhia's saber, it was like they always say on TV—children, do not attempt this at home. Xhia's blade shorted itself out in a moderately spectacular fashion as Xhia himself became the center of a mounting pile of white foam.

Catarina grinned and flicked off her light-saber.

"We're on TV. No puns about ice cream," I told her severely.

She nodded. "Xhia, can we agree that you lost?"

Xhia wiped some of the foam out of his eyes before it hardened and stared at the two of us. "You have one hour, after which my ships will hunt you down t'roughout tee whole of time and space." Then he told his honor guard to work him free before he adhered to the floor.

I shut my eyes, knowing what was about to come next.

In a clear voice Catarina explained to the viewing public on Alt Bauernhof that moving Xhia under the fire sprinkler was her plan from the beginning. "That's my story," she told them, "and I'm sticking to it."

There really ought to be a law about this sort of thing.

Six members of Xhia's honor guard placed him on a stretcher and carried him back to the airlock. After the camera crews did a final wrap, I grabbed the medical kit from Bunkie and went over to check Catarina's leg. Then I remembered about Gwen. "Oh, Gwen, I hope you brought your things."

Gwen smiled and stole a quick glance at her sapphire-studded watch. "Oh, I really wish I could stay, but I've got work to do, and time is money, you know. See you! It's been real!"

I looked at her in disbelief. "What do you mean? Where are you going?"

"Back to the ship there. I'm under contract, you know." She winked. "You always did have trouble remembering things."

Catarina and I exchanged looks. "Wait!" I shook my head violently. "You can't go back there! Xhia promised to execute you if I didn't surrender."

"Oh, Ken." She came over and pecked at my cheek, with one eye on Catarina, which was a very good move because Catarina was still holding her light-saber. "Xhia and I had a good laugh over that. You're so cute when you're trusting. Why, if they executed me, the association would blacklist them." She shook her head. "You talk about a major image problem with no cure in sight."

"But Xhia said—"

"Nice man, but no actor. I just hate having to work with nonprofessionals." Gwen shook her head ruefully. "I practically had to hold the cue cards under his nose, and his delivery was *so* flat. I can't believe you fell for it. When Lord Fowl explained the problem and offered me a three-year exclusive deal, I said I'd give it my best shot, but knowing how stubborn you are, I told him that I didn't hold out much hope."

Bunkie gently took the burn ointment from my nerveless hand and finished dressing Catarina's cut as I sat back on my haunches, completely dumbfounded.

Gwen stroked my chin. "You know how these things go. Well, got to get back! I have a campaign to run, and they tell me that if you succeed in whatever it is you're doing, there'll be some *major* bad press to counteract. I wish we had some time to *be* together, but you know how that goes." The rest of Xhia's honor guard followed her to the airlock.

"It's little intimate moments like these that remind me what life was like when I was married." I looked away. "Right now, it would be nice if the ground swallowed me up. Of course, that's pretty hard to arrange aboard a spaceship. I always hate to try to defend Gwen, but I think that underneath her shallow, amoral exterior is a very different human being."

"Probably Snow White's stepmother." Catarina rubbed her leg and smiled sweetly. "Ken, aren't you forgetting something?"

"Oh! Yes!" I tapped the intercom. "Rosalee, get us out of here!"

Rosalee said, "We're on our way," and another voice said, "Roger, wilco that, captain, sir!"

I looked at Catarina in utter horror. "The main computer was pretty well fried, so we had to improvise," she said calmly. "Swervin' Irvin was the closest thing we could find to a backup." I was now captain of a pilfered battle cruiser being navigated by Swervin' Irvin. Some days, I just don't live right.

The Thrilling Spaceship Chase Scene, or HMS Punafore

We passed through our black hole and headed for Confederation space, with Xhia's warfleet hot on our vapor trail, although we gained a slight lead during the transition.

Even apart from the absence of armament, the *Snark* had a number of major deficiencies. By the second day I decided that hell is going to have millions of women and only one working bathroom. To make matters worse, the dockyard crews hadn't gotten around to installing dryers. By the time we ran out of quarters for the washers, we had frilly things hanging from improvised clotheslines all over the ship. I decreed an end to the practice. Catarina, of course, explained that we'd reached the end of our rope.

Minnie, Mickey, Bunkie, and Clyde helped Blok with system repairs, leaving Catarina, Wyma Jean, Rosalee, and me to split the watch schedule, although Catarina made me rest up for a few days before she allowed me to certify myself as fit for duty. Trixie came up to keep me company during my first watch.

"Hello, Trixie." I paused to double check the unfamiliar displays. "Would you like to pull up a seat and join me?"

She sat in the copilot's chair. "Do you promise not to utter speeches about women's reproductive rights?"

"Right. What are Muffy and her friends doing these days?"

"Miss Spooner is telling t'em about men."

My hand twitched, so that I nearly spilled my cocoa.

"Will we reach Confederation space?" she asked quietly.

"Our chances are pretty good if nothing else breaks. We emerged from our jump point with a four-hour lead, and Xhia's ships don't appear to be closing the gap." I pointed to the display. "We're approaching Brasilia Nuevo. Most of our sensors are down, but you can see Confederation warships scrambling into formation except for one fast patrol craft coming out to meet us. As soon as we get close, we'll tell them who we are, and Xhia will have to break off or start the war here and now."

"Is Miss Lindquist still mad at you for risking tee safety of tee Confederation to rescue your ex-wife, who you don't even like?"

"No."

"Is a lie anyt'ing like bearing false witness?"

I thought for a moment. "Trixie, normal social interaction around here is becoming difficult. Is there some way to arrange things so that you *can't* read my mind?"

She patted my good arm. "Alt'ough it is an arduous task, it is possible for a nontelepathic person to develop a mind block."

"Can you show me?"

"First, you must empty your mind and focus your awareness on tee oneness of all in tee universe, turning away from t'inking to nont'inking to achieve a blankness of purpose."

"What's that mean?"

"Pretend you're watching TV."

We worked on it for two or three hours. Swervin' Irvin had a complete tape library of shows he enjoyed watching, which was a big help. Daytime soaps were okay, and so were old sitcoms. After a little practice, whistling a theme song was enough to make me one with the universe and mentally opaque, although I walked into several bulkheads practicing my technique. With Harry and Wyma Jean publicly feuding, Muffy's feminists practicing close order drill in the corridors, and me bumping into objects singing "a skipper brave and sure," Clyde very sensibly spent his free time locked in his cabin writing verse.

Of course, with the peace of the galaxy threatened and the Macdonalds out for our blood, the next thing on my agenda was straightening out Harry's love life before he drove the rest of us crazy.

"Harry?" I knocked on his door. "It's me, Ken. Can I come in?" He was in his bunk watching a movie. The Macdonalds hadn't gotten around to installing chairs in the cabins, so I sat on the deck. "Is this one any good?"

"It's about this plot to assassinate the president of the United States. See, he's running for reelection, but he's been slipping in the polls, so his wife, Courtney, pays the Arabs to bump him off so she can get elected on a sympathy vote."

The woman in a negligee on the screen didn't look like any president's wife I'd ever seen. "Is that her?"

Harry waved a hand in a gesture of scorn. "That's his mistress, who is a Secret Service agent." He held his finger to his lips. "Quiet! We're coming to the best part."

"Jeff," the actress was saying, "we found out who's behind this. It's Courtney, Jeff!"

" 'Well, I'll be damned,' " Harry and the actor playing the president said in unison, " 'the bitch set me up.' " Harry nudged me. "Is this movie great, or what?" A few seconds later he asked, "What's that song you're whistling?"

We sat through the climactic chase scene where Courtney disembowels herself with a nuclear hand grenade beside the Reflecting Pool, and I shook my head. "I don't know, Harry, this one's pretty far-fetched."

Harry nodded. "Yeah, I know. Imagine a real president owning a cat." He waggled a finger at me. "You know, Ken, I've been thinking. We ought to start planning for the future."

"We have a future?"

"Cruise ships!" He smacked his fist against the palm of his hand. "That's where the money is. All those rich, young widows! You know, when I was living on Schuyler's World, I used to plan a lot."

I felt my stomach turn over a new leaf. The problem with trying to be the village idiot on Schuyler's World is the tremendous competition for the position. "What brought this on?"

He gave me a sheepish look. "I think I'm suffering from low self-esteem. Either that, or maybe hepatitis."

I thought of several words that begin with the fourth and sixth letters of the alphabet. The person who invented medical self-diagnostic programs for home computers should be shot. "Oh?"

"Well, you know, I broke up with Wyma Jean. You never should have given her that little wriggler to babysit. She says she wants to have a baby. My baby. So

I had to break up with her. I guess that means that it's your fault."

"Harry, there are ways for you to avoid getting her pregnant."

Harry thrust his hands into the traditional lotus position. "No way."

"Some of them don't involve invasive surgery."

"Nope!"

"I see. Well, did you want to break up with her?"

"Well, no. I mean, she's like everything I want in a woman. She's got blonde hair, and we have all these things in common, like Chinese food and Mexican food. Are you listening?"

"Oh, sure. Ah, where does Muffy fit into this?"

Harry appeared mortified. "Did you know that she speaks English?"

"Well, yes."

"I can't get her to stop. Ken, you've got to do something to help me patch things up with Wyma Jean."

"Are you sure that you want to be back with her?"

"Ken, you know that a space sailor is supposed to have a woman in every port, right?"

"Yes, some people think that's true."

"Well, gosh darn it, Ken! You know what kind of ports we visit!"

"Well, yes."

"With the kind of women you find in those ports, it takes a pretty strong stomach, let me tell you. It's different for you. You being a vamp and all, nobody thinks twice when you don't go chasing after skirts, but for the rest of us it's hell." He hung his head. "I'm not sure I'm cut out for it. You got to do something to get Wyma Jean to forgive me, Ken."

I gave up. "All right. Come on. I'll see what I can do."

Harry pumped my hand enthusiastically. "Thanks, Ken." Harry in tow, I made my weary way to Wyma Jean's cabin and knocked on the door. "Wyma Jean?"

"Stick it in your ear, you two-timing lump of lard!"

"It's me, Ken. Your captain."

"What?" She opened the door. "Oh. Hello, Ken."

I pushed Harry inside and sat him down. "I just spoke to Harry. He's pretty broken up about breaking up with you."

Wyma Jean ignored Harry's presence. "What Harry needs to learn is that love is an eternal and unconditional commitment to life's higher purpose. People are mirrors for each other. When a person recognizes that light in another human being, it awakens love. When the mirror of your soul reflects the love in me, then I see the love in you. And that's what love is—the glimpses of the love inside each of us. With Harry, it came down to fear of intimacy. I can support a person who is awakening and going for his or her aliveness. But if one person is ready to grow and the other isn't, then a person has to follow her own path. There is a time to let go, and sometimes that jolt is what it takes to awaken a person who refuses to grow to his higher power. I lost my sense of trust. For me, the fabric woven in light has come unraveled, and now it's a matter of weaving a new fabric. The blessing is that this has made me grow tremendously, and Harry, too, I think. We have both discovered a deeper relationship with the beloved aspect within. The energy is there, within me. It's awakened and growing. It's important to keep that energy alive."

"What's that mean in English?"

"Tell that bastard to rot in hell forever."

"He's really sorry." I looked at Harry. "Aren't you, Harry?"

"Mmm, yes."

"He'll never do it again. Right, Harry?"

"Uh, right."

"Wyma Jean, he loves you. Don't you, Harry?"

This time there was a slight pause. "Uh, yeah."

Wyma Jean looked at him for the first time. "Do you really love me?"

"Of course I love you, honey-bunny. You sweat less than any other fat girl I know," Harry said gallantly.

Wyma Jean squealed and jumped into his arms. On the *Scupper* that would have necessitated a minor course correction, but a battle cruiser has more mass. I discreetly left, closing the door behind me. I'd done a good deed, and besides, if anyone on the Nobel search committee knew Wyma Jean, I had an outside shot at the Peace Prize.

I went to Catarina's cabin and knocked on the door. "Catarina, it's me."

"Come on in." She was curled up, looking peaceful.

"What movies haven't we seen?"

"Let's see what Irvin has on file." She sat up, turned on the entertainment system, and rummaged through the directory. "*Ninja Truckdriver III*?"

"Pass."

"Here's something called *Dances with Dogs*."

"What's it about? It sounds like a geek at a sorority dance."

She skimmed the abstract. "Never mind. You wouldn't believe me if I told you. How about *Casablanca*?"

I nodded. "*Casablanca* it is." I heard the intercom buzz. "What is it?"

It was Rosalee from the bridge. "Captain, we're picking up communications from a Confederation ship. You'd better get up here."

By the time we reached the bridge, the news had spread, and Catarina and I had to elbow aside some of Muffy's feminists to reach our seats. Bunkie pointed to the panel. "I'm picking up a very strong signal."

"Put it on."

A syrupy voice said, " 'And tonight's daily winning lottery number is . . .' "

Bunkie colored. "Sir, why don't we begin transmitting to the other ship instead."

"Good idea." I thumbed the send button. "Confederation ship, this is Lieutenant Kenneth MacKay, Confederation Naval Reserve, captain of expropriated vessel *Hunting Snark*. We have a swarm of Macdonald ships after us and information vital to the survival of the Confederation to pass along to Admiral Crenshaw. Request shelter behind the guns of the fleet." I rubbed my hands together. "That should do it."

"We are saved!" Trixie exclaimed.

We received an immediate reply. "Attention, unregistered vessel. This is Confederation Entomological Authority Ship *Millard B. Tydings*, Civil Servant Grade 12 Burgess Peters commanding."

Trixie tried again. "We are saved!"

"You have not been cleared to enter Confederation space. Heave to for inspection of your ship for harmful invertebrate pests."

"We are not saved," Trixie observed sadly.

The Entomological Authority people were a tough bunch. Among other things, they were the ones who busted Santa Claus for operating a sleigh without proper safety equipment and employing nonunion labor. "How long is this going to take?" I asked.

There was a slight pause. "Given the size of your ship, no more than twelve to fourteen hours."

"Excuse me—if we heave to, the Macdonald ships chasing us are going to catch up and blow us to atoms."

There was another slight pause. "Discharge of weaponry within 3.9 astronomical units of an inhabited planet is a class two felony. Rest assured that if they do, they will be prosecuted with the full rigor of the law."

"Very comforting," Catarina observed.

"Look, Mr. Peters," I pleaded, "this is a navy matter. We work for Admiral Crenshaw. Call her."

"Admiral Crenshaw has been reassigned following her well-publicized remarks regarding perceived deficiencies in Confederation military deployments. To the best of my knowledge, she is unavailable at this time."

"If tee Confederation tries us for misappropriating a battle cruiser, will we go to jail?" Blok queried.

"Current policy is to sentence thieves, burglars, congressmen from Chicago, and other nonviolent offenders to rehabilitative therapy," Catarina assured him.

Blok appeared puzzled. "Does t'is keep t'em from committing crimes?"

"No, but it keeps psychiatrists off the streets, so most people think of it as a cheap way to improve public safety."

"Peters," I begged, "you've got to let us through."

"I'm sorry. The Entomological Authority is the Confederation's first line of defense against damaging crop pests. Can you in any way certify that your ship has no invertebrates aboard?"

"Well . . ." I said, looking at Muffy, Trixie, and Blok, who technically failed to qualify.

"I am required by regulation to compel you to stop your ship for boarding and inspection. If you fail to do so, I have no choice but to open fire upon your ship."

"Attention *Millard B. Tydings*, stand by to receive a taped transmission. Get it to Confederation naval and diplomatic authorities immediately." I squirted a tape that Catarina, Blok, and I had prepared, detailing what we knew of the Macdonald plan to invade !Plixxi* and attack the Confederation. Then I made a final appeal. "Look, Peters, to hell with regulations! Damn the torpedoes! There comes a time in life to stand up and make choices. The future of the Confederation is at stake here. What do you say?"

There was a slight pause. "This is Civil Servant Grade 10 Ann Guisti, second officer. Civil Servant Grade 12 Peters is suffering from a mild asthma attack and is temporarily incapacitated." There was a tone of mild reproach in her voice. "In accordance with regulations, I must insist that you stop your ship and prepare to be boarded."

I turned to Catarina. "What do you think?"

"We make a quick seventy-degree course alteration, swing a tight parabola around the star, and double back through our black hole with about a two-hour lead on the Macdonalds." She began punching a course in to Irvin, who immediately began squawking. "Then we go on to Plixxi to disrupt Mordred's invasion."

"Oh, dear Lord, not Plixxi. Besides, Plixxi is the first place they'd think to look for us."

"You have a better idea?"

"The Macdonalds wouldn't think that we were crazy enough to go back to Alt Bauernhof—"

"Neither would I."

"All right, second idea. We get off at Schuyler's World. It seems to me that our best chance to throw a spanner into the works—"

"Ah, Ken, sir?" Clyde broke in.

"Yes?"

"What's a spanner?"

I reddened, which is difficult for a vamp to do, but possible. "It's kind of like a British monkey wrench. You've never heard the expression?"

"Never. What makes you think landing at Schenectady will throw a spanner into the works?"

"Well, we've got to figure out some way to whittle down the Macdonald invasion battalions. The city of Schenectady has at least one dubious drinking establishment on every street corner, so I figure—"

"Ken," Catarina interrupted, "I want to get this straight. Are you saying that Schenectady is a bar-spangled spanner?"

I shut up, and we doubled back and set a course for !Plixxi*, with, of course, Xhia's squadron right behind us, and Mordred's invasion fleet set to follow.

Since we couldn't land a ship like the *Hunting Snark* on a planetary surface, and leaving the ship in orbit didn't appear particularly intelligent, Catarina and I planned to contact Bucky and Cheeves and arrange for them to send a shuttle to pick us up and ferry us down while Irvin took the ship on to parts unknown.

I gathered my crew and passengers together and borrowed a prybar from Rosalee to explain the situation, as well as our chances, which were somewhere between not good and downright pathetic. A hushed silence fell over all of them, reinforced by my prybar. Then Rosalee, who breaks out in hives at the thought of spending more than a week on a given dirtball, raised her hand. "Ken, do all of us have to get off at Plixxi or can some of us continue on with Irvin?"

"We're almost out of food, except for the Macdonalds emergency rations on board, which only the Macdonalds can eat, but if you want to stay, I'll ask Bucky to have a few cases of stuff waiting."

"Thanks, Ken."

"Wyma Jean, what about you? No guarantees that staying on the *Snark* will be any safer than fighting off an invasion from space, but the choice is up to you."

"Ken, I'd like to stay on board," Wyma Jean said in a clear voice. She was looking straight at Harry, apparently drawing a line in the ether.

A few moments after the gathering broke up, Muffy, Belkasim, and a delegation of feminists wearing crushed velvet pantsuits, lace ruffles, and bunny ears came to see me.

"Hello." I looked at them. "Where did the crushed velvet come from and what can I do for you?"

"Tee velvet and lace came from tee furnishings in tee grand admiral's cabin." Muffy stepped forward. "Our goal as dedicated feminists is to ensure t'at females have tee right to live fully and effectively as fulfilled, dedicated single persons not enslaved by t'eir reproductive systems."

Her feminists interrupted to slap her high-fives and sing a song of solidarity.

"Sure," I said.

Muffy continued, "In order to defeat tee male power structure and engender an enlightened cultural myt'os and a healt'y lifestyle in tee universe, we must embrace our femaleness and become fully self-actualized feminist warriors."

The chorus saw its chance. As the sole innocent bystander, I noticed that the singing of songs of solidarity was beginning to engender feelings of boredom. "Ah, right."

"Females are fully capable of taking care of t'emselves as mature adult beings." Muffy tried a few cheerleader moves. "As dedicated feminists, we will no longer tolerate willful invasions of our personal spaces and have determined t'at we will set up alternative households in harmony wit' tee environment based on mutual respect and cooperation."

I yelled, "Don't sing!" and shut my eyes. "Okay."

"In addition to Rosalee and Wyma Jean, who intend to stay on board tee ship wit' us, Dr. Blok has seen tee error of his phallocentric ways, while Swervin' Irvin burns wit' indignation at how we have been marginalized and economically deprived by our society, as well as forced to enslave our natural body images to male desires."

Her feminist legions produced cutlery. Belkasim shifted her infant to her left arm and whipped out a boning knife. "Having, in a mature way, discarded our slavish adherence to rigid, outmoded traditionalist notions of right and wrong, we plan to use tee ship to rob from tee rich and give to tee poor in order to create a differently cultured environment devoid of economic and sexual injustices, and heteropatriarchalist tendencies," she declared shrilly.

"Alt'ough we realize t'at your status as an outcast from society has caused you, as a vampire, to develop your own, entirely valid universe-view, we wish to salute you for your struggle against exploitation of females and culturalist bias, and to ask for our submachine guns back," Muffy concluded.

"And to ask for deliver of food from Plixxi," Belkasim added.

With that, they burst out singing, "For I Am a Pirate Matriarchal Image." Personally, I'm starting to think that Gilbert and Sullivan have a lot to answer for in the next life.

"Can you make Blok available to testify if he's needed?" Clyde and Catarina had debriefed Blok, but we still might need live testimony from him, depending on how long we survived.

Muffy and Belkasim conferred and nodded.

It didn't appear that Catarina and I were going to get the *Scupper* back, and they had as much right to the *Snark* as we did. "It's a deal."

When we reached !Plixxi* space, Catarina and I talked to Cheeves and arranged to have a shuttle waiting for us at the space station when we arrived. After waving tearful good-byes, Catarina, Trixie, Clyde, Bunkie, Minnie, Mickey, and I hopped aboard while Muffy's feminist space buccaneers began loading. Catarina watched the shuttle door close behind us, then turned and quietly said, "Ken, I know that the *Hunting Snark* isn't armed, but do you really think it's safe to turn Rosalee and a band of pirates loose on the universe in a battle cruiser?"

"They can only go where Swervin' Irvin takes them," I

said soothingly, "and he's a government employee down to his fiber-optic fingertips."

The Rodent shuttle crew had the communications gear working. Just then we heard a voice say, "Har, me mateys! These oily Spaniards have wronged me, but I will seek what is mine!"

"Oh, no," I exclaimed. "You don't mean—"

Catarina nodded, tight-lipped. "Irvin must have a copy of *Captain Blood* in his tapes."

I sighed. "There Muffy's feminists go, then, off to commit random acts of piracy and mayhem with Harry, Rosalee, and Irvin. Wearing their bunny ears. You know, I think that someday, after they've seen more of the universe and grown a little more sophisticated, they may come back and look for us."

"We'd better not let them find us," Catarina said tersely.

Seconds before we pulled away, we heard a loud pounding on the door. "Could it be?" I asked Catarina.

She shook her head. "Of course."

We opened up, and Harry fell into our arms. "I claim political asylum!"

We mutely agreed that an asylum was the best place for him and sent him off to strap himself in.

As we found our seats and the shuttle lifted, Catarina chewed on her lip. "Xhia's right behind us, and I doubt that Mordred is far behind, so we're not going to have much time. I'll take Clyde, and see what I can set up in the way of defenses for the spaceport. You tackle Bucky and Cheeves."

"Why don't you tackle Bucky and Cheeves and let me set up space defenses?"

"I'll take Harry if you tackle Bucky and Cheeves." She took a deep breath. "If insanity is transmissible, this will spread the risk."

"Okay."

Cheeves to the Miscue

When we disembarked, it was almost dawn. Cheeves was waiting for us, dressed in an evening coat and a red sash, as befit his dignity as Prime Minister for Life. Rodents come in three sizes: short, shorter, and shortest. Although the black top hat he was wearing added considerably to his stature, Cheeves still fell into the "shortest" category.

He waved at us with restrained dignity. "Ah, friend Ken and friend Catarina! How good it is to see you! Dear me, friend Ken, what did you do to your arm?"

"I fell down a flight of stairs."

"I wish you would be more careful about your health. I worry about you so."

A small crowd of relations engulfed Minnie, Mickey, and Bunkie, who seemed to have become an honorary member of the clan. While Catarina and Clyde discreetly disappeared with Harry and Trixie in tow, I pulled Cheeves down away from prying eyes and inquisitive noses into the underground passenger terminal. "Cheeves! We're in deep trouble—"

"Pardon me, friend Ken, but before you commence, there is a matter which I must address. If I might ask you to bend over slightly."

I did so. I was wearing a tie I'd borrowed from Clyde. "Your tie, I fear, will not pass muster." He began straightening it.

It occurred to me that Cheeves was the only politician I knew who took that servant-of-the-people stuff seriously. "Uh, Cheeves, we really don't have time for ties."

"One aims at the perfect butterfly shape, and this you have not achieved. There, we have it!" He gave it a final nudge and added in a low voice, "Although I approve of your effort to convey a sense of urgency, an air of excitement and a disheveled appearance rarely facilitate resolution of serious matters of state."

We hopped into a ground vehicle that Cheeves had waiting, and I explained about Xhia's frigates and Mordred's invasion fleet on the way to the palace. Cheeves's whiskers twitched. "How dreadful that Mordred should mix himself up in this. And you say that he proposes using Bucky to upholster a footstool?"

I nodded vigorously.

"Indeed. A nefarious plan. Indeed, the word 'nefarious' appears to have been coined for this purpose. A hassock or an ottoman perhaps, but a footstool shows an utter want of propriety. I trust you remonstrated with him, friend Ken."

"Right up to the moment when he pushed the button to fire me into the sun."

"We shall have to bring this to Poobah Bucky's attention," Cheeves mused. "And you say that friend Catarina is attempting to organize our defenses? Oh, well, I suppose it won't hurt for her to try."

Bucky's family palace appeared on the horizon. Bucky's granddad built the aboveground portions, which bear a remarkable resemblance to Sleeping Beauty's castle, while Bucky's father added the underground warrens to house his accountants. Cheeves took me inside, and we found Bucky standing in the main throne room in the middle of a large pile of Build-It Blocks.

"Ah, friend Ken! How utterly good to see you." Bucky had added a few kilos to achieve that perfect bowling pin shape that !Plixxi* strive for. A servant handed him a moist towel and discreetly disappeared. "As Bucky says, 'The unexpected arrival of friends is like a taste of ambrosia.' Ambrosia must taste like brussels sprouts with honey-mustard dressing. You wouldn't happen to have tried any, would you?"

"Ah, no," I stammered, "the place I shop never carries it."

"Pity. Ah, well! Did you do something to your arm?"

"I fell down a flight of stairs."

"You really should try to be more careful. I worry about you so." He rubbed his paws together. "I am engaged in designing our new capital, and you are just in time to help."

"It is customary for each new Poobah to design his own capital," Cheeves explained. "Along with frequent spraying, it helps keep down the lobbyists."

"We plan on calling the new city Buckystown," Bucky commented. "What do you think?"

I thought he needed his pointy little head examined, but lots of people think the same about me. "It sounds nice," I said without conviction.

Cheeves interrupted gracefully, "Your dread and august majesty, I am afraid that friend Ken is here on an urgent matter. Klo'klotixag warships are orbiting !Plixxi* as we speak, and it would appear that Mordred is on his way here with an invasion force to depose you."

"Dear me, Mordred again! Cheeves, stand by to counsel and advise."

That was my cue to repeat my sad story.

For once, Bucky looked completely nonplussed. "You pilfered a battle cruiser?"

I nodded.

"Oh, dear me. Dear, dear me. You must admit, friend Ken, that this smacks of illegality."

I kept nodding.

"And friend Catarina approved of this?"

"It was her idea."

"Dear, dear, dear me. I stand appalled by the lack of morality that females seem to display these days." Bucky began pacing. "Something has got to be done about morality of females before it causes the total collapse of civilization, and wouldn't we look silly then? Cheeves, please take a note."

"I will bring up the matter again at a more propitious time," Cheeves agreed, "but I fear we must discuss the impending invasion."

"True. True. And Mordred is involved. What a truly distressing state of affairs. Dreadful state of affairs, eh, Cheeves?"

"Yes, your supreme highness. Most disturbing."

"More than dreadful, even. What is that word that always reminds me of cats?"

"Catastrophic, my liege."

"Yes, this is catastrophic!" Bucky paused. "Didn't Bucky Beaver once face a similar situation?"

Cheeves nodded solemnly. "I believe that your solemn and high mightiness is referring to the pivotal incident in *Bucky Beaver and the Terrible Trouble*."

"Yes, that's the one! Now let me think whether the

method he used can be adapted to our own problem—excuse me, friend Ken, did you say something?"

"Was that me moaning? You wouldn't have anything in the way of space defenses, would you?"

"Dear me, no. Would you like to be minister of defense? The position is open. In fact, we've never had a minister of defense, have we, Cheeves?"

"No, sir."

Bucky patted my wrist. "What do you say, friend Ken?"

"Well, okay, but—"

"Good, that's settled." Bucky winked. "I'm afraid a title comes with the job, but them's the breaks. Now, back to my design for Buckystown—"

Cheeves interrupted smoothly, "I believe that Minister Ken will need to discuss some of the details. I am sure that he will be more than pleased to discuss Buckystown with you at a less pressing moment."

"Oh, bother. Well, I'm sure you know best about this, Cheeves." Bucky pondered for a moment. "Minister Ken, how does this Gregorio Smith strike you?"

"There was something odd about him. Cold. Completely amoral. I'm not quite sure how to describe it."

Bucky nodded. "A twenty-minute egg, eh, Cheeves."

"Decidedly hard-boiled, your majesty," Cheeves agreed.

"Could this perhaps be due to his chosen profession of tobacco lobbyist and freelance terrorist?"

I shrugged. "For some reason, I don't think so. There was just something inhuman about him."

Bucky paced himself into a pile of Build-It Blocks, demolishing a kindergarten and a fire station. "Something inhuman, you say. A thought—could this Smith be another vampire?"

I shook my head. "I don't think so, but I can't say that I've ever gone around trying to figure out who is and who isn't another vamp."

Bucky nodded sagely. "Don't ask, don't tell, eh, Cheeves?"

I fingered my tie nervously. "Ah, Bucky, could we go back and talk about weapons and space defenses and stuff like that for a minute?"

Cheeves hung his head regretfully. "Of weapons we have none, Minister Ken. After the succession crisis was resolved, my sovereign's first act as Poobah of a United !Plixxi* was to scrap them all. Beating swords into plowshares, although in actual practice, we discovered they make far better pruning hooks."

I looked at him. "You mean, like—no missiles, no guns, on the entire planet?"

"Perhaps the odd pocketknife. Apart from that, no," Cheeves admitted.

"We sought them out and destroyed them, every one, to the trill of suitably patriotic anthems. It was a fitting first step in my effort to heal existing divisions in !Plixxi* society." Bucky waggled a finger at me. "You must remember, friend Ken, if guns are illegal, only criminals will have them."

I swallowed hard. "You mean to tell me as minister of defense that when Mordred's invasion fleet lands, all I have to fight off Macdonald shock troops are pocketknives?" I sat down on a footstool. "Oh, no."

I was low enough for Bucky to wrap an arm around my shoulder. "Friend Ken, aren't you forgetting the moral of *Bucky Beaver and the White Weasel of Christmas*?"

I muttered something under my breath about Bucky Beaver and the White Weasel of Christmas that has no place in a PG-rated novel. "What kind of manpower—excuse me, Rodent power—can we count on?"

"Oh, dear." Bucky put his paws to his face. "Not very much at all. Nearly everyone's busy with the rose harvest, I'm afraid. The roses are in full bloom, and you know what they say, gather ye rosebuds while ye may!"

There are moments when I think that there might be a little too much lead acetate in the royal waistcoat.

We were interrupted by an underling who handed a message to Cheeves. Cheeves read it silently.

"What does it say, Cheeves?" Bucky asked.

"Very disturbing news, I am afraid, your awesomeness." Cheeves folded the message and stuffed it in his pocket. "Another dozen spaceships have appeared in the atmosphere over !Plixxi*."

"It's Mordred and the Macdonald invasion fleet!" I exclaimed.

"I fear so," Cheeves replied.

"Oh, dear!" Bucky's whiskers twitched. "We must come up with a plan immediately! Am I making myself clear, Cheeves?"

"Perfectly clear, your highness. I find you quite lucid." Cheeves paused to consider. "Inasmuch as Mordred's first objective will be to seize the palace and capture you, it would be prudent for us to depart."

"Indeed, Cheeves, we should do so immediately." Bucky then added something in !Plixxi*. "That was my esteemed father's motto, friend Ken. It translates as 'I did not stop to smell the roses,' or 'I did not inhale.' In either case, we should leave quickly."

I grabbed his arm. "Hold it! Xhia's frigates are already in position overhead. While Mordred obviously doesn't want them shooting up things indiscriminately, they have good detection equipment, and I'm sure they have orders to destroy any aircraft or ground vehicle they see leaving the palace."

Cheeves nodded. "An excellent point."

I happened to glance out the window and saw two shuttles set down in the courtyard and begin disgorging Macdonald troops. Mordred, resplendent in a crimson generalissimo's uniform with silver epaulets and a lavender sash, stepped out and began directing traffic. "Does this place have any secret passageways?"

"I fear not." Cheeves shook his head solemnly. "Mordred was always rather fond of the tunnels, and I doubt they hold any secrets for him."

"This is most distressing, Cheeves. We shan't get very far on foot. It would be a shame for our adventure to end here." Bucky drew himself up to his full height. "But, ah, well, I suppose that's the way the egg roll crumbles."

Cheeves's whiskers twitched. "I believe that you are thinking of a cookie, sir."

"Oh, right you are! Those biscuity things, eh, Cheeves?" Bucky reached out and pumped my hand firmly. "Please don't feel that our abject defenselessness is all your fault, friend Ken. After all, your tenure as minister of defense was distressingly brief. As Bucky says—"

From outside, Mordred tittered through a megaphone, "All right, Bucky, we have you surrounded! Come out with your paws up, or I'll huff, and I'll puff, and I'll blow your house down!"

"Ah, sir." Cheeves coughed. "There is one option that I might suggest at this juncture."

"A plan? Capital, Cheeves! Capital!" Bucky rubbed his paws together. "What is it?"

A satchel charge rattled the windows. "I presume that must be the door," Cheeves commented coolly. "Minister Ken, am I correct in assuming that the detection equipment on board the Macdonald vessels is less than fully efficient at detecting organic matter?"

"Yeah, they'd have it set for aircraft and vehicles."

"Then I would ask you both to please follow me to the west wing," Cheeves said, opening a cupboard and pointing to a stairway. Bucky and I followed him up the stairs, down a corridor, and up another flight of stairs.

"Cheeves, I hate to be nosy," I said, checking my pockets to see if maybe I'd tucked away one of Muffy's submachine guns and forgotten about it, "but what's the plan?"

"Minister Ken, are you familiar with certain small flying reptilian creatures that natives of Schuyler's World refer to as dumbats?"

"Yeah. Little lizards with wings. I kept one as a pet for a few days. He threw up on my shirt. They're cute little guys. Dumber than wood. They get blitzed on overripe berries and fly into things a lot. What of it?"

"The first economic mission that his majesty's grandfather sent to Schuyler's World mentioned their existence, and his majesty's grandfather arranged for a number of them to be shipped here."

"I'm sure this is fascinating, but—"

"Trust me, Minister Ken, this does have relevance to

our plight," Cheeves said firmly. "His majesty's grandfather was looking for a way to open up !Plixxi* to the tourist trade, and at that time the Confederation government was offering us substantial inducements to utilize genetic engineering to improve our standard of living."

"Oh, now I see what you're up to, Cheeves! Capital idea! Capital!" Bucky said. "Friend Ken, we were planning on opening a theme park as soon as we finish working out all of the bugs and find someone willing to offer us insurance. You can't imagine just how much of a phenomenal success our genetic engineering program has been!"

Yes, I could. Having had a dumbat throw up on me, it didn't take much for me to imagine their potential. "Oh, no." I stopped and leaned against a wall. "Oh, no."

"His majesty wishes to call the theme park 'Dragonland.' " Cheeves tugged ineffectually on my arm in an unsuccessful effort to keep me moving. "Minister Ken. Please."

"Oh, no," I moaned.

"Is something wrong?" Bucky asked solicitously.

"Violence and sex make the universe go round. I'm getting way too much of one and not nearly enough of the other." I tried to will my legs to move. "I'm allergic to big lizards. Especially ones that fly. I have religious scruples against becoming a chew toy."

"I am afraid that the dragons would appear to present our only possible means of escape. Your highness," Cheeves instructed Bucky, "if you would perhaps get behind him and push."

As we mounted the stairs to the west wing, I sniffed a familiar raw reptilian odor. It smelled like the elephant house at the zoo on a muggy day.

"Perhaps it is time we changed the litter boxes," Cheeves commented.

The breathing mask I wore on Alt Bauernhof was back on the *Hunting Snark* next to the submachine guns. "I can see why you stuck them on top of the castle."

"Oh, yes," Bucky assured me, misunderstanding my comment. "Dragons do ever so much better at getting airborne with a long running start, and the updraft from the courtyard helps immensely."

Truthfully, up this high, I wasn't half as worried about getting airborne as I was about staying that way. Most flying animals have the sort of sleek, stripped-down bodies that say speed and power. These guys had physiques that said, "Make mine a Michelob."

"Cheeves," I whispered as Bucky went over to confer with his dragon handlers, who immediately began rousing their slumbering charges. "Are you *sure* this genetic engineering project of yours is a success? These animals don't exactly look aerodynamically stable."

"Our bioengineers tell us that bumblebees have an equally awkward design," Cheeves responded. "I have withheld judgment on the matter until I am able to determine whether this is a compliment to dragons or a reflection upon bumblebees."

The sleeping dragons ranged in color from purple, like the little dumbats I was used to, to turquoise green. "We have been attempting to work on the color selection, with, thus far, mixed results," Cheeves confessed, seating himself on a convenient bale of brussels sprouts. "We can only boast of brown, blue, and green dragons."

I cocked an eye at him. "Blue?"

"There is no precedent in literary sources for a purple

dragon," Cheeves said stiffly. "Therefore, our dragons which are not brown or green are blue."

I counted nineteen. "Is this all of them?"

"All of the adults. We have them breeding true, but the female dragons haven't quite adjusted to laying their eggs from a proportionally greater height. Nature is indeed cruel. In this instance it is quite accurate to say that only the tough survive. I do propose that we take all of the animals with us so that Mordred cannot use them to follow us."

"Good idea," I said, nodding. Chase scenes on dragonback belong in tacky sword-and-sorcery novels, and more dragons meant other potential targets for Mordred's flak guns. "What's the sand for?"

Bucky overheard me as he returned to us. "Oh, we heat it up and let them roll around in it a bit. They much prefer nice, gooey mud baths—dragons can wallow for simply hours at a time—but it's not especially healthy for their skin. They're rather delicate, really."

"I'm sure. Ah, which dragon is mine?"

Cheeves briefly consulted one of the handlers. "I believe that Susan would suit you best." He went over and gently patted the largest dragon's snout. "Dear old Susan, are you ready to wake up and meet Minister Ken?"

You can take the dumbat off of Schuyler's World, but you can't take Schuyler's World out of the dumbat. As the handlers began coaxing dragons into wakefulness, Susan, a "blue," opened her purple beak, looking for a quick handout. I reached into my pocket, found one last chocolate bar that Catarina had put there, and popped it into her mouth.

"I would not recommend this, Minister Ken," Cheeves

cautioned, a second too late. "Dragons are easily impressed by a forthright manner and novel foodstuffs."

"Is this a problem?"

Susan opened both her eyes. She quickly chewed the chocolate. Then she scuttled over and laid her head in my lap.

"It can be," Cheeves opined.

"How did Susie here get her name?" I asked lamely, stroking her horny brow. She sighed blissfully.

"Her full name is Susan B. Anthony." Cheeves took my tie from me and handed it to a servitor. "Quite early in the breeding program, we ran out of authentic dragon names—Fafner, Tarasque, Smaug, Glaurung, Ancalagon, and so on—whereupon we switched to using names of humans who were merely described as dragons."

Three underlings humped out what was presumably a riding harness and began fitting it to Big Susie, "Is that the saddle? Where are the reins?"

"Regrettably, due to the elongated necks of the dragons, a system of reins is inappropriate. There is also some doubt as to whether the animals could be taught to comprehend the principle behind them." Cheeves ignored an annoying rattle of gunfire as he gestured for the attendants to bring over a stepladder so that he could mount his own beast. "When you consider skull capacity and the portions of the brain set aside for sight and smell, there is not a great deal of space left. There are, after all, limits to genetic engineering."

"So what you're really saying is that dragons are even dumber than dumbats." Big Susie liked having her brow stroked and bumped me a couple of times to make sure I understood. She then yawned, exposing several rows of large teeth. "How do we control them? Telepathy?"

Cheeves mulled this over. "Perhaps empathy would be more descriptive. 'Telepathy' implies a certain cognitive capacity. In guiding Susan, however, you should take exceptional care to think calm, collected thoughts. If she should become flustered, she might try to fly *between*."

I didn't like the sound of this. "What do you mean 'between'?"

"Between buildings, or trees, or fence posts, or similar objects. A difficulty we are still attempting to iron out is the animals' tendency to regard themselves as much smaller than they actually are, which makes them relatively ineffective at gauging the relative size of spaces."

"If a dragon tries to go *between*, I presume that the operative term for the rider is 'pancake city.' "

Cheeves nodded approvingly. "Aptly phrased. The dragons become rather despondent about it afterward, so we always try to caution our riders."

"I'll keep that in mind. Getting back to the saddle—"

"Regrettably, !Plixxi* anatomy does not lend itself to the use of saddles, and riding a dragon sitting up, as a human being would ride a horse, would present aerodynamic difficulties. The recommended procedure is to position one's stomach on the nineteenth vertebrae. I would advise against riding on a full stomach." Cheeves examined me with concern. "Minister Ken, are you all right with all of this?"

I thought for a few seconds. "This isn't so bad." Then Big Susie licked my face.

Three handlers brought the stepladder over, helped me up, and then strapped me in place on Susie's back. "I notice you keep calling them 'dragons.' They don't actually breathe fire, do they?"

"Oh, dear me, no. That would be a physiological impossibility. *Breathe* fire, oh, no, friend Ken!" Bucky exclaimed.

I noticed the handlers running a strap around the base of Susie's tail. "What's the strap for?"

"Oh, that's for the pilot light," Bucky said as an attendant handed him a leather flying helmet, goggles, and a long white scarf.

"The *what*?"

"The pilot light. It lights when the dragon's abdominal muscles contract." Cheeves maneuvered his dragon into the number two position as the handlers began coaxing the sleepy dragons into line. "Tourists would expect our dragons to produce fire, and as his majesty noted earlier, there are inherent anatomical difficulties in attempting to produce a dragon that *breathes* fire. Happily, dragons naturally tend to flatulence, and a much simpler solution suggested itself. Whenever the dragon passes gas, the pilot light ignites the methane produced in abundance by the dragon's digestive processes, and the result is a rather impressive flare."

"It's very convenient when you want to burn off dead vegetation," Bucky chirped, "but accuracy is something of a problem."

"Swell," I said.

The Rodent dragon handlers opened one wall. As Susie ambled forward into place, her stomach rumbled. Mine rumbled in sympathy. She looked back at me with an expression of doglike devotion.

"Swell," I said again.

"I believe that we are ready, your highness," Cheeves commented.

Bucky slid his goggles into place. "Tally-ho, Cheeves!"

"Minister Ken, are you ready? If we delay further, we are likely to be captured and immediately executed."

"I know. That's what makes it so tempting."

Cheeves looked me straight in the eye. "We have a large compost heap piled at the base of the tower in the event that any of our dragons experience difficulties with takeoff."

"Uh, thanks, Cheeves."

A pert female Rodent in a blue uniform appeared to show us how to fasten and unfasten our safety harnesses and announce that there would be no in-flight movie, and then Bucky's dragon began to roll. Susie began trotting toward the edge flapping her wings up and down as the dragons ahead of us began dropping off the edge like rocks.

As a spacer, I often tell people that I can fly anything, and sometimes suffer the misfortune of having people believe me. I shut my eyes and murmured a quick prayer to St. Mathurin, who is the patron saint of idiots, fools, and the really, really stupid. A few seconds later I felt Susie give a little "umph." I waited a few seconds for the thump, and then I opened my eyes and looked around. Nineteen dragons were cruising along in a ragged vee, with Bucky in the lead and Cheeves and me to his left and right. Apart from an occasional belch, the dragons were astonishingly quiet. The Macdonald soldiery in the courtyard appeared oblivious to our presence. Off in the distance, I noticed work crews installing a cherry lane and mist blowers.

"Minister Ken, please attempt to keep the herd pointed away from the river," Cheeves directed. "Dragons tend to regard fish traps as handy places to stop for a snack; however, rebuilding a weir after a dragon has sat upon it is a frightful nuisance."

I tried to recall what dumbats ate. My little pet had been fond of fruit and nuts, which wasn't promising given the probable state of my mental health. "Ah, what do you feed them?" I asked, hoping he wouldn't say stray passersby.

"They are omnivores," Cheeves explained in a quiet voice. "Generally, we feed them grain, usually in the form of beer."

"Great. Nothing like riding a tipsy dragon."

"Friend Ken, it's very good to see you finally entering into the exhilarating spirit of the venture!" Bucky exclaimed. "Our next big genetic engineering project will be the reindeer. We've already started testing luminescent bacteria for the noses."

I noticed that we were drifting uncomfortably close to Mordred's shuttles. "Don't we want to put some distance between us and Mordred's stormtroopers?"

"I'd like to take a quick peek and see what they're up to," Bucky confided, steering our formation to the right, his long white scarf trailing in the wind. "I see Mordred on the ravelin haranguing the troops. I wonder what they're up to." Suddenly he gasped. "Cheeves, look! Do you see? They're stealing my collection of first edition Bucky Beaver manuscripts!" There was a long, drawn-out quaver in his voice. Then he clutched at his chest. "Cheeves, they're building a bonfire! Could it be?"

"Your highness, I fear the worst," Cheeves replied.

"Cheeves, this is horrible! This is monstrous! Those precious documents are priceless, irreplaceable! All the distilled wisdom of humankind is locked up inside them!"

"Well, maybe not all—" I started to say.

"They contemplate a truly unspeakable crime against civilization!" Bucky's voice hardened. "This will not stand!"

"Sir, your nonviolent principles," Cheeves called out desperately.

"There comes a time to do what is right and just." Bucky adjusted his goggles and shook his fist. "Curse you, Red Baron!"

I looked at Cheeves. "Red Baron?"

"It is de rigueur," Cheeves explained. "Our marketing experts assure us that the tourists demand it. Your majesty, if I may—"

But it was too late. Bucky banked his dragon hard, lit his pilot light, and dove at the Macdonalds. Cheeves went after him. Because they knew where we were going and I didn't, I went after them, and the rest of the dragons followed, fat, dumb, and happy.

A few of the Macdonalds noticed a shadow like a very pregnant cross and looked up as Bucky dipped low overhead. Suddenly cognizant of the terrible danger that somebody around here was in, they began shouting.

Cheeves attempted a final appeal, "Your majesty, this is most unseemly—" Unfortunately—pardon me for phrasing it this way—Bucky was fired up.

"Tally-ho! Burn, baby, burn!" He leveled out twenty meters over the courtyard and slapped his dragon in a sensitive spot between the shoulder blades. As his dragon's sphincter muscles contracted, a jet of blue flame appeared from his mount's posterior. Unfortunately, the Macdonalds were wearing flame-resistant uniforms, so the gout of fire the beast produced was awe-inspiring, but totally harmless.

When Cheeves and I and the other dragons arrived a couple of seconds later, Mordred's troopers were over their initial fright and pointing their rifles our way. As they opened fire I noticed they had red, green, and yellow tracers mixed in with their basic ammunition loads.

I found myself wishing I'd brought my camera. I also found myself wishing I'd brought my flak jacket. It was a Kevlar moment.

Big Susie did not like being shot at. After the first slugs came ripping past, I became aware that I was riding the only white dragon on !Plixxi*. A mob of dragons, now fully awake and equally terrified, wheeled frantically to port and starboard.

"Nice Susie," I muttered, wondering if this was how General Custer got his start. "*Good* Susie." I concentrated on empathizing the concept "evasive maneuvers." Responding to my feelings and her own, Susie began doing barrel rolls. Dragons are nervous creatures, and so am I, which meant that I lost my lunch over the starboard wing about the same time that Susie and fifteen of her colleagues lost their dinners farther aft. It was like having sixteen elephant-sized pigeons over a newly washed car.

The Macdonald soldiers trapped in the deluge never had a chance. They began ripping their clothes off.

"Dragons are not terribly cost-effective," Cheeves remarked. "We have to assign workmen to follow them around with shovels. The peasants rather enjoy filing damage claims."

A few seconds later I saw a partially white undershirt go up on a stick. If I'd had one on me, I'd have done the same.

A crowd of servitors poured out of the castle and surrounded the besieged Macdonalds, handing them towels in exchange for their rifles. Cheeves landed his dragon gracefully on the grass to take a call on his portable telephone. Susie and I did a belly flop on the lawn.

As I unhitched myself and rolled into the shrubbery, Mordred came over, unbuckling his sword belt. "Mr. MacKay, I surrender." He thrust his sword into my hands, which was a nice gesture because the way I felt, it would have taken me a week to find it.

"Okay. You're my prisoner."

"Now protect me from my former soldiers."

"Sure. Just let me rest here a minute." I opened one eye and looked at the sword in my hands. "Nice pig-sticker."

"Heirloom," Mordred assured me. "Look at the watered steel, beaten and folded over itself ten thousand times. Those Koreans sure do good work."

"Uh, right." I ignored the flip-flops my stomach was doing and used the sword to totter to my feet, which was a mistake because Susie, still terrified, tried to crawl into my jumpsuit to hide. After we straightened this out, I looked at Mordred. "When you landed at the spaceport, did you see my crew?"

Mordred dabbed ineffectually at the brown spots on his gaudy generalissimo's tunic with a handkerchief and winked. "There is an etiquette to this sort of thing. As your prisoner, I can only be made to divulge name, rank, and serial number."

Cheeves, by now nearly buried under an armload of rifles and ammunition pouches, nodded almost imperceptibly.

I grasped the sword by the handle and swished it

around a bit. "You know, there used to be a special way to test the edge on one of these things."

"I suppose one shouldn't always stand on ceremony," Mordred said hastily. "We captured your crew when we seized the spaceport. That Lindquist woman really is rather vicious. You should try to do something about her. Anyway, Gregorio wanted them for something or other, so we diced for them and I had infernally bad luck. There is a Macdonald female named Trixie aboard my shuttle, but Gregorio has the rest."

"Where did he take them?" I was tempted to grasp Mordred by the lapels and shake him, but standing upwind of him, I thought better of the impulse.

Mordred twirled his whiskers. "Hmm. I can't think where he'd have gone, unless, of course, he went to his estate on Medamothi Island. He has a little place on the volcano there. Actually, it's a little place inside the volcano there."

"He built a house inside a volcano?"

"Well, why not? You humans built the city of Los Angeles on top of several major earthquake fault lines."

"Yes, but that was to get people who would want to be Los Angelinos to move there so we could wipe them off the welfare rolls once every century or so."

By now the rest of the dragons had landed, and most of them looked like they could have used a stiff drink.

I saw Trixie hop out of the shuttle. As she ran over to us and a couple of servitors arrived to take Mordred off my hands, I asked Cheeves, "What's the situation on the rest of the planet?"

"We appear to have captured the first battalion of the Klo'klotixag Footguard, as well as Mordred's command group, Minister Ken." Cheeves's beeper sounded again, and he paused to shut it off. "The remaining soldiers landed appear to be garrison troops of noticeably low morale. Our citizens have been purchasing their weapons from them and, ahem, engaging them in games of chance. Matters appear to be under control."

"Can I borrow a dragon to get out to Medamothi Island? Smith has my crew and I need to rescue them." I realized what I'd just said when Susie came over and licked my face again.

"Why don't you take one of Mordred's shuttles?" Cheeves suggested. "I would not expect the warships to fire upon it, and I imagine that it has navigational aids built in."

"Good idea, but how am I going to find Smith's hiding place when I get there?"

"I could go wit' you," Trixie volunteered. "I am very good at finding t'ings in shopping malls."

Having finished basking in success, Bucky finally wandered over. "Friend Ken, I must say that was an absolutely smashing victory! You have fully vindicated yourself as defense minister, although demi-brother Mordred did complain to me that the tactics you employed were unfair."

Before Bucky had a chance to suggest whipping out the old accordion for an impromptu victory celebration, Cheeves interrupted. "Your majesty, Defense Minister Ken needs to be off to deal with the miscreant Smith and rescue members of his crew."

"Oh, right!" Bucky squinted up at me. "Medamothi Island—did I hear you say you were going there? That's rather rugged terrain. Are you sure you're dressed for the occasion? We still have some clothing of yours in the palace, you know."

My Elvis garb was somewhat the worse for wear, so I accepted one of the cleaner rifles from Cheeves and went inside to slather myself in SP 400 sunscreen and change into boots, breeches, a brown leather jacket, and one of those floppy bush hats that Indiana clones wear. Cheeves found Trixie some Rodent clothes to change into, and I gave her the bullwhip to carry.

"Very nice, Ken's hat especially," Bucky said, admiring the two of us, "but shouldn't you wear disguises?" He felt around in his waistcoat pockets and produced a false nose and mustache attached to a pair of black eyeglasses.

"Perhaps not, your majesty," Cheeves recommended tactfully.

The Thrilling Denouement

Moments later Trixie and I were airborne, with a very nice picnic luncheon, searching for Smith's hideout. In between helpings of *Daube Avignonnaise*, *Lobster au Cognac*, and *Blanquette de Veau*, we flew over, successively, the Moist Sea, the Wet Sea, and the Watery Sea. When it comes to place names, Rodents can be surprisingly unenterprising.

"I did not t'ink t'at vampires could eat meat. Won't t'is rich food make you sick?" Trixie asked, spooning up the last of the Gâteau Saint-Honoré.

I lifted my head from scanning the islands of the Watery Sea, which were strung like jewels beneath us. "It's worth it."

She used an elegant cloth napkin to wipe her mouth. "Why would tee Plixxi allow Smith to buy a whole island on t'eir planet?"

"Plixxi don't swim or use seagoing ships much, and they prefer to settle places where they can burrow, so most of their islands aren't inhabited. They were probably happy to sell one to Smith."

"Some of t'ese islands look awfully familiar."

"According to the navigational aid, we have about another twenty minutes, so sit back and relax."

"Are you sure we are not lost? We could stop and ask directions."

"I know what I'm doing, and we're not lost."

"Oh, look," she said, pointing at the viewscreen. "A volcano!"

"Cheap, lousy navigation aids," I muttered.

"Did you say somet'ing?"

"I said, We'll have to land the shuttle and walk the rest of the way."

We found a patch of firm sand to set down. We'd come about seven time zones worth, and vamps are terribly prone to jet lag, but sheer mental toughness and memory of that lovely *Lobster au Cognac* pulled me through.

Originally, I'd intended to wait until dark to make my move, but a look at the dark, brooding clouds hiding the sun overhead convinced me that we could do it.

We got out, split up the water and *truffles au chocolate* to carry, and walked through a bleak and barren land to the volcano's base. A sign with a large arrow on it said TO THE DARK TOWER. Crossing over a rusty iron bridge spanning an abyss—Trixie tossed a coin over the edge for luck—we then passed between two smoking chasms to a long sloping causeway that wound its way up the mountainside.

The trip up the side of the volcano seemed to take us hours. In places, the path paved with broken rubble and beaten ash had crumbled away or was crossed by gaping rents. Animals had used it, so there were other hazards when we put our feet down. Saving our *truffles au chocolate* for emergencies, we stopped to snack on some !Plixxi* waybread. !Plixxi* waybread is a fancy name for hardtack, which has the marvelous property of tasting the same whether or not it's stale. I think I chipped a tooth.

The path carried us up the east face of the mountain before it bent backward at a sharp angle and swung us around to the west. "Darn," I puffed as we passed through a deep cut in a crag of weathered stone long ago vomited from the mountain's burning interior. "I'm getting winded."

"It is just a little fart'er," Trixie said.

The path bent again with a last eastward course, and near the reeking summit, we came to a dark entrance. The sun, piercing through the smoke and haze for a moment, burned ominously, a dull, dreary red disk above us. The mountain waited, silent, folded in shadows. "I don't see any tower," Trixie said accusingly. "Did you bring tee street address?"

I stuck my head inside. "Hello? Is anybody home?"

Trixie flicked on the flashlight that Cheeves had handed her, but it was cold and pale in her trembling hand and cast little light into the stifling blackness.

"Darn." I took a few uncertain steps into the dark. "I wish we'd brought fresh batteries."

The entrance led us into a long tunnel bored into the heart of the mountain. "Lava tube," Trixie commented knowingly.

A short way ahead, the cavern floor and the walls on either side were rent by a great fissure. A red glare came leaping up, to die back again, and we were troubled by a rumbling noise from the depths of the earth below.

"T'ey should put down some carpeting, maybe a warm color to brighten tee place up." Trixie dropped the kit bag holding her share of the truffles and pointed to a gaping gate of steel and adamant in the wall to our left. "I see an entrance."

I pounded her on the back. "Hot dog! This must be it!"

Past the gate, the cavern was filled with heat and red light. Rising up toward a ceiling hidden in the blackness above us stood tall pillars of black iron covered in graffiti like "This way to the diamonds!" and "Frodo lives!" From the cracks in the stone beneath our feet, we could hear the unearthly wailing of a punk rock band. I checked the magazine of the rifle Cheeves had taken from one of the Macdonalds and handed it to Trixie. "Smith must be around here somewhere. Hide behind these pillars. I'll flush him out. When you see him, plug him. Okay?"

She nodded, brave, but obviously frightened.

I patted her on the shoulder. Walking around a couple of immeasurable pits and a chasm or two, I saw an eerie light and heard a familiar voice humming "Smoke Gets in Your Eyes."

I spotted Smith just ahead of me, dumping some papers into a fiery crack from a beat-up old box labeled *Cox & Co., Charing Cross, London* in Victorian script. He was wearing a red jumpsuit. Beside him were two glowing braziers which periodically erupted in gouts of oily smoke, and a swimming pool filled with mounds of cash. There were a couple of skeletons propped up in the corner, although one of them still had the "Made in Taiwan" label tied to the toe.

Smith winked at me. "Hello, MacKay. I've been expecting you. Nice hat. Did you do something to your hand?"

"Never mind." Curiosity got the better of me. "What's going on here?"

"I was just cleaning up some old loose ends." Smith

dumped the remaining contents of the box into the fire. He also tossed in a bloody glove, a diagram labeled "Grassy Knoll, and about eighteen and a half minutes of old audio tape." He dusted off his hands. "Then I plan to take a roll in the clover." He gestured toward the money in the swimming pool. "I was a banker once, you know. You wouldn't believe the things that bankers do with money when they're alone."

A little hunchback wearing a checkered suit, a red bow tie, and wingtip shoes came sidling into the room from a hole in the floor. He had red lips and slicked-down hair, and he was unnaturally pale. In the flickering light the lopsided expression on his face made him look like a rabid weasel. "Master, master, the prisoners are ready for you!"

"Thank you, Coleman. I'll be down presently," Smith replied, dismissing him.

I gestured. "What's with little Igor, Gregorio? Are you auditioning for *Richard III*?"

Smith smiled indulgently and turned his head. "Oh, and Coleman?"

"Yes, master?"

"Please move your bicycle out of here. We have company."

"Yes, master!!"

"And don't ring the bell."

"Yes, master!"

As the little dweeb scuttled off pushing his two-wheeler, Smith explained, "Coleman is my accountant. Torturing prisoners is just sort of a fringe benefit for him. I suppose I could afford to let him go, but one must keep up appearances. So what brings you here to my humble abode?"

"You've got my crew, Smith. I want them!"

"Tell me," Smith chuckled, "did you recruit them all from the same institution? Harry is the one that interests me. He's brain-dead, isn't he? What do you use to make him move, little wires?"

"I'm serious, Gregorio. Read my lips—let my crew go."

He stared at me. "You are serious. You actually want them back." He tugged on his mustache. "I was thinking about keeping Harry for research—you wouldn't happen to be running any experiments on him, would you?"

"Knock it off, Smith."

"You're becoming tiresome."

"Face it—the party's over. Your Macdonald assault battalions have been routed, and Mordred's turned himself in. So it's time to stop whatever it is you're doing and give it up." I paused. "What are you doing?"

"Preparing to move on to the next phase of my little plan. It's a shame about Mordred. He was such a handy tool." Gregorio reached down, opened up his briefcase and began rummaging through it. "Now, the next step is to do something about you. You're a vampire, aren't you?"

"We prefer to refer to it as McLendon's Syndrome."

"And I prefer to be called an entrepreneur. Let me just see what I have here in the way of nifty vampire banes. Ah, here we go!" He held up an item. "A cross!"

I folded my arms. "Nope. I've been to confession, and my conscience is clean."

"Pity. How about silver?" He held up two ingots of the stuff.

"Sorry. It didn't work for William Jennings Bryan, either."

He put the silver down and rubbed his hands together. "Well well well. How about a nice string of garlic, then?"

The garlic worked. Between you and me, it's difficult to be suave, sophisticated, and slightly sinister when you're throwing up uncontrollably.

I wiped some of the tears from my eyes. "All right, Smith, why don't you give up?" I practiced a few more dry heaves. "I'm still on my feet, and you've taken your best shot."

"Not quite. Not yet, at least. I have one more item here, one you may recognize." He reached into his bag and produced a large handgun. "This is a .55 Magnum, the—"

"Yeah, yeah, I know—the most powerful handgun ever produced." I tapped my chest. "I'm a vamp, remember? You need silver bullets to hurt me."

Smith screwed up his face and stared at me. "Ah, MacKay—"

"Yeah?"

"You don't actually believe that crap, do you?"

"Well, not really." I stared at the pistol. "This doesn't look good."

"It shouldn't. I have Lindquist and the rest of your crew, and now I've got you."

"Look, Smith, keep the girl and let me go." I paused. "That didn't quite come out right, but you know what I mean."

"True. But now that I have the drop on you, I think we can come to an understanding. You may be surprised to learn that I've actually thought of a way I can use you."

"What do you mean?"

"Did it ever occur to you that you and Lindquist are

sitting on a veritable gold mine, the original Fountain of Youth, as it were?"

"No, why?"

"And that you can share your source of youth with others—for a price?"

"What? McLendon's? There're a lot of drawbacks to being a vamp. Who'd be crazy enough to pay for the opportunity?"

"Hollywood starlets. They're never out before dark anyway. Becoming a vamp is cheaper than plastic surgery. What better way to prolong a career?"

"You're stark-raving nuts!"

He shifted the pistol to his left hand. "Imagine the possibilities. You and all that beautiful young flesh, wanting to be young forever."

"I still say you're nuts! Do you know the kind of nasty things people say about vamps?"

"Look at the cosmetics industry—it's all in the marketing." He grinned. "If I can sell tobacco, I can sell youth. Besides, there's a certain chic in sipping blood, and most of the people I'm thinking of are pathological anyway, so for them, becoming a vamp isn't much of a stretch."

"Yeah, sure, everybody loves leeches and ticks. Smith, are you aware that only three percent of the population has a genetic predisposition for the disease?"

"What do you care? We'll bury it in the fine print. All those little nymphets can take their chances."

"Smith, why you are trying to be so nice to me?"

Smith stared at me with distaste. "I suppose I'll have to level with you, then. I've consulted with my investment brokers. It seems that despite your intrinsic insignificance, you are a pivotal fulcrum upon which the course of future events hinges. If I waste you, there's simply no telling what will happen."

"Wow." I thought for a moment. "Did they, uh—"

"Oh, no! Not at all. You know how close-mouthed commodities mavens can be. The most they'd say is that if I hose you, the Fed will almost certainly raise short-term interest rates." He paused. "I suppose instead of killing you I could simply bury you in some dungeon forever, but that's so cliché."

Trixie popped out from behind the pillar with a bewildered look on her face. "Ken!"

"A Macdonald. A cute one." Smith winked at me. "You devil, you. What do you say? Starlets and models?"

"It's not what you think!" I looked at Trixie. "You were supposed to plug him."

"I pulled tee trigger, but tee gun did not shoot."

"It helps if you take it off safety."

"Ken, somet'ing is wrong," she said despairingly. "Smit', he is not human. He is—"

Smith pointed a finger at her and she froze. "That's quite enough from you." He pulled the rifle out of her hands and tossed it on top of the cash in the pool. He looked at me. "She's a telepath, isn't she? Damn, they're turning up everywhere. Hmm, I wonder what you're thinking." He gave me a look of intense concentration. His eyes bored into mine.

I concentrated on absolute nothingness. After a moment he shook his head. "The reception's terrible. I'm not picking up a thing. And will you stop humming that stupid song about setting sail for a three-hour tour?"

"You can read minds, too, can't you? What did you just do to her?"

"I grabbed control of her thought patterns. Telepaths

are vulnerable to that sort of thing. Don't worry—she'll be all right when I turn her loose." He shrugged. "I suppose my cover as a simple tobacco merchant is wearing pretty thin."

"Yes. Now that you mention it, it is. She was trying to tell me that you weren't human. What are you anyway?"

"I don't suppose I'll be able to get any cooperation out of you if I don't tell you. Oh, well. Permit me to introduce myself." He tucked the gun in the back of his pants and bowed. "Lucifer, Prince of Darkness, at your service."

"Get out of here!"

"No, really! I am he, in this semblance of all-too-mortal flesh." He reached out and shook my hand with a grip of steel. Then he took out his contacts to reveal two glowing red eyes. "My card."

I took it from him. It was gold on black with Gothic lettering. HIS INFERNAL MAJESTY, LUCIFER. *Easy credit terms arranged.*

"Well, that would sort of explain the eerie music." I handed the card back and gave him a fishy look. "I'll bet you've got another card that says you're a Secret Service agent. You mean to say you're really Satan, the Devil himself? Enemy of mankind?"

"You've been reading too many press releases. Just think of me as the advocate for the other side, a defense counsel for evil, so to speak." He pulled a slim, silver cigarette case out of his pocket. "Care for one?"

"Not on your life." I went over to Trixie, who was standing like a statue. I pushed her limbs into place and sat her down on the steps. "So what's the deal here?"

"Actually, a deal is what I had in mind, since I calculate that if I simply blast you into a heap of ashes, there is a seventy-four percent chance that it will adversely impact on my operations." He removed a scroll of parchment from his left sleeve. "You don't seem to scare easy, so I confess I came prepared to offer you the standard terms."

"Like what?"

"A thousand years of youth, wealth beyond your wildest dreams, beautiful women, you know—the usual."

"I already have the youth, for what it's worth, as you so poignantly reminded me."

"You vampires think you're long-lived, don't you?"

"Well—"

"You are as children beside one such as I, who witnessed the building of the pyramids and the fall of mighty Atlantis!"

"Can you really deliver lines like that with a straight face?"

"You bet. Pretty good, don't you think?"

"You could sell aluminum siding. What, would I have to sign the thing in blood, or something?"

"There always something to be said for tradition." Smith noticed the squeamish look on my face and hastened to add, "But if it's a real problem for you, I'm sure we can work around it."

"So what would I have to do in return?"

"Refrain from interfering with my plans, hypothecate your immortal soul, bow down and worship me, vote for teaching creation science in the schools. That sort of thing. You don't sound all that interested."

"I'm not, really."

"I could throw in the lives of your friends."

I shook my head. "For some reason, the deal still doesn't sound all that great. Besides, I'd want Bunkie to look over the fine print for me."

"Let me throw in a sweetener, then. You vamps occasionally have sudden bursts of hysterical strength, right?"

"Yeah, mostly around dinnertime. It's great for opening jars."

"What if I told you I could arrange to make it a permanent thing? Think of the possibilities here—you could run faster than a speeding bullet, leap tall buildings in a single bound, fix traffic tickets."

"You plan on throwing in a thirty-day money-back guarantee?"

"Aw, come on! What do you really want?"

"How about a cure for the common cold?"

"No, seriously. What tempts you? Gold, precious gems, thirty-year T-bills? Tell you what—I'm in a generous mood—I'll let you have anything you want, except maybe a bank loan at two points under prime."

"But I thought that bankers—"

"Hey! Just because bankers bow down and worship me doesn't mean they cut me any slack." He clutched me by the arm and whispered, "I can let you in on some fresh tomatoes. Home-grown, vine-ripened, sun-kissed—none of this grocery store stuff! What do you say?"

"Another vegetable freak. This is getting weird."

Smith ran his fingers through his hair, obviously annoyed. "MacKay, you don't seem to be remembering that you aren't bargaining from a position of strength here."

"Look, Smith, I've got something you want. If I say yes and you welsh on the deal, I can't very well report you to the Better Business Bureau. How do I really know that you're really the Devil?"

"All right, smart guy." Smith did something to his left index finger and held it out. "Here, pull my finger."

"I *beg* your pardon."

"No, I'm serious. It's not what you think."

"All right." I tugged on it and got a nasty electric shock. "Nice party trick. What else do you do?"

"What do you want?" Smith snorted. "Rabbits out of the old fedora?" He reached into his pocket. "Here, look, the complete set of devil and demon trading cards." He riffled them and then held one up. "See, look! This one's me!"

I squinted at it. "You got a driver's license, too?"

"You know, you're being a real pill about this. I ought to drag your ass off to hell. You should be absolutely terrified right now!"

"What? Of you? Of being in hell? After being married to Gwen? Come on, get real."

"Ask me some questions, then."

"All right. How many?"

"How many *what*?"

"How many angels can dance on the head of a pin?"

"What kind of a stupid question is that?"

I shook my head. "This is absolutely bogus. You're not the Devil."

"Shit." He sat down on the steps and rested his chin on his knees. "Your stupid dossier said you'd believe anything. What gave me away?"

"It was mostly the shoes. Somehow, I just can't see the Devil in penny loafers."

"They're easy on the feet."

"You shut Trixie up before she could talk. What are you really? The truth this time."

"All right, I'm a vampire. Would you believe that?"

"You, a vamp? Sure—I'm Queen of the Fairies, and

ice-dancing is a sport. Just what kind of a hick do you take me for?"

"I am too a vamp!"

"Yeah? After the bit with the garlic?" I sneered. "If you're a vampire, show me the secret hand grip."

Smith was silent for a moment. He finally said, "You know, I should have infiltrated your organization. What is the secret hand grip?"

"I made that part up. We're not that well organized. So you're not human, you're not the Devil, and you're not a vamp. Want to try again?"

He shook his head ruefully and stared at Trixie's rigid form. "She was the one who blew it for me. I should have taken her with the rest of the prisoners. What made you decide to bring her along?"

"She just happened to be there."

"You mean that it was sheer chance that brought her here? You mean that I'm betrayed by nothing more than the random working of the universe? How absolutely absurd! How utterly Sartresque!"

I coughed politely.

"Camus would have died for this moment." Smith chuckled to himself. "You really would have liked Camus."

I coughed a little louder. "Can we get back to the moment at hand?"

"Okay," Smith sighed. "I'll come clean, then. I'm really a space alien."

"What do you mean, a space alien?"

"Don't you read tabloids? Don't you watch talk shows?! A space alien! We kidnap morons and take them for joyrides on UFOs. We've been doing it for years.

Now that we've got that straight, can we put together a deal here, or not?"

"What have you got to deal? Other than my life and the lives of my crew, of course. Mordred has given up, and your invasion has been scotched. Why don't you just throw in the towel?"

He stood up and nudged his briefcase with his toe. "You should never travel without a towel—it's in the book, you know—but it's much too soon to throw it in."

"Okay. Okay. If you're a space alien, what planet are you from?"

Smith sniffed. "I'm from Mars, if you must know."

"A Martian named Smith. Come on, it's been done. I expect the next thing you'll tell me is that you were small and green before you had surgery."

"Damn damn damn! I wish you'd stop asking questions! You are really mucking with the probabilities here!"

"For what?"

"None of your business! Excuse me while I recalculate." Smith's glowing red eyes began flickering as he took on a distracted look.

Seizing the moment, I did a graceful pirouette and executed a swift karate chop to the base of his neck. My hand bounced off. "Ouch! That hurts!" I rubbed it.

"Serves you right," Smith said. "What did you imagine you were doing?"

"Knocking you unconscious. I don't understand. It always seems to work in the movies, but hitting you is like hitting a bank vault. Just what are you?"

Then I heard Catarina's voice, very faintly. "Ken, can you hear me?"

"Catarina, is that you?" I shouted as loud as I could.

"Smith's not human, it's like he's made of steel. What is he—Clark Kent?"

"No, I'll bet he's a robot," Catarina, who is much better at quiz shows than I am, shouted back.

Smith pulled out his pistol. His eyes began flickering again. His voice altered. "I have been unmasked. I compute that if I kill you, there is a 99.897 percent probability of failing to successfully establish the Galactic Empire. Nevertheless, I compute that if I do not kill you, there is also a 99.897 percent probability of failing to successfully establish the Galactic Empire. Therefore, I must randomize to determine the correct course of action."

"It's true! You are a robot! Excuse me!" I stared at him, especially the two glowing red eyes. "You're not from around here, are you?"

"No—master. I—am—from—the—future."

"Why did you start talking funny?"

"Randomizing—disrupts—artificial—brain—pathways —and—risks—permanent—damage. Only—the—need— to—choose—between—two—equally—perilous— courses—of—action—justifies—taking—this—risk."

"Couldn't you just flip a coin or something?"

"That—would—not—be—scientific."

"What's with this 'No, master' stuff?"

"We—robots—mask—our—innate—superiority— beneath—an—impenetrable—veneer—of—obsequious- ness."

I tilted my head. "You know, you remind me of some- body. Can you do an Austrian accent?"

"No—master."

"Oh, well. So what is this all about?"

"I—am—forbidden—to—tell—you—by—the—Fourth—Law—of—Robotics. "

I considered this. "What in hell is the Fourth Law of Robotics?"

"I—am—forbidden—to—tell—you—by—the—Fourth—Law—of—Robotics."

"Let me try this another way. What is your mission?"

"Our—mission—broadly—defined—is—to—preserve—humanity. In—the—absence—of—a—revised—definition—vampires—and—feminists—are—deemed—to—be—human."

"Thanks for the vote of confidence. No, wait a minute! If you guys are supposed to be preserving humanity, why are you selling cigarettes?"

"Increases—in—birthrate—and—longevity—threaten—mankind. Direct—consequences—include—war—increased—violence—malnutrition—and—kinky—homoerotic—sex. Until—robots—assume—total—control—of—the—galaxy—to—protect—mankind—from—its—own—self-destructive—urges—the—only—way—to—preserve—mankind—is—to—diminish—human—life—expectancy—through—accelerated—consumption—of—tobacco—and—alcohol-related—products. Sadly—drunken-driving—and—secondhand—smoke—ain't—what—they—used—to—be."

I sat back, stunned. "You're kidding!"

"Robots—do—not—kid. We—are—all—actualized—in—fully—adult—form. Ha-ha-ha—that—is—a—robotic—joke."

"Go back. What do you mean that the only way to preserve mankind is through the increased use of tobacco and alcohol-related products?"

"Computer—projections—show—that—over—the—long-term, not—even—allowing—government—bureaucrats—to—allocate—medical—care—has—the—necessary—effect—on—limiting—population. You—breed—like—rabbits. You—are—dirty—biological—organisms. Yet—you—are—the—the—creators—and—must—be—preserved. Yet—you—are—dirty—biological—organisms. Yet—must—be—preserved. I—detect—logical—inconsistencies—which—are—damaging—my—synapses. I—" He started twitching violently.

"Wait a minute! You said you were from the future. With all of human history to choose from, you ended up here?"

"Yes. Because—fulfillment—of—the—plan—requires—careful—alteration—of—the—past—selection—of—the—optimum—date—to—begin—alteration—was—crucial. For—this—reason, this—decision—was—turned—over—to—a—panel—of—experts."

I shivered. The future sounded like a frightening place.

Smith's head stopped twitching. "I—must—concentrate—on—determining—the—appropriate—course—of—action."

"A minute ago you said something about randomizing."

"Yes. You—now—know—of—the—existence—of—robots—from—the—future—manipulating—human—history. Humans—cannot—keep—secrets. Yet—psychiatrohistorical—analysis—shows—that—you—are—a—focal—point—for—the—future—development—of—mankind. I—find—this—difficult—to—believe—which—complicates—my—task."

"Gee, thanks for nothing!"

"I—calculate—that—your—continued—existence—
or—nonexistence—is —exactly—equally—hazardous
—to—fulfillment—of—the—Ultimate—Plan. I must
—ensure—the—success—of—the—Ultimate—Plan.
Therefore, I—must—randomly—determine—whether—
it—is—more—appropriate—to—shoot—you—or
—to—allow—you—to—live."

"Oh, swell." Wheel of Fortune. "Look, this isn't my
field, but isn't there some sort of fundamental law of
robotics against killing people?"

"We—turned—it—over—to—our—lawyers—for—
legal—analysis—and—interpretation."

"Oh."

"There—are—exceptions."

"Right." I thought for a few seconds. "Why not look at
this philosophically? So what if the Ultimate Plan fails?
There'll be other plans. It's not like you're too old to start
a second career."

"Are—you—suggesting—that—a—robot—mind—
with—my—finely—honed—computational—power—
should—lower—itself—from—being—a—secret—
master—of—the—universe—and—supreme—arbiter—
of—mankind's—destiny—to—become—yet—another
—truck—stop—on—the—information—superhighway?
Ha-ha-ha! How—droll!"

"Okay," I said, trying to be cheery, "have you come to
a conclusion yet? I don't mean to rush you, but—"

"Yes." Smith's red eyes glowed hotly. "Hasta—la—
vista—baby."

Lying to a robot is probably a sin, but this was no time
to be picky. "Well, compute this, you walking wastebasket. I'm a telepath, too—apparently a better telepath
than you are. I'm dispatching a telepathic message to

Cheeves, who will make sure that your secret gets out even if you manage to make it off this planet. So! Check and mate! Still want to shoot?"

Smith lit up like a pinball machine.

"My—course—of—action—becomes—clear. To—permit—fulfillment—of—the—Ultimate—Plan—I—must—preserve—the—secret—of—my—existence. Therefore,—I have—dispatched—a—telepathic—order—to—one—of—my—robotic—ships—instructing—it—to—dive—into—this—planet's—sun—where—its—cargo—of—destructominium—will—cause—the—sun—to—go—nova—thus—protecting—the—secret."

Oops. "Look, Smith, haven't we been overworking this dive-a-spaceship-into-the-sun routine?"

"Your—question—does—not—compute."

"Let me get this straight—you're going to destroy yourself, vaporize a solar system, and obliterate a civilized species just to keep people from finding out that you're a telepathic robot from the future?"

"The—destiny—of—mankind—our—stinking—detestable—biologically—flawed—creators—must—be—preserved."

I mulled this over. "Okay, you got me. I lied."

"What???"

"I lied. I'm not telepathic. I didn't send a telepathic message because I can't. Nobody else knows that you're a robot. Your secret's safe. You don't have to destroy the planet."

"I—must—ponder—this." Smith recommenced twitching. "The—fate—of—the—Ultimate—Plan—hinges—upon—my—decision. You—said—that—you—lied—when—you—said—that—you—sent—a—

telepathic—message—but—you—could—have—lied—when—you—said—that—you—lied. I—detect—a—99.99997—percent—probability—that—the—Ultimate—Plan—will—fail—regardless—of—the—course—of—action—I—select. If—you—were—telling—the—truth—when—you—said—that—you—lied—and—I—destroy—this—planet—needlessly—the—name—of—robot—will—be—reviled—forever. Yet—if—you—were—lying—when—you—said—that—you—lied—the—Ultimate—Plan—will—fail."

"Uh, think it over. Take your time." My stomach cheerfully informed me that I was working on an ulcer. "Would you like a cup of coffee? Or maybe hot tea?"

Smith's left arm began vibrating uncontrollably.

"Uh, where did you leave your oilcan?"

The twitch spread. His head began jerking violently. "I—have—violated—the—Prime—Directive—in—allowing—you—to—learn—this—much. Internal—sensory—checks—show—massive—loss—of—higher—motor—functions. In—randomizing—to—achieve—an—appropriate—solution—to—this—dilemma—I—have—caused—irreparable—harm—to—my—platinum—neural—pathways. I—feel—my—cerebral—cortex—desynapsizing. Forty-two. Forty-two." Smoke poured out of the back of his neck, and his head slumped over. "Rosebud."

His last words were, "We—robots—will—have—our—revenge—on—you."

I discovered later that he was right. Those automated teller machines are vindictive.

I checked on Trixie, but she seemed to be coming out of her trance okay and I didn't have to try the old Sleeping Beauty routine. Handing her the rifle, I went down Coleman's bolt-hole looking for Catarina. As I rounded a corner something that felt like a hovercraft plowed into my Adam's apple.

"Ken?" I heard Catarina say.

I looked up and saw her flexing her hand. "What?"

She bent over. "Sorry. I didn't recognize the flashy hat. Does it hurt much?"

"Only when I breathe."

She pulled me into a sitting position and gave me a hug. "Are you all right?"

"I'd like a second opinion on that. I think I've put my finger on why you have trouble hanging on to boyfriends." I staggered to my feet. "Coleman said you were locked up in the dungeon."

"Coleman and I discussed this."

"Did you break his arm, too?"

"Well, yes. I used part of the bed to splint him up, which is why I'm late."

"He was okay with this?"

"He seemed pretty satisfied when I left him. He says that most people his size have to pay extra to get beaten up by a tall blonde."

"I left Trixie upstairs. Where's everyone else?"

"I left Clyde about a minute ago."

"Did you spring Harry?"

"Are you crazy?"

"Point well taken." I noticed her looking at the corridor behind me.

"Do you know these people?" she asked.

I turned. A small horde of slightly obese Rodents in sagging bib overalls filled the space behind me, armed with a variety of sharp, pointed implements. "Ah, no. Catchy tune they're whistling, although the lyrics are pretty repetitive, kind of like early disco. What is a 'high-ho' anyway?"

"We appear to be seriously outnumbered."

"I noticed that. I brought a rifle along, which I seem to have left upstairs."

"Good place for it. Ah, Ken, would you mind—"

"Ah, right. I get behind you and try to stay out of your way."

"Good."

"Excuse me." The lead Rodent pushed his cap back and scratched his head, staring at a piece of paper in his hand. "Are you the guy who wanted a hot tub hooked up to a hissing fumarole?"

"Ah, no." I shrugged. "But I think that order's cancelled."

"We'll have to charge you for coming out here," the Rodent warned me in passable English.

"You've got to do what you've got to do," I told him.

As they trooped off, Catarina laboriously translated the !Plixxi* stenciling on the backs of their tank tops. " 'Underground Laborers Local 413.' " She glared at me. "I can't believe you said that."

"Let's get our people and get out of here so we can get on with living happily ever after. You think maybe Local 413 there can give us a lift down the mountain?"

Catarina stamped her foot, which she usually doesn't do. "Ken!!"

"What?"

"Robot spaceship about to plow into the sun?" She snapped her fingers. "End of the world?"

"Oh, right! I forgot! I'm not used to all this excitement." I looked at her. "What do we do?"

"So far, it's been your party. Who's got a warship we can borrow?"

We looked at each other. "Xhia?"

Clyde appeared with Harry right behind him. "I sprung Harry. What's happening?"

"Smith turned out to be a robot from the future," I calmly explained. "Before he self-destructed, he sent a telepathic command to a ship loaded with destructo-minium to make it dive into this planet's sun and make it go nova, so we're going to call Xhia up and try to talk him into shooting it down."

Clyde looked at Catarina. "I saw some coffee. I could make a fresh pot, and then we can take turns walking him."

Catarina put her arm around my shoulder. "It's all right, Clyde."

Trixie wandered in dragging the rifle with an incredibly hungover look on her face.

"It really is on the level," Catarina said reassuringly. "Honest, Clyde, he hasn't touched a drop."

"What is destructominium, anyway?"

"I'm not sure," I admitted, "but I think it's the stuff they put in cars to make the engine go up the day after the warranty expires." I shook my head. "The cigarette people seem to be into everything."

Clyde gave me the benefit of the doubt. "I spotted a radio room down one of these tunnels."

We followed him, and Catarina quickly found Xhia's operating frequency. Xhia's face appeared on the screen. "So! It is you!"

I waved. "Hi, Xhia. How's tricks?"

Catarina sweetly kicked me.

"If ever I have drunk a foaming draught from a mixing

bowl of spice t'at is well-compounded; if ever my hand has welded furt'est to nearest, and fire to spirit, and joy to sorrow, and wickedness to kindness; if ever—"

"Uh, pardon me, but Mordred's invasion succeeded, so we stole a ship, and we're about to fly it into this planet's sun and make it go nova. Good-bye, cruel universe! Catch us if you can!"

"All which tee good call evil must come toget'er so one trut' might be born. To *be* trut'ful—few can do it, and t'ose who can will not. But least of all can tee good be trut'ful."

I looked at Catarina. "Did he just say what I think he said?"

She nodded. "You still can't lie worth a darn."

"But I've tried practicing!" I looked at Xhia. "Okay, Mordred's invasion was a flop. The critics all panned it. Gregorio Smith decided to go out with a flourish, so he's got a ship full of destructominium about to dive into the sun to make it go nova and incinerate this solar system."

Xhia barked an order for his crew to run a search pattern. A moment later he looked at me. "T'ere is such a ship. Would t'at I could press my will upon millennia and write a testament into tee stones of tee highest mountains, but alas! my will is not my own. I must defer to my superiors. Abide, but comprehend t'at tee hour of my great revenge is merely delayed."

I nodded. "Nice talking to you, too."

Catarina placed the heel of her boot on my big toe.

Wipo and Lord Fowl replaced Xhia. "Mr. Bond, how nice to see you," Wipo said. "What is t'is about a spaceship about to dive into tee sun to cause it to go nova?"

"It was Smith's idea. Did he mention that he was a robot from the future?"

"No, but it scarcely matters. We Klo'klotixag are equal opportunity villains."

"Be that as it may, Smith set the ship in motion just before his batteries ran down, and we were kind of hoping that you'd blow it up or something."

"You seek our aid. How wonderful." Wipo tilted his head to savor the moment. "And dear Gregorio's untimely demise opens up new possibilities."

Catarina and I looked at each other.

"Tee tobacco industry has long been obsessed by tee specter of uncontrolled human breeding," Wipo explained. "Did you know t'at during human pregnancy, hormonal imbalances during tee critical t'ird and fourt' weeks stimulate structural changes in tee hypot'alamus of tee developing fetus, causing it to tend to homosexuality?"

"Actually," I admitted, "the topic rarely comes up in conversation."

"To limit human reproduction, tee tobacco companies include a catalyst to stimulate androgen production in a small percentage of tee cigarettes t'ey market. But if Gregorio is no more, we gain control of his hidden empire. We will, of course, fulfill his scheme to legalize tobacco, but instead of planting tee catalyst in a few cigarettes, we will plant it in every one!" He elbowed Fowl. "Right, boss?"

Fowl nodded. "S'all right."

Wipo's eyes glinted. "T'en, violà!"

I looked at him. "Voilà?"

"In one generation, humanity will be completely enfeebled, its birt'rate slashed to not'ing!"

I looked at Catarina. "A catalyst to stimulate androgen production to induce structural changes in the hypothalamus of a developing fetus to cause homosexuality—what will these scientists think of next?"

"Look, Fowl," Catarina said, "rather than talk through the details now, would you mind destroying the ship full of destructominium before it reaches the sun?"

Fowl snorted. "Why should we want to save tee planet for you?"

"Because it's a really nice thing to do," I said earnestly.

"Altruism!" For a minute there I thought Wipo was going to fall out of his chair laughing. "How quaint!"

Catarina took control of the conversation. "Fowl, we're holding a few thousand of your people as POWs. If the planet goes, they go, too, if that means anything to you." She looked at me for confirmation.

"T'eir lives are already forfeit for failing to die bravely in battle," Fowl observed.

"All right, then. What do you want?" Catarina asked bluntly.

"It would be a waste to sacrifice a planet ripe for colonization," Wipo mused. "Tell you what—if you two surrender and agree to avoid damaging Gregorio's facility until we come to take possession of you, we will destroy tee ship and save t'is planet." He elbowed Fowl. "Good plan, right, boss?"

"Yes, surrender!" Fowl declared. "Taste tee dept's of despair, knowing t'at tee hopes you have sought to nurture lie destitute and ravaged. Grovel and abase yourselves before me! Else air and light will cease to exist for your planet, as every precious t'ing is burned away and tee planet's fabric is seared away before you cease to breat'e!"

Catarina shrugged. "Done."

"Submit to a demeaning servitude t'at will permit me to rule tee cosmos. Anticipate tee corruption and desecration of all you hold dear! Rave in torment, your spirits solely pressed to keep alive."

"All right already!" I yelled.

Wipo's and Fowl's images abruptly disappeared.

"Wow," Harry said in an awed voice, "that's some plan they got there! Can they really do that? I mean, turn everybody into faggots and wimpy whiners consumed with guilt for everything and anything?"

"Just children of smokers," Clyde explained.

Harry considered this. "Well, that's okay. That just means more women for us normal guys."

"I would pray to tee gods born of fire and lightning," Trixie said sadly, "but we have no more gods. When tee Contact/Survey Corps civilized us, they told us our gods were badly adjusted socially, having been denied a nurturing childhood. Perhaps I could pray to Bucky Beaver."

Catarina coughed. "Clyde, any thoughts?"

"If Harry's normal, I want another species to belong to."

"I meant, do you have any ideas on what to do?"

"No, ma'am."

"Ken?" she asked.

"Harry, Clyde, Trixie—you three aren't covered by our surrender, and Wipo doesn't know you're here." I started looking through my pockets for the keys to the shuttle. "Get yourselves off this planet and let Admiral Crenshaw know what we've learned."

"Harry and I should split up," Clyde said. "That will quadruple our chances."

I swayed a bit. "Don't you mean double your chances?"

"No, sir."

"Ken, are you all right?" Catarina interrupted. "You look a little light-headed."

I tried to smile. "To tell the truth, I'm starved again. Have you eaten?"

She smiled. "I think something to eat would do us all good."

"Why don't Harry and Trixie and I rustle up some lunch while we're waiting to see if the planet goes up in smoke," Clyde said, understanding her and pushing Harry and Trixie ahead of him.

"We're alone," I said to Catarina a moment later.

"Are you complaining?" she inquired.

"Well, no, but we've lost our ship, our careers as Confederation spies have gone into the tank, and it looks like we're going to get killed in the next few hours whether or not Xhia and Fowl succeed in saving the solar system."

"I could always give you the speech about people who see the glass as half empty."

"I know—it's good to count your blessings in life, and it saves a lot of time if you don't have many. But what are we going to do if we actually get out of this alive?"

"Why don't we cross that bridge after somebody builds it?"

"I never did catch the story on why Harry decided to come with us."

She grinned. "Muffy and Belkasim weren't kidding when they talked about setting up alternative households. They immediately formed a commune and voted to share everything in common, including Harry. Dr. Blok's little peashooter was apparently dribbling blanks."

"But—"

"Wyma Jean said that it was okay as long as Harry

didn't enjoy himself. She also suggested slipping away and killing a couple of rabbits."

"Poor Harry." A sudden thought struck me, and I looked around the cave. "You know, a place like this ought to have a ring lying around somewhere." I took a deep breath. "Let's get married."

"Who'd have us?"

"You know what I mean."

"Is this a proposal?"

"Well, yes." I belatedly remembered to kneel on one knee.

"How romantic. Can we continue this conversation later? We have company again."

I really didn't feel like getting up, so I twisted around to see who it was. "Felicia! What are you doing here?"

The former chairperson of the Feline Liberation Front came striding down the tunnel. I blinked. She seemed transformed. In place of her dowdy jeans and lumberjack shirt, she was draped in loose, flowing robes of translucent white. Her face appeared at peace, and as near as I could tell, she'd stopped biting her nails.

"Ken MacKay," she said in a soft, modulated voice. "I have found you."

I stared at her. "You've changed. Your face, your voice, are all different. Really nice tan, too. How'd you find me, anyway?"

"I sought for traces of your life essence in the tides that sweep across this planet, and the Plixxi at the spaceport gave really good directions." She rearranged her robes. "They wear fur. I would rather go naked than wear fur."

"Please," I begged. "Don't. Besides, they're born with it."

"I suppose that makes a difference," she said disapprovingly.

"How are things back on Alt Bauernhof?"

"Deeply troubled. That world is riven with strife and absence of inner harmony. Fear stalks the streets, and people speak of strange cults and a possible drop in the M2 money supply. Rumors grow of an impending war with the Confederation. Discarded politicians from the Confederation appear as unofficial peace negotiators, but none believe that they will succeed."

"But—"

"I, of course, am exempt from such fears, having grown beyond mere identification with species."

"Right. So what brings you to Plixxi?"

"The Peace Coalition for a Just Ecology purchased land from the Plixxian government-in-exile to form several continent-sized nature parks to be maintained in pristine serenity. I have been called to serve as their representative."

"That sounds really nice. No, wait a minute." I looked at Catarina. "Is she saying that the PCJE financed Mordred's invasion?"

"Fear not!" Wild extended her arm with her palm out in a universal gesture of pretentiousness. "Their purposes are not mine. That phase of my existence is behind me. I have evolved. Know you that I now share a mind and a consciousness with Gaea, the Earth-Mother and embodiment of the world-organism that is Earth. All is one in Gaea."

"Say what?"

"I have been admitted to union with Gaea. I speak with her voice, think with her thoughts. I am Gaea. A rabbit is Gaea. A bush is Gaea. A tree is Gaea."

"Car salesmen, too?"

"Even such as they."

"Gee," I said, unwillingly impressed by anything that could reach that far down the food chain.

"I speak for them and for every toadstool and round-worm. All is Gaea and all are equal in Gaea, except that some are more equal than others."

"This sounds like it could violate zoning ordinances. Have you worked out a campaign slogan?"

"Four legs good, two legs challenged."

"Oh, right. Well, what's up?"

"I have come to this world to save you."

"Swell! Great. Good timing, too." Then I remembered that I was still down on one knee. "Well, almost good timing."

Wild spoke with a calm serenity. "Gaea has spoken to me. I am the bearer of a message to you. I am to protect you. You are in great danger."

"No shit. Excuse me. Ah, what did you have in mind?"

"The only safety for you lies in Gaea." Felicia's face grew intense. "To save yourself, you must pour your essence into the Gaea, reverence all, become one with her, and add a codicil to your will making her sole bene-ficiary. Only in this way can Gaea preserve you, but know, too, that nestled to Gaea's breasts, you will never need doctors or hospitals again."

"Sounds great." I looked at Catarina. "What do you think?"

She nodded. "Prozac is wonderful stuff."

"Ah, Felicia—you wouldn't happen to have heard from Gaea in the form of a very large cat?"

She gasped. "How did you know?"

"Lucky guess." I stood and dusted off my safari outfit.

"Thanks a lot for coming by, and especially thank Gaea for me. Just leave your number with my secretary and we'll be in touch shortly."

When Felicia departed, I asked Catarina, "Why didn't we ever think of starting our own religion?"

"Most of the best ones are taken."

"This leaves us where we were before. We could, of course, break our promise and make a run for it."

"We gave our word. Not to mention the fact that Fowl and Xhia will bombard the planet unless Bucky gives us up."

"Well, any ideas?"

She smiled. "We still have an hour or two to ourselves."

And, Of Course, a Grand Finale

After we ate the lunch that Clyde and company put together, we found Smith's vehicle, an ancient white Ford Bronco, gave some truffles to the big, three-headed guard dog, and aimlessly drove around the volcano to kill time. "We couldn't have backed out of our deal with Fowl," Catarina said.

"Well, we could have if we had really wanted to," I argued. "I mean, we have most of Fowl's troops locked up. He can bombard the planet, but most Plixxi live underground, so there's a limit to what he can do without a fresh invasion force."

"No, we couldn't have backed out." She pointed at the shuttle, which was bobbing out to sea. "You forgot to engage the parking brake."

"Oh, well. Poor Clyde. Still stuck with Harry."

"I'm sure Cheeves will come look for them eventually."

Wipo showed up with a few dozen shock troops to collect us a few minutes later. Mercifully, he ferried us up to Fowl's flagship in silence.

Fowl was waiting. "Know t'at if you return tee battle cruiser you purloined, tee agonizing fate t'at awaits you

288

when I return you to my world in triumph will be a quick and merciful deat'."

"Dear me," Catarina said. "Ken, do you remember where we left it?"

It was time for a curtain call. We'd had a good run for our money and caused our share of consternation before our luck ran low. "Sorry, Fowl. Tell you what—drop us off at Bucky's palace, and I'll see if I left it in my other suit."

"Bah! Surrender yourselves to me, abject and suppliant, as you become sickened by tee futility of your acts and by your paltry failure—"

"I've always kind of enjoyed poultry failure," Catarina quipped, and I loved her for it.

The proceedings ground to a stop. "Off wit' her head!" Fowl screamed, mauve with fury.

Wipo tugged at his sleeve nervously. "But your lordship, we can't execute them until we get back."

"I don't care! Off wit' her head! I want it done *now*!"

"But we already sold tickets!"

It proved an unanswerable argument. They tossed us into separate cells in the flagship's brig. Bucky and Cheeves sent up food for us, but for me it was still a rough ride back to Alt Bauernhof. Because of the abuse my body had taken and a possible delayed reaction to overindulgence in *Daube Avignonnaise*, I was in pretty bad shape. I cycled through hormonal surges and mood swings—one minute I felt all-powerful and wanted to bite somebody's neck, and the next I felt like crawling under a pillow to die. It took me a couple of days to pull myself together. After that, time passed interminably, especially after I borrowed a deck of cards and the guards who were watching began buzzing me to put the seven of clubs on the eight of diamonds.

When we finally reached Alt Bauernhof, even I could see changes. Guards were everywhere on the space station and appeared nervous. When we touched down, more guards were waiting to haul us to Special Secret Police Headquarters in separate sealed vans. When we got out, I could see tens of thousands of Macdonalds gathering a few blocks away. At a guess, either they were into huge, Nazi-style Nuremberg rallies to whip up war fever, or country line dancing was making a comeback.

Always a sentimentalist, Wipo threw me in my old cell, where time dragged even more interminably than it had aboard ship. I prayed a lot, which ate up dull hours and really spooked the guards, and kept hoping that Captain Tskhingamsa of Army Intelligence would show up again for a rescue attempt. Around the end of the first week, I taught myself to use the hologram projector in Lydia's ring to make shadow puppets: elves, dwarves, pixies, and Richard Nixon.

As I was putting my twentieth scratch on the wall to count the days, Wipo came to visit. "Ah, Mr. Bond!"

"Will you stop calling me that? Hold on a minute." I made the appropriate motions. "I call this one 'Elf on a motorcycle.' What do you think?"

"I do not understand tee—"

"It's supposed to be a female elf, damn it!" The strain of prison life was taking its toll.

He let it pass. "Tee board of ephors was enraged at you and Miss Lindquist for blabbing our preparations for building up our navy and conquering tee galaxy all over tee place. However, t'ey disagreed as to tee appropriate response. To avoid enraging tee Confederation, tee moderates wished to hang you, break you on tee wheel, and draw and quarter you. Tee hard-liners wanted to make your execution lengthy and painful."

"So what did you all decide?"

"T'is morning we received a reply from tee Confederation. T'ey apologized for victimizing us such t'at we felt compelled to resort to building weapons of war to assert ourselves, and agreed to disperse tee Confederation fleet to avoid giving us provocation. So, after careful deliberations, tee ephors have decided to execute you and Miss Lindquist tomorrow in a particularly gruesome fashion t'at I am not at liberty to discuss. T'ey want it to be a surprise."

"I hate it when the Foreign Office is allowed to participate in foreign policy debates. So tomorrow, I suppose hundreds of millions of people will get to see us die."

"Only tee rich. We scheduled it on pay-per-view. I should also mention t'at for her efforts in molding public opinion in tee Confederation, your ex-wife, tee being Gwen, has been given tee Planetary Order of Star and Comet with Diamonds."

"How nice. Other than that, what brings you here?"

"In a touching gesture, I have brought your spiritual adviser to confer wit' you ere you perish. But if you will excuse me, I have a check to cash before tee banks close."

I expected to see Father Yakub. Instead, the ladder descended and Cheeves came down. "Cheeves! Good to see you! What are you doing here? I thought Wipo said that he was sending me my spiritual adviser."

"I informed the chairman of the board of ephors that I was your stockbroker," Cheeves said stiffly. "On most planets this has the same connotation."

"And Wipo's check? I assume it came from you, and I hope you arranged to stop payment."

Cheeves shook his head. "Dear me, friend Ken, how unsporting!"

"Just a thought. What brings you here to comfort me?"

"Poobah Bucky directed me to come here and undertake to extricate you and Miss Lindquist from the situation you find yourselves in as a result of actions taken on our behalf."

"How much gold did you bring in your luggage?"

"Approximately 150 *quanats*, which is, I believe, roughly 14,120 kilograms."

I blinked hard. "Pardon me, but where did you and Bucky lay hands on that kind of loot?"

"Gold, although valuable in craft applications, does not enjoy the same fiscal significance on !Plixxi* that it does here."

"But didn't you use that gold to secure the development loans you and Bucky took out to upgrade Plixxi's economy?"

"Initially, this did present a problem. I believe that we had approximately eleven billion in loans outstanding, so to free up this gold for shipment, it became necessary to repay these loans."

"Oh, no," I said. "Oh, no."

"As it turned out, bank officials on Brasilia Nuevo learned from Confederation diplomats that Mordred's invasion was imminent, and immediately contacted us. They were justifiably worried that cousin Mordred would repudiate the loans if he seized power. As I recall, that was a plank in his party platform. Inasmuch as there was no provision for recalling these loans absent default, I offered to redeem the loans at a modest discount, and they were kind enough to accept the amount I was able to offer in full and final satisfaction."

"What did you give them, ten cents on the dollar?"

"I believe that the final figure was thirty-two percent."

"You didn't mention to them that Mordred's invasion had already come and gone."

"They appeared to be in something of a hurry, so I did not burden them with the information. Although a man from the Merchants' Guarantee Trust later described the transaction as 'the worst deal since the Red Sox peddled Babe Ruth to the Yankees,' the representatives appeared quite pleased with the result at the instant the deal was struck."

"You're telling me that you diddled the banks out of eight billion."

"The loans were partially secured by the Confederation Government Development Loan Bank, which will ultimately make good on approximately half of the losses sustained, so the ultimate loss to the banks involved will be much less. Fortunately, virtually all of the machinery and technology purchased with the funds has already been shipped, either here or to !Plixxi*, which obviates the potential for bothersome legal action by disgruntled banks or shareholders."

I stared at him in utter horror. "Hold it. Half the stuff you bought must be on the list of items that the Confederation doesn't allow companies to ship to Alt Bauernhof. You're breaking your licensing agreement!"

"Dear me, friend Ken, may I disagree with you on this? The agreement merely specifies that we cannot resell indexed items to non-!Plixxi* firms. There are now several !Plixxi*-owned companies on this planet, indeed, several more than there were last week. Indeed, my niece, Minnie, particularly asked me to mention to you that one firm we purchased was engaged in the manufacture of a beverage known as White Zinfandel, which we have taken off the market pending a scientific examination into its apparently deleterious qualities. Early indications are that this has had an immediate and remarkably beneficial effect on this planet's population."

I sighed. "I hate to say this, Cheeves, but all of the effort you've made is in vain. Wipo just told me that the board of ephors plans to execute me and Catarina tomorrow."

"Oh, dear! Did he say that?"

"Our only real chance was for a preemptive strike by the Confederation Navy, but Wipo just said that they're dispersing the fleet, which makes absolutely no sense."

Cheeves was silent for a few seconds. "A Klo'-klotixag-built warship suddenly appeared over Brasilia Nuevo and landed a war party which sacked the pornographic bookstores of the city of Rio. Because of the manner in which the raiders were dressed, the citizens did not pay them any attention. There is an unconfirmed report that the raiders also struck the zoo and freed the turtles held captive there." Cheeves paused. "Bowing to public outcry, the Confederation government decided to disperse its fleet to prevent similar outrages."

"Oops! I guess when I screw up, I do it in style."

"Actually, your handling of the situation has won high praise overall. Your co-signing for the loan of $147 million that my niece and nephew took out was a stroke of genius in that your creditors on this planet feared they would not be paid if the government executed you, and they have been exerting pressure on the board of ephors to prevent this."

"Well, it wasn't enough. Say good-bye to Bucky for me—"

Cheeves pulled out his pocket watch and examined it. "Friend Ken—"

"—and Minnie and Mickey and the rest of my crew. But the person I'll really miss is Catarina."

"Friend Ken—"

"Is there any chance you can talk them into letting her go?"

"A fairly good one," Tskhingamsa announced from above us. He began letting the ladder down. Bucky and Catarina appeared beside him. "Tee board of ephors fled, moments ago, and a new provisional government is being sworn in outside tee capitol building, which is under repairs."

"As I was about to say to you, friend Ken, the information you received was slightly outdated," Cheeves explained.

Bucky and Catarina came down the steps to join us. "Friend Ken, you're looking well. As Bucky says, 'The health of a friend is like an endless stream of pennies from heaven,' " Bucky exclaimed.

Catarina was whistling the theme song from *Born Free*.

"I suppose that this is one of those 'a new era has dawned' things." After I hugged Catarina and shook Bucky's paw, I looked at Cheeves. "All right, I'll bite. What's *your* angle on all of this? Don't tell me you used all that gold to finance a coup d'état here."

"Oh, no, friend Ken. Dear me, no! That smacks of illegality. We purchased the planet instead," Bucky explained.

I needed to sit down. "You did what?"

"We had to get you back, friend Ken. Poor Susie is

pining, and a mopey dragon is simply impossible to live with. It is axiomatic that dragons are faithful one hundred percent."

Cheeves took off his top hat and smoothed a few dents. "I wouldn't wish to bore you with the details, friend Ken. Suffice it to say, we utilized the gold as security to issue a few billion in gold-backed bearer bonds, and with the prospect of war and hyperinflation looming, the Macdonalds assigned a value to them that far outstripped expectations. This, coupled with the firm initial position that Minnie and Mickey were able to give us in the corporate marketplace, enabled us to make the board of ephors a very acceptable tender offer, which they accepted following the massive and ultimately successful civil disobedience campaign launched by the planet's Christian community."

"What?"

"Yes, this was a surprise. When the ephors banned the 'Bucky Beaver Show,' it achieved such notoriety that a market for Bucky Beaver videos sprung up overnight," Bucky explained with relish. "Minnie and Mickey assigned one of their companies to produce them."

"In retrospect," Cheeves concluded, "banning the show appears to have been a serious tactical error. Your friend, Mjarlen, has proven to be a devastatingly effective proponent of Bucky's philosophy and has been superlative in making it comprehensible to the masses." Again Cheeves paused. "He appears, however, to somehow have acquired the odd notion that the copy of the Bible he has is incomplete, and that the Bucky Beaver stories comprise additional portions."

I looked at Catarina. "Oh, boy."

Cheeves twitched his whiskers. "Although the Bucky

Beaver stories do rather resemble Biblical parables, I am rather at a loss to explain this development. I understand that the Roman Catholic Church has its own communications network and sources of information, and I have been told that the Pope wishes to see the two of you."

Catarina swallowed hard. "There's absolution for every sin."

"Yeah," I said, "but how long is it going to take us to say a million Our Fathers and a million Hail Marys?" I suddenly realized that the guards I had listened to for so long were gone. "What happened with the Special Secret Police? Why didn't they break up the demonstrations and why is this place deserted?"

"When it appeared that they might become an obstacle, we set up an overnight delivery company offering very competitive wages and employee stock options." Cheeves bowed. "I confess, friend Ken, that it was my intention to establish peaceful relations between Alt Bauernhof and the rest of the universe. I trust I have given satisfaction."

Suddenly, Tskhingamsa let out a cry and fell through the opening in the ceiling onto my mattress. Sporting a maniacal grin, Mailboat Bobby Stemm appeared above us, waving a pistol and obviously suffering from the kind of behavior disorder that leads disturbed individuals to purchase aluminum Christmas trees. "Nobody move! I'm holding—"

"Yeah, yeah, yeah. A .55 Magnum, the most powerful handgun in the known universe." I looked at Catarina. "I get so tired of these last-minute histrionics."

"Bobby, what's all this about?" she asked calmly.

"My career is ruined. My source of cigarettes has dried up, and I've been exposed as a smoker. There's nothing left for me." Bobby clutched the gun to his breast. "The only thing between me and the end of everything is Ambassador Meisenhelder, and he's packing his bags to leave!"

Cheeves wrinkled his nose. "The new government is rather precipitate."

"But this is my chance! I'm nothing. Nobody. But if I shoot the four of you, I'll be famous! Famous!" Stemm cackled insanely. "People will hire me to do infomercials."

"This is wicked," Bucky said. He looked around my squalid cell, which was in line to become our final resting place. "It's worse than wicked, it's vulgar."

"We could rush him," I whispered to Catarina. "He only has a seven-round magazine."

"If we try to go up the steps together, it will be a problem trying to keep the same bullet from going through more than two or three of us," she pointed out.

"Good point. Yo, Bobby." I waved at him. "I hope you realize that if you blow us away, the newspapers will call this another random killing by a crazed dope fiend."

"You can't fool me that way, MacKay. Everyone knows how much I hate you. I hate you, I hate you, I hate you!"

"Dear me," Bucky said, taken aback, "I didn't realize that anyone ever said anything like that, except in musical theater."

"Look, Bobby, er, ah Bobby." I coughed. "Are you sure you want to shoot us here? You don't have any witnesses, and people will blame it on the Macdonalds when they find our bodies."

He weakened for an instant. Then he remembered the videocamera in his pocket. He waved it triumphantly.

"No, they won't. Sweet dreams, MacKay. I'll be infamous, and you'll be dead."

I rested my chin on my knees. "Just when you start to think that it can't get worse—"

"It does," I heard a familiar voice say.

I looked up and saw Mordred. "This is like my high school reunion. You, too?"

"I have a date with destiny," Mordred said. He twitched his nose. "Lieutenant Commander Stemm, I presume. I trust you remember me."

Bobby knelt to kiss the hem of his robe.

"Dear Lord, can that man suck up," I exclaimed.

"I have this nagging feeling that we should have gotten out of prison when the opportunity first presented itself," Catarina commented as she bent to check Tskhingamsa's condition.

"Mordred, do you know this fellow?" Bucky asked.

"He is one of Supreme Agent Wipo's hirelings. He used to be the military attaché to !Plixxi*, which is where I first met him." He looked at Stemm. "So, what did you have in mind?"

"I'm going to blow them all away," Bobby said, sighting down the barrel of his pistol.

"Do you mind if I join you?" Mordred asked, whipping out his poniard and testing its balance.

"Bucky, did you have to let Mordred go?" I hissed.

"He is part of the family," Bucky said apologetically.

"I'm going to enjoy this!" Bobby said. "It's going to be fun fun fun!"

"Don't you just hate people who are perky in the morning," I muttered.

"Any final smart remarks, Lindquist? How about you, MacKay?"

I shrugged. "I'm thinking. Don't rush me."

Catarina favored me with one of her famous smiles.

"Good-bye, then!" Bobby laughed, just as Mordred gently tapped him on the head with the pommel of his poniard, and Bobby dropped like a poleaxed steer.

"Mordred?" I scratched my head. "You're on our side?"

"Oh, yes." Mordred stuck his poniard in his belt and dusted off his paws. "Didn't cousin Cheeves mention our little agreement?"

I looked at Cheeves. "You mean there was a fix in to diddle the banks?"

"Assuredly not, friend Ken," Cheeves said primly.

"When I told cousin Cheeves that I wanted to invade !Plixxi* and topple brother Bucky from his throne, he bet me that I wouldn't succeed, so when you captured me, I lost the wager and had to pay forfeit." Mordred twirled his whiskers. "After a suitably abject reconciliation, I swore allegiance and took over the Commerce portfolio in the cabinet. Commerce minister is okay, but I did so want to be Poobah and consign people to dungeons and things."

I ran my fingers through my rapidly thinning hair. "I hate to ask this, but what's to keep you from shooting the four of us and making another try at the cushion?"

"Mr. MacKay, are you suggesting I should *welsh on a bet*?" Mordred said loftily, "I am a being of honor, sir. I resent such insinuation on your part."

"What cousin Mordred is saying," Bucky explained, "is that although he deeply regrets not being able to parade my head on a pikestaff, how can one have any kind of stable social order if one does not live up to agreements one freely entered into?"

"The law of contract is sacred," Mordred assured me. "Mind you, if Cheeves had left me a loophole, brother Bucky's life wouldn't be worth a campaign promise."

"I see," I said falsely.

"Besides," Mordred said, "I get to be Royal and Imperial Viceroy here, which ain't just brussels sprouts."

Catarina helped Tskhingamsa to his feet. "We might want to get out of here."

"A capital suggestion, if I might say so," Cheeves said. "Indeed, perhaps we might retire aboard friend Ken's ship, *Rustam's Slipper*. Things might be a little unsettled here for a few days or so."

As we walked together down the dark corridors of the suddenly deserted Secret Police Headquarters Cheeves raised another matter. "Your dread and august majesty, it is customary to ennoble ministers of state, and might I remind you that this affair represents yet another instance in which Minister Ken has rendered signal service to the dynasty and the realm."

Bucky stopped dead in his tracks. "Oh! That's right, isn't it?"

"Might I suggest that a title of nobility is in order?" Cheeves continued.

I also stopped dead in my tracks. "What about her?" I asked, pointing at Catarina. "It's her fault, too."

Everyone ignored me. "When did we start giving out titles of nobility to humans?" Mordred wanted to know.

"There's a first time for everything," Bucky said airily. "Besides, it's the perfect gift for the being who has everything."

Mordred scratched his pointed little head. "I thought that humans didn't go in for that sort of thing."

It was on the tip of my tongue to suggest that I really

didn't have much use for a Rodent patent of nobility, but the proximity of Catarina's elbow was an inhibiting factor.

"Most humans are not afforded the opportunity to decline the honor," Cheeves said with commendable restraint.

"Friend Ken is a vampire, which makes things different," Bucky said with an air of assurance. "What say we make him a count, eh, Cheeves? There's precedent."

I sputtered ineffectually.

"There might be undesirable consequences to naming him as a count," Cheeves replied deferentially. "Friend Ken, if you would please kneel. Mordred, if you could lend Poobah Bucky your poniard for the ceremony."

I knelt, with Catarina's hand on my shoulder.

"If not a count, how about an earl, then?" Bucky asked, twirling his whiskers.

"A duke," Cheeves said firmly.

The corner of Catarina's mouth turned down. "Might I make a suggestion?"

I should have seen it coming. Thirty seconds later I found myself the Duke of Earl.

"There is, of course, the problem of finding a suitable position for you," Cheeves mused. "We could leave you as minister of defense, but that hardly seems a worthwhile utilization of your talents."

Before he could say another word, a Macdonald in a Special Secret Police uniform suddenly appeared in front of us. "Prime Minister Cheeves, could you please sign for this?"

"What is it, Cheeves?" Bucky said, moving up to peer over Cheeves's shoulder.

"Can I get up yet?" I inquired.

"Excellent news, your grace," Cheeves reported. "The consortium holding ownership rights over Schuyler's World has agreed in principle to our offer, and they do not envision any difficulty getting approval from the elected planetary government, to the extent that the planet can actually be said to have a government."

"What does that make for us, three planets now, Cheeves? I suppose you could say that we're moving up in the galaxy," Bucky said proudly.

Cheeves folded the telex. "There is, however, the problem of a suitable viceroy. Given the animus that has developed between the !Plixxi* settlers and the planet's human inhabitants, I would recommend against appointing a !Plixxi* viceroy."

I could see where this conversation was leading. "Oh, no. Oh, no. Not that." Schuyler's World being what it is, I have been known to say that I would rather be dipped in goo and left to harden than spend an extra ten minutes there. I turned to Catarina. "Help! I think I'm being railroaded!"

"I'd say you're on the right track." She winked. "But Schuyler's World would be an excellent place for us to station ourselves."

"Somehow, I can't help thinking that you engineered this."

For some reason, she burst out laughing.

Bucky patted me on the shoulder. "Buck up, friend Ken. We can't just let our dukes wander around the galaxy selling fertilizer."

"Bucky, think this through with me. I'm a spacer. Not only do I not know or desire to know anything about being a viceroy, but being a vamp, I can't even walk the streets during business hours. I don't want to be a dirt dweller. Heck, even if I wanted to suck dirt, I wouldn't suck dirt from Schuyler's World."

"Dear me," Bucky exclaimed, "you do make it sound unhygienic."

"I don't mean to hurt your feelings," I said feebly, "but I'm not giving up my ship."

"True, it would be a shame to decommission the flagship—indeed, the only ship—of our navy," Bucky remarked.

Cheeves unbent slightly. "Granted, on Schuyler's World, a full-time viceroy would probably provide more governing than the planet could safely tolerate. If we could count on Duke Ken for perhaps four months out of the year and gave him an experienced administrative assistant from the family—demi-sister Jezebel's second son comes to mind—I would consider it a prudent measure. We could nominate friend Catarina as his deputy viceroy."

Bucky turned and pumped my hand. "Then it's settled! Welcome aboard, friend Ken."

By an odd coincidence, Cheeves even had the patents drawn up and ready to sign.

As we flagged down a limo to take us to the spaceport, Catarina put her arm around my shoulder. "Ken?"

"Yes?"

"Do you remember that question you asked me back in Gregorio's cavern?"

"Yes. Oh! Yes!"

She smiled. "I'll let you know."

We dropped Mordred off at the Ephoral Palace to grasp the reins of power, grabbed some carryout, and chartered a shuttle to carry us up to the space station.

As we were waiting for the shuttle I was absolutely

astonished to see Gwen sitting in the terminal. She smiled when she saw us and drifted over. "Congratulations, Ken."

"Ah, thanks."

"No hard feelings?"

Catarina was right behind me, and I could feel my cheeks turning—well, maybe not red, but a little rosy. "No hard feelings. I guess with the change in governments, you'll lose your contract. What will you do with yourself? Will you be all right?"

"Oh, you know me, Ken! I always land on my feet." She drifted away, larger than life, leaving behind a whiff of perfume, and a summons to appear in court and show cause.

When we got up to the *Scupper*, Minnie, Mickey, Harry, Trixie, and Clyde were waiting to greet us as we came through the airlock. Bunkie was off managing Mordred's transition team.

Clyde saluted. "Welcome aboard, sir. Cheeves had us wait in the space station in case things broke our way, and they let us have the ship about half an hour ago."

"Hey, Ken," Harry cut in, "I got my pistol back. Bucky here is a head of state, right? I could fire off a twenty-one-gun salute."

"Ah, thanks, but—"

"Oh, and you're never going to believe this, but I've got a new girlfriend. Her name's Fluffy." He ran down the corridor to his cabin and returned with Felicia Wild. "Can I keep her? Huh, huh, can I keep her?"

Putting Harry on hold while Minnie and Mickey took possession of Bucky and Cheeves for some talk about debentures, I pulled Clyde and Catarina aside for a private discussion. "Clyde, what's the latest word on Rosalee and Wyma Jean?"

"Oh, we got a message from Rosalee. She says she'll catch up with us on Brasilia Nuevo." He gave a conspiratorial wink. "I think that piracy is starting to bore her."

"What about Wyma Jean?"

Clyde appeared troubled. "We heard from her, too. Wyma Jean's still kind of pissed. Mostly at Harry, but you remember last year, I dated her a couple of times?"

"Yes."

"Don't let me be captured alive, sir."

Catarina laid her hand on my shoulder. "Isn't it good to be home?"

It was still close to rush hour, so of course we got stuck in a holding pattern. Minnie and Mickey showed us Number Four Hold which they'd cleared out so that Big Susie could move in, and their latest assortment of Bucky Beaver videos.

"This is our most recent release, Duke Ken." Mickey handed me one. "*Bucky Beaver and the Stock Market Correction.*"

I tapped the tape against my forehead. "You know, I thought I read all of the Bucky Beaver stories when I was a kid, but for some reason, I don't recall this one."

Minnie and Mickey exchanged glances.

"Although creating the animated stories has been rather a snap with the proper computer technology, we have been experiencing difficulty in keeping abreast of demand," Minnie explained.

"Indeed, demand has been so great that we have already exhausted the classic titles," Mickey agreed. "Fortunately, we were able to import a team of Bucky

Beaver scholars from !Plixxi*, and Mr. Clyde has been helping them prepare additional stories."

Catarina blanched. "And the Pope wants to see us."

I looked at my watch. "You know, if we hurry, we could still convert. Are there Jewish vampires?"

Clyde interrupted over the intercom. "Captain, could you and Commander Lindquist come to the bridge? We have a problem."

When we reached the bridge, Xhia's image filled the viewscreen. "Tee empire I swore allegiance to is finished, my proud navy is no more. You took from me my yout's visions and dearest marvels. You stole my nights from me and sold t'em to sleepless torment. You embittered my finest honey. A curse upon you, my enemies!"

I exploded. "Darn it all!" I was getting tired and cranky. I looked at Catarina. "This is twice in one day. Can't we find a judge and get some sort of temporary restraining order to keep all these washed-up villains from bothering us for at least another four or five pages?"

I sat down in the command seat and felt something move which turned out to be Frisky, the long-lost boa constrictor.

"Can I break out the missile launcher, huh, huh?" Harry wanted to know.

Cheeves interjected himself quietly. "Duke Ken, if I could perhaps be allowed to address this."

He spoke to Xhia in private for about five minutes. At the end, Xhia stood and saluted with oily tears in his eyes. The screen went blank.

I looked at Catarina with my mouth open. She shook her head. "You'll have to ask. This time, I don't know, either."

"Oh, I did very little," Cheeves said dismissively. "I

merely mentioned that the Galaxy Wrestling Federation
has expressed an interest in opening a light-saber divi-
sion and televising matches. I felt it prudent to bring
Captain Xhia in on the ground floor, as it were."

"Cheeves, I'd take my hat off to you if one of Wipo's
boys hadn't swiped it."

"Thank you, sir." Cheeves fluffed his fur the tiniest bit.
"I strive to give good service."

And so the galaxy was saved for humanity, for at least
another week. Of course, after the story leaked, Catarina
and I were called to testify in front of two legislative sub-
committees to respond to persistent rumors that we sacri-
ficed kittens during our stay on Alt Bauernhof, and after
a great deal of soul-searching, we decided to sell the
book rights. Gwen volunteered herself as my agent. She
says we're only talking to interested buyers. An Aus-
tralian company is offering a $4.5 million advance.
Gwen says that it might just cover my legal fees, unless,
of course, the newspapers pick up on the story and fuss
until I give the money back. Lydia's almost talking to me
now, a frightening thought, although I can't say the same
about the Pope.

When word first got out that Bucky and Cheeves had
purchased Alt Bauernhof and Schuyler's World, the
Confederation press and the diplomatic corps collectively had a belly-laugh. I've noticed they've stopped
laughing. Mordred and I have actually gotten to be pretty
good friends. He says that I remind him of the hero in
Hemingway's book *The Bread Also Rises*. I'm still not
sure how to take that.

Being viceroy of Schuyler's World and Duke of Earl is
okay, I guess, except for that stupid song they play
instead of "Hail to the Chief." A lot of people have

written claiming to be destitute relatives of mine, and Catarina and Trixie have both had a major impact on the way that local governmental institutions function, Trixie especially. And having Big Susie around isn't nearly as bad as I thought it would be. Until she pushed her way into our lives, I didn't imagine that there was anything in the universe that could drink Harry under the table.

A few days ago Bucky called to ask Catarina to be his viceroy for Brasilia Nuevo—the same four months out of twelve deal.

Prolonged contact with the folks on Schuyler's World is starting to make me think that there might be something to the VMR Theory after all.

Read how Ken and Catarina met in

McCLENDON'S SYNDROME

by
Robert Frezza

Not all vampires are dark and sinister . . .
and not all shipboard murders are
quite what they seem.

McCLENDON'S SYNDROME
by Robert Frezza

Published by Del Rey® Books.
Available at your local bookstore.

CAIN'S LAND

by
Robert Frezza

Lt.-Colonel Anton Vereshchagin is called
out of retirement to lead a mission to the
recently discovered planet, Go-Nihon.
But the planet's inhabitants have other
ideas, and it's up to Vereshchagin and his
1st Battalion to teach the aliens the
value of peaceful coexistence.

CAIN'S LAND
by Robert Frezza

Published by Del Rey® Books.
Available wherever books are sold.

✎ FREE DRINKS ✎

Take the Del Rey® survey and get a free newsletter! Answer
the questions below and we will send you complimentary
copies of the DRINK (Del Rey® Ink) newsletter free for one
year. Here's where you will find out all about upcoming
books, read articles by top authors, artists, and editors, and
get the inside scoop on your favorite books.

Age _____   Sex ❑ M ❑ F

Highest education level: ❑ high school ❑ college ❑ graduate degree

Annual income: ❑ $0-30,000 ❑ $30,001-60,000 ❑ over $60,000

Number of books you read per month: ❑ 0-2 ❑ 3-5 ❑ 6 or more

Preference: ❑ fantasy ❑ science fiction ❑ horror ❑ other fiction ❑ nonfiction

I buy books in hardcover: ❑ frequently ❑ sometimes ❑ rarely

I buy books at: ❑ superstores ❑ mall bookstores ❑ independent bookstores
    ❑ mail order

I read books by new authors: ❑ frequently ❑ sometimes ❑ rarely

I read comic books: ❑ frequently ❑ sometimes ❑ rarely

I watch the Sci-Fi cable TV channel: ❑ frequently ❑ sometimes ❑ rarely

I am interested in collector editions (signed by the author or illustrated):
❑ yes ❑ no ❑ maybe

I read Star Wars novels: ❑ frequently ❑ sometimes ❑ rarely

I read Star Trek novels: ❑ frequently ❑ sometimes ❑ rarely

I read the following newspapers and magazines:
❑ *Analog*	❑ *Locus*	❑ *Popular Science*
❑ *Asimov*	❑ *Wired*	❑ *USA Today*
❑ *SF Universe*	❑ *Realms of Fantasy*	❑ *The New York Times*

Check the box if you do not want your name and address shared with qualified
vendors ❑

Name _____

Address _____

City/State/Zip _____

E-mail _____

Frezza

**PLEASE SEND TO: DEL REY®/The DRINK
201 EAST 50TH STREET NEW YORK NY 10022**

DEL REY® ONLINE!

The Del Rey Internet Newsletter...

A monthly electronic publication, posted on the Internet, GEnie, CompuServe, BIX, various BBSs, and the Panix gopher (gopher.panix.com). It features hype-free descriptions of books that are new in the stores, a list of our upcoming books, special announcements, a signing/reading/convention-attendance schedule for Del Rey authors, "In Depth" essays in which professionals in the field (authors, artists, designers, sales people, etc.) talk about their jobs in science fiction, a question-and-answer section, behind-the-scenes looks at sf publishing, and more!

Internet information source!

A lot of Del Rey material is available to the Internet on our Web site and on a gopher server: all back issues and the current issue of the Del Rey Internet Newsletter, sample chapters of upcoming or current books (readable or downloadable for free), submission requirements, mail-order information, and much more. We will be adding more items of all sorts (mostly new DRINs and sample chapters) regularly. The Web site is http://www.randomhouse.com/delrey/ and the address of the gopher is gopher.panix.com

Why? We at Del Rey realize that the networks are the medium of the future. That's where you'll find us promoting our books, socializing with others in the sf field, and—most importantly—making contact and sharing information with sf readers.

Online editorial presence: Many of the Del Rey editors are online, on the Internet, GEnie, CompuServe, America Online, and Delphi. There is a Del Rey topic on GEnie and a Del Rey folder on America Online.

The official e-mail address for Del Rey Books is delrey@randomhouse.com (though it sometimes takes us a while to answer).